REALM OF THE WOLF II

Kevin,

Wow!! 41 years old!! Happy Birthday. I hope you really enjoy this book and story. Wish you could have picked it up yourself.

Your friend,

David L. Falconer

MAY 3, 2008

REALM OF THE WOLF II
LAW OF THE WOLF

David L. Falconer

authorHOUSE®

AuthorHouse™
1663 Liberty Drive, Suite 200
Bloomington, IN 47403
www.authorhouse.com
Phone: 1-800-839-8640

This book is a work of fiction. People, places, events, and situations are the product of the author's imagination. Any resemblance to actual persons, living or dead, or historical events, is purely coincidental.

First published by AuthorHouse   4/9/2008

ISBN: 978-1-4343-7213-0 (sc)

Printed in the United States of America
Bloomington, Indiana

This book is printed on acid-free paper.

DEDICATION

To my friends, Kevin Thomas and Joe Wells, both of which passed on in the same year. They were the kind of friends that always watched your back and they would show up if they just thought you needed help. Some people make your life better for being part of it. That is an apt description of these two men.

REALM OF THE WOLF:
LAW OF THE WOLF

The sun glared in his eyes as he drove the green Chevy truck with the matching fiberglass camper shell down the lonely country road. Pulling out on the state highway, he adjusted the visor with his right hand as his eyes strayed to the farmhouses in the distance. This part of Southeastern Oklahoma reminded him of home though the soil and vegetation was slightly different from the mountains in the east.

It was the chicken houses that stood out the most in the green of the forest as he drove north on Highway 259. The long, silver buildings reflected the sunlight at almost every angle due to the ridges in the sheet iron that covered them. In his opinion, they scarred the land, but they were a necessary means of survival for the people in this region. Industrialization was not an ecological problem in this part of Oklahoma. There were no gray smokestack arrowing up to the sky while belching the new Black Death of acid rain. Without the factories though, it meant that people had to look for other means to support a family. The clear-cuts marked the other industry in the area, logging. This too served to mar the forest, but he knew it served the wildlife too. It gave the deer a place to hide, turkey a place to nest, and the quail a place to roost.

He stopped the truck on top of the highest mountain beside a monument that had three sticks pointing to the sky. The lookout overlooked a massive valley that was beautifully clothed in the summer green of early June. There were a few clouds in the sky and the radio station out of Mena, Arkansas was calling for torrential rains and thunderstorms for a few days starting late this evening. It was possible to see the dual stations at the small crossroads community of Big Cedar where President John F. Kennedy once gave a speech as the guest of Oklahoma Senator Bob Kerr, a brief time in the spotlight for a community that soon faded into the obscurity that claimed many little backwoods towns.

Rubbing the palms of his hands against his jeans, he sneezed twice. The pollen always caused his allergies to act up. He frowned a little when he noticed crusty, red dirt under his fingernails. Reaching into his pocket, he retrieved the knife that was always there. Flicking open the longest blade, he used the point to scrape the dirt from under his nails. When he finished, he closed the knife and put it back in his pocket, a small jingle reaching his ears as it slid into the small amount of change at the bottom.

A shiver ran through him as though he had a sudden chill. It wouldn't be long now. It was never very long after he start getting the itching palms and the shivers that would course through his body.

Nervously, he got back into the pick-up. He couldn't believe that it would call so soon after being satiated.

He had disposed of the last body only a few hours before on a hillside beside an abandoned logging road. She had been dead almost three days and decomposition had set in on her dismembered body. She had started to stink two days ago.

The stirring of an erection began as he thought about the fear in her eyes when he had advanced on her with the short hand axe. Her eyes had held that fear as he had raped her repeatedly in an empty house in Denison, Texas. He had picked the girl up in Dallas at a bar in the West End. She had probably been a prostitute.

The thought of her being a prostitute sickened him. The unclean body of a whore was not his usual choice when the hunger called, but that night it had been too strong to deny. The woman had not been the first whore to succumb to the hunger though. She had been drunk and an easy mark. Her long, dark hair had been enticing in the gloomy light of the bar. He had suggested they leave and find a motel room. The woman agreed readily, not knowing that she had sealed her fate as soon as she walked out of the bar with him. They went to a cheap motel and he'd had sex with her twice before trying to force her into the act of sodomy. When she refused, he knocked her out with a short club he carried in the waistband of his pants. He had tied and gagged her, loaded her into the back of his truck and covered her with a tarp. They drove north on Highway 75 to Denison where he felt the need to take her again.

He drove around the much smaller city and found a house that looked deserted. Pulling his truck into an alley, he took the woman inside and dumped her in the empty room that had been the living room at one time. He walked back to his truck and went to a motel, checking in with a name that was not his own.

The man was average height with no characteristics that made him stand out. He had the kind of face that did not draw undue attention and the desk clerk forgot him as soon as he walked out with the key to his room.

Going to his room, he showered and dressed in clean clothes. He hated the feel of sweat-dried clothes on his body and took special pains to keep clean clothes handy at all times. Lying down on the bed, he slept for a couple hours and looked outside. It would be a few hours before the sun would come up. The house was in walking distance, but he knew he would be more conspicuous as a walker at this hour than he would in his truck. He got in his truck and drove to the parking lot of a small business that looked to have gone out of business and left it. The house was less than a block away and he made it without being seen by cutting through the alleyway.

The woman was looking at him in fear as he walked into the room. He picked up the small hand axe he had brought in earlier and laid it close to hand. Then he had used the woman until he had tired of her and the hunger had been satisfied. The feel of power when he snapped her neck while looking into her eyes was god-like. His veins had throbbed with that power for hours after the deed had been done.

He looked at the scar on his hand. At least this woman hadn't bitten him like the bitch before her. He had picked up a girl on the campus of Texas A&M on the pretext of giving her a ride to Waco and they had talked while he drove. She had been talking when she stopped in mid-sentence and looked at him strangely. He decided he better make his move. He clubbed her hard across the forehead with the back of his knuckles and the back of her head almost cracked the rear window. She had slumped forward and he started to push her into the floor when she suddenly bit him. His feet slammed on the brakes and she flew forward into the dashboard as he pulled the hand axe from under the seat of the truck and decapitated her in one fell swoop. Her blood saturating the seat of the truck and pooling on the floor mat was deep red.

He had found it strange that her teeth had looked misshapen in death. They had seemed so white and even before. Her face seemed darker too, but he didn't look any closer at it. It wasn't good luck to look into the face of the dead after the eyes had glazed over.

He had taken two days to clean out all traces of blood in his truck, even going to the extent of purchasing a new bench seat and installing it himself. The old one had been burned, leaving only the charred springs and melted vinyl as evidence to the death of the young girl.

This delay and the unsatisfying death of the girl had frustrated him and the hunger had only gotten worse. That was why he had chosen to try to find a hooker in Dallas for his next kill.

He drove through the community of Big Cedar and kept going north. It was next to a little road stop beside the Poteau River that he saw the woman walking the little French poodle. The short blue shorts and a white halter-top that did little more than cover her ample bosom beautifully accented her lithe tanned legs. She looked to be in her late twenties or early thirties and her figure was very attractive. The red foreign sports car was the only vehicle parked in the small rest stop as he turned in. The woman seemed to be alone.

He stopped close to the car and got out. Not much traffic had been on the highway and there wasn't a single car in sight. He smiled at the woman as she walked back to her car. His teeth were white and even as he said hello to the woman.

CHAPTER ONE

Scott Hale looked at the remains of the woman. She had been dismembered and buried in a shallow grave southwest of Heavener, Oklahoma on State Highway 271 near the community of Summerfield. The body had been found by 'coon hunters out running their dogs for exercise and to "get away from the womenfolk" on a summer night. The woman had been missing for sixteen days. No sign of her car had been seen either. No one had even been sure of where she had disappeared.

The grave had been less than a hundred yards off the road near a small creek, but it was almost a miracle that it had been found so soon after the murder occurred. The county Sheriff had been notified, but he had been on vacation in Idaho and wouldn't arrive back until sometime in the evening. His team had worked tediously on maintaining what remained of the integrity of the site after the hunters found the body. They had been here all night and through the morning.

Scott had seen enough bodies of this nature in the four years he had spent in the FBI division dealing with serial killers that they no longer made him puke every time. His stomach had almost lost it though when a tanned, bloated leg severed above the knee and splattered with dry blood fell out of the bag when it was opened

The sound of a truck coming up the road averted his attention from the woman's dismembered cadaver and made him watch expectantly as a dark blue, Ford four-wheel drive with a county Sheriff emblem on the door pulled up beside his rental car. It looked like the Sheriff had caught an early flight.

He was surprised as the tall man got out of the truck. Dark brown hair, a mustache of the same color outlined a face that looked more like twenty-eight than the thirty-eight years of age this man was supposed to be. Scott

1

had a dossier on this man. It had been pulled up immediately when the report of the murder had came in late last night and he had readied for the helicopter trip from Austin, Texas. He always liked to know the names and background of the local officials that he would be dealing with on a case like this one.

The man's name was Logan Denton and he was not a typical southern sheriff as portrayed by television. He was an ex-Special Forces Sergeant that had been injured in a training mission that resulted in the loss of one of his feet. The injury had been sufficient to warrant his discharge from the Army. He had been a private detective for several years in Dallas/Ft. Worth and specialized in dangerous situations. It was noted that he had killed a man while serving in that capacity. He was an expert in two forms of martial arts and was one of the survivors of a horrible massacre that occurred in the mountains of Idaho almost ten years ago with a white supremacist group. He had disappeared for almost four years before mysteriously returning to his hometown in western Oklahoma. He had married his high school sweetheart, also a survivor of that massacre, and they had lived in their hometown for two years.

Miranda Denton had taken a job in the small town of Cantonville between Poteau and Talihina as junior high school principal and the computer science teacher. They had enough money from selling Logan's business and the death of Miranda's first husband that Logan did not have to work more than part time. They had lived in Leflore County for three years before Logan ran for county Sheriff. In a very close campaign, he had won by a small majority.

They had two children. Logan's daughter, Tana, from Logan's first marriage to classmate Sandy Trent was a teenager and a son, Logan Daniel from their marriage was a healthy nine-year-old.

The man walking towards him was slim, yet muscular and Scott recognized the weapon on his hip as a government style .45 auto. In a world that advocated the high capacity semi-auto handguns for police use, his choice was a throwback to the men who had cut their teeth on the venerable old 1911 war-horse in the service of the US Military. Logan had on blue jeans, a light green T-shirt tucked neat within his jeans, and a pair of hiking boots on his feet. The badge denoting him as the County Sheriff was pinned to his shirt.

"Sheriff Denton, I'm Agent Hale with the Federal Bureau of Investigation, Department of Behavioral Science. That's the department of investigation concerning serial homicide. I was notified almost as soon as you were of this tragic event."

Logan shook the man's hand and moved downwind of him. The agent's scent was one of a normal man. None of the warning signs that flagged when Logan was dealing with someone untrustworthy came up either and he decided the agent could probably be trusted. His assessment took less time than it took to shake the man's hand.

"Nice to meet you, Agent Hale." He walked over to the plastic cadaver bag that contained the dismembered body of the woman. Opening the zipper slowly, he didn't see Agent Hill cringe in expectation of a falling limb from the grisly contents of the bag. The examination was expertly done and Agent Hale remained quiet as Sheriff Denton shook his head angrily.

"Know who she is?"

Agent Hale nodded his head. "Melinda Anderson, age twenty-nine, beautiful and she had quite a bit of money from a divorce settlement. She was the owner of a glamour shop in Tulsa and had been to Smithville visiting some family that moved there recently. She drove a mint Mercedes 500 E, red and it is still missing. She was reported missing sixteen days ago."

He paused as he nodded his head towards the body. "Some of the marks on her body were done by animals, scavengers, but there are human teeth marks as well on her neck and her breasts. They may be good enough we can get a mold of this maniac's teeth and check some dental records. This guy has the same MO as a guy that's been operating in Texas most recently, New Mexico, and Louisiana, but this is the first time we've seen bite marks. I think he thought that the body would be too decomposed for any evidence to be found by the time the body was discovered."

"He raped her." It was a statement, not a question, but Agent Hale misunderstood.

"I imagine he did, but we haven't ran any tests so right now it's just hypothesis. If it is the same guy, then he did rape her."

Logan looked up at him and then back to the body. His right hand rested on the butt of the pistol and Agent Hale figured this was a natural position for a man that pulled guard in a top-secret military installation armed with a sidearm.

Looking up from the body as he zipped the body bag closed, he asked, "Where was the burial site?"

Agent Hale pointed into the woods and said, "It's in that direction. I have some people in there wrapping up the scene. The dogs disturbed it a lot, but there is rarely anything useable found after this amount of time."

Logan turned to face the man. "She was in the ground a while. I'll expect a copy of any findings and your full report on this incidence to assist in my investigation of this crime. My people will cooperate completely as long as we are kept abreast of your findings."

Hale shrugged his shoulders and said, "No problem Sheriff. It is our policy to cooperate with the local authorities when at all possible. We are in this together and we want him as badly as you do."

The Sheriff walked into the woods without commenting and Scott watched him disappear. Logan Denton looked like the type of man that it would be a smart idea to stay on his good side. He was not unfriendly, but there was an aloofness about him that marked him as a man that would be hard to get to know, to become close to.

Logan had surveyed the scene and found that the Feds were very efficient in their job. They had disturbed the crime scene very little and were buttoning up their investigation while Logan looked the area over on his own.

With the senses of the werewolf, Logan had determined that the man involved in this was a normal human, though his scent was very faint on the mutilated body of the woman; it was almost indistinguishable with the scent of the federal investigators. It would be impossible to find the perpetrator by scent alone. The scent of semen had been slightly easier to detect and the smell of it combined with the rotting inner body fluids had almost made him nauseous. With the rain that had been pouring down in this area for the past week, it was impossible to pick up the scent of the man that had committed this crime in the area of the gravesite. The scent of the investigators would mask the much fainter scent anyway.

One of the agents had lingered for a few seconds while Logan finished up. The man was not tall, though lanky, his face very serious as though humor would be an affront to his personality, he was somewhere around five feet, ten inches in height and around thirty-five years of age. Logan looked up expectantly at the agent.

Taking the look as a cue to speak, the man said, "Name is Phill Sturgis. The man dismembered the body somewhere other than here and then carried it to this point for burial. He carried the body parts in a plastic trash sack and placed it in the grave too. We have sent it to the lab for any type of data we might get from it, though I doubt that it's much. That's about all we could tell here."

Logan nodded his head as though he was in thought before speaking. "Thanks. I appreciate the information, Agent Sturgis."

The man nodded his head, leaving to join his companions. Logan waited until the man disappeared, kneeling to the ground where the body had been buried. He inhaled deeply and the scent of rotting death almost overpowered him, but he knew there might still be a clue here. Moving over to the other side of the shallow grave, he inhaled again as he heard the footsteps coming through the woods. He stood up straight, walking to a post oak tree and sat down beside it as Agent Hale approached him.

"Find anything my men missed?"

He broke a dead twig between his fingers before answering. "No I didn't. Your people have covered everything that I could think of." He looked directly at the federal agent for a second. "That is as long as we're given all the information you've uncovered."

Scott nodded his head. "I've already agreed to that once Sheriff. I won't try to keep anything from you. Remember that it was your people who asked us to assist. In fact, I would be delighted if you could shed some insight into this after you receive our report. Our leads are not overly strong and we've been aware of this particular killer's activity for well over a year."

"How many people has he killed?"

"We have seven murders over a three year period with bodies scattered throughout New Mexico, Louisiana and south Texas in the rural areas with the same MO before he headed north. We believe we have discovered less than half of the people he has actually killed. There was a young black girl's body found outside of Texarkanna, Arkansas and the disappearance of another girl - white this time - on the Texas side. Both occurred within a couple of days of each other. The one body that was recovered seemed to be the work of the same man that killed a waitress near Shreveport two and a half weeks prior. We believe he started killing over five years ago."

The agent pulled his jacket off revealing a white shirt and a shoulder-holstered Combat Commander in .45 caliber. Logan decided that Agent Hale must be smarter than most agents. He carried a gun that had a good track record for stopping a man instead of those snub-nosed .38's that he had seen some of the spooks carry when he had associated with them in the Special Forces and he seemed to have the natural aversion to the plastic handguns many of the police forces were issuing nowadays.

Scott loosened his tie and said, "I don't know if he will strike here again or if he's already moved on. He kills more in one area than he does in another with no apparent reason. It may simply be opportunity. Hell if I know, but I intend to catch the son-of-a-bitch!"

"Understand the feeling." Logan stood and brushed off his pants. "If you need a place to make or take some calls, my office is free for your use. I suppose that you fellows still ban the use of cell phones for certain types of communications?"

Smiling, Hale nodded his head. "Our phones are secure nowadays, Sheriff. I appreciate the offer though. You're used to security details where encryption is necessary. We don't need it in our department and if we did, we have cells that do that."

Logan shrugged as they started back to their vehicles.

"This man seems to be highly intelligent. It was only the purest chance that the body of the girl was found so quickly. A couple more weeks in this weather and there wouldn't have been anything left of her remains except the skeleton."

"He is very smart in maniacal sense, though a lot of serial killers do possess a higher than average I.Q. Ted Bundy had an I.Q. of 150."

"Read that somewhere myself." They reached the vehicles and Logan motioned for the only one of his deputies that was still at the scene. The serious, lanky man walked over to the Sheriff, glancing at the FBI agent with a look that carried little concern. Obviously, the federal agent didn't impress this man.

"Bill, hire out a couple of boats to drag the Poteau for a mile to a mile and a half down river from the road stop south of Heavener. There was a report filed in the office two weeks ago about tire tracks leading into the river and flood waters may have carried the car down the river."

Bill Jackson nodded his head. He was a no-nonsense man of forty-three that had been a county deputy for twelve of the fourteen years he had lived in Leflore county. Before that he had been a city policeman in Miami, Oklahoma and he had a good solid record. Logan had decided he was going to name Bill as his assistant Sheriff, but was waiting for the retirement of the man that currently filled the position. This was the man that had called the FBI for help. Logan had not fired a single deputy when he took the job as Sheriff, but he had made it clear as to how his policies would be obeyed. One man had quit, but most of the men liked the man that had filled the position of their previous boss.

Logan had managed to wrangle lightweight body armor and budgeted a training schedule in which every officer under him, including himself, had to qualify with a high enough score at the pistol range before he would be allowed for fieldwork. Men that had been working for six to eight years found themselves scheduled for schooling that would help them in their investigations as well as training that might someday save their lives. His men were impressed when their Sheriff turned out for a charity function for the police that resulted in a standard issue Ruger Mini-Thirty in 7.62 X 39 mm in each car or truck. The men also qualified with this weapon on a monthly basis.

They heard that Logan had been chewed out several times for almost exceeding or even slightly exceeding his monthly budget. The county commissioners were constantly on his back about whether the things he asked for were necessary. He took the ass chewing with the veneer of a career military man that had seen many of them and went ahead and did what he planned to do anyway. Logan had not been a career soldier, but that certainly wasn't held against him.

Bill and the rest of the men that he worked with respected Logan Denton because they realized he had nothing, but respect for them. Logan was a straight shooter with his men and that was exactly what Bill liked about him.

"I've got three boats standing by in case you wanted to do that. I suspected that the report might be useful in this investigation, but Ralph didn't think so."

A frown briefly crossed Logan's face at the mention of the assistant Sheriff. The man had obtained his position by being kin to one of the previous county commissioners. Logan hated to fire a man, but the inefficient manner in which Ralph did his job could not be tolerated much longer without some type of action being taken.

"I'll have a talk with Ralph. Get those boats on the water. Make that search two miles." He glanced back at the FBI agent. "Do you want one of your people with them?"

Scott shook his head. "No. I believe your people know more about that kind of work than the people I have with me. If you think you need some assistance, I'll be glad to make a call or two."

"Appreciate it, but we'll pass for now."

Bill nodded his head and walked back to his vehicle. Logan watched as the car disappeared. Turning back to his truck, he stopped as the FBI agent began to speak.

"Sheriff Denton?"

Scott was walking closer to Logan and the older man stood impassively.

Scott continued, "I was wondering if you could suggest a good motel for my people and me to stay in for a couple of days?"

Logan nodded. "There's several good motels in Poteau that should meet your needs. We don't have any deluxe accommodations, but they will be utilitarian. It's not that big a town but it is growing."

Nodding in understanding, Agent Hale yawned. "I haven't had any sleep in over twenty-four hours and damned little to eat. It'll be several hours at the earliest, a couple of days at the latest before the initial analysis will be completed on what evidence we've found and I think I'll use that time to get some rest."

"Don't blame you. I'm going to swing by the courthouse in Poteau and check some records after I eat some lunch at home. I'm still officially on vacation for a couple of days, but I'm going to take an active hand in this investigation so I guess it has been cut short." He looked up at Agent Hale. "Your welcome to come to the house and eat lunch with me. I'd like some more information on the MO of this killer."

"That would be fine and I appreciate it." He rubbed his neck as he watched his people close everything up to leave the area. It had been hard to believe that the press had not sniffed out the story yet.

Scott walked over to the lanky man that had spoken to Logan earlier and spoke with him for a few seconds. Then he walked back to Logan's truck.

"Be alright if I ride with you?"

Logan flipped the power locks on the door and the passenger side door lock flipped up. The Agent stepped inside the cab of the truck and settled into the seat. The Sheriff said wryly, "Latch your seatbelt Agent Hale. It's the law in Oklahoma and I'd hate to have to ticket you in my own vehicle."

Smiling, the agent belted himself in place as the four-wheel drive followed the dirt road out to the highway.

Miranda "Randy" Denton looked out the window to check on her son as he played in the back yard in a large wooden tree house in a huge red oak at the edge of their lawn. The boy's father had built it the first month they had lived at the house.

She was cutting up a yellow onion under the running water faucet to prevent it from causing her eyes to water. Logan loved onions and she intended to put some in the tuna salad she had made for his lunch. Big red slices of garden fresh tomato and green leaves of lettuce already adorned a plate. The onion would join the tuna and the pickle already mixed together in a bowl.

She dried her hands off on her apron. A noise upstairs let her know that her daughter was up from her nap. Tana wasn't really Miranda's daughter, but she was as close to the girl as her biological mother and Tana had called her mom since Logan and her had married. Tana had caught a cold on the last day of their trip and had felt miserable this morning when they arrived at the Ft. Smith, Arkansas airport. She hadn't even fussed when Miranda had told her to take the nap.

The pretty, sandy-blonde topped head of the teenager appeared at the door. The girl looked a lot like her mother and whatever else Sandy Trent had been in the past, she had been a beautiful girl and was even now a very beautiful woman. Her daughter would have much the same looks, though her personality was more her dad's. Tana's eyes were puffy and a little red from the congestion in her head, but she looked somewhat perkier than what she had looked before the nap.

"Dad back yet?"

"No, but he should be here for lunch in a few minutes. How are you feeling?"

"Better," she replied as she stepped up to the bar that came out from the wall. Pulling one of the oak stools out, she sat down and put her chin in her hands.

Miranda had been working as she talked and had added all of her ingredients together except for the mayonnaise. Getting the jar out of the refrigerator, she dipped out an eye-calculated amount and plopped it into the bowl. She added a little more for good measure and then stirred it up. Satisfied with the consistency of the tuna salad, she set it on the bar beside the condiments plate.

Tana smiled as she watched her stepmother work. She loved Randy, that's what her dad called Miranda, and felt as if she had been as much of a mother as her real mom had ever been. It had never bothered Tana that her father had married Randy and she understood why he loved her.

Randy was a beautiful woman and lacked one inch being six feet tall. Dressed in a pair of faded Levi's and a bright blue T-shirt, she didn't look near as professional as she could when she wanted. Dark brown hair in a ponytail draped her shoulders and gave her a youthful appearance that belied her age. Her eyes were a deep green that flashed emerald when she was angered. Her slender, yet well-rounded body was in excellent shape as she and Logan jogged two miles each weekday morning. Tana knew Logan enjoyed this ritual with his wife in the mornings.

Tana also knew that Randy had been in love with her father as far back as high school. Randy had freely told her that several times as Tana had grown older and started asking questions of that nature. Randy had also told her that Logan and her had been friends all through school from grade school. Only during the life and death struggle with the rogue werewolf cult in Idaho did they express their love to each other.

Tana knew the true story of most of what happened in the mountains. At eighteen years of age, she had known the actual events for the last five years. She knew her father was a werewolf. It didn't bother her any, he was a good dad and that was what counted. Besides, he had not chosen to become a werewolf. Her Aunt Vivian, a beautiful blond woman and werewolf that had befriended her dad and later married her Uncle Corrie, had been forced to give him the power of the wolf or watch him die. She had chosen to make him a wolf and for that Tana has been very thankful.

It had been a good thing that she had done it because only in the form of a wolf was he able to save Randy from death by the cult leader, a werewolf named Madden. In a battle that had resulted in the death of the cult leader, Logan had almost doomed himself to a life as a monster caught in the unforgiving grip of lycanthropy as he had forced the change early to be able to save Randy. It was four years of relentlessly working to force the change to a human before he was finally successful. He had found Randy in their hometown with his son that he had not been aware of. The child was the result of a single lovemaking session in the mountains. Logan and Randy were married before the next Christmas.

Randy had chosen to become a werewolf, as Corrie had done after marrying Vivian. The power of the wolf bestowed upon those who received it a near-immortality. Aging decreased to a snail's pace and sickness was nearly unknown. A limb removed from the body would be regenerated during the change from man to man-beast. The microbes that created the stimulus to change a man into a wolf wanted a perfect host.

There was only two ways to kill a werewolf: silver and decapitation. Silver acted as a deadly kind of poison when it entered the blood stream and decapitation separated the brain from the body. Any other wound would heal in seconds while in the form of the man-beast, minutes in the form of a wolf, and minutes to hours in a human. Internal organs always repaired themselves first. A devastating injury to the brain, as from a close shotgun blast, could also kill a werewolf as the survivors of the Idaho massacre could attest to.

The two forms of the werewolf are the man-beast or first form and the wolf or the second form. Tana had only seen her dad in the second form twice. She had never seen him in the first form or Randy in either form. The third form or host form was, of course, human.

Randy had the table set and smiled at Tana from the dining room as she heard the familiar sound of the four-wheel drive truck pulling into the circle drive in front of their home. Looking out the window, she saw that there were two men in the truck. Removing her apron, she tossed it on the counter while walking to the front door to greet her husband and their guest.

The truck door opened and the tall, handsome man that was her husband stepped out. She watched as he removed his pistol and belt, setting them inside the truck before shutting the door. The second man removed a shoulder-holster and left it inside the vehicle as well. Randy approved when she saw Logan hit the button to secure the locks. He and the man in the suit were talking quietly as they headed for the door.

Scott was impressed with the extra large log cabin-style, two-story home and the beautiful landscaped yard with the flowers in the different flowerbeds. It looked like more than what a county Sheriff could afford, but then he remembered that the couple had quite a sum to begin with in their marriage. There was a bicycle in front of the garage that had to belong to Logan's son. Scott remembered that the man's daughter was older.

Logan looked up, he scented him almost as soon as he heard the sounds of his son coming around the corner of the house. The dark-haired nine year-old jogged up to him. He looked at the man with his father, being especially attentive to the man's wrists. It was obvious he was looking for handcuffs.

"Hey Dad! Did ya' catch the bad guy?"

Scott grinned at the confidence in the voice of Logan's son. It had been amusing that the boy thought his father might have brought the criminal home for lunch with him.

"Yeah and I brought him home to eat lunch with us," Logan said with an amused look on his face.

"No way!!" Logan Daniel exclaimed. "You haven't caught him yet have you?"

"Not yet Dan-o, but I will."

That made the boy grin as he fell in behind the two men for the lunch that he knew was waiting.

Logan opened the door for Scott and a very tall and beautiful woman met him. Scott decided the woman wasn't exactly in the runway model class, but she had a dignity about her that radiated from within. She, like her husband, looked to be in her late twenties or early thirties as opposed to being in her late thirties.

He felt Logan steps in behind him.

"Agent Scott Hale, this is my wife Miranda and," he noticed his daughter step in behind Miranda, "behind her is my daughter Tana. You've already met Logan Daniel."

Glancing at the grinning nine-year-old beside him, Scott had to smile back. He looked up at Logan's wife and held out his hand.

"I'm pleased to meet you Mrs. Denton, Tana."

Her smile was warm and genuine. "Please, call me Miranda." Looking back at her husband expectantly, it served to cue him to continue the introduction.

"Agent Hale is with the Federal Bureau of Investigation and is looking into this case too. I invited him to lunch."

Miranda smiled. "Well Lord knows I've made enough! Y'all wash up. The table is already ready." Gesturing to her son's face, she added, "And wash your face."

Logan waited until everyone had finished before he washed his hands. Logan Daniel had sounded like a motor boat when he ran the wash cloth over his mouth and Logan ended up helping him get his face clean enough to pass his mother's inspection. He and Scott walked together to the table.

The FBI agent removed his jacket before sitting at the table. He sighed audibly as the comfortable cushions in the oak-framed chair seemed to absorb some of his fatigue. Watching as Miranda moved to take her place after having set dining ware at his seat, he couldn't help, but admire the calm beauty of the woman. In his opinion, Logan Denton had picked himself a hell of a good-looking woman.

He took the clear glass bowl of tuna salad as it was passed around the table, careful to keep the large plastic spoon away from his hands where he could knock it out of the bowl before he served himself. After he had fixed his plate, he took a drink of the tea in his glass. It was good.

Scott had not paid any attention when he met her previously, but now he noticed that Logan's daughter Tana was a very beautiful young girl. She looked older and prettier than the sixteen or eighteen years of age that she had to be. That she would be even a more beautiful woman was certain.

Logan asked, "How long have you been with the FBI, Scott?"

They had gotten on a first name basis while driving over from the burial site of the deceased woman.

"A little over six years. I was a Navy SEAL for three years before that."

He noticed Logan's daughter staring at him and he realized the girl knew what a SEAL was.

"SEAL huh? That's pretty impressive. SEAL training was one of the hardest P.T.'s that could be accomplished," Logan said as he took a bite of his tuna salad sandwich.

Nodding his head, Scott ventured a question of his own in the form of a statement. "I understand you were in a Special Forces unit yourself."

Logan grinned. "I imagine they have quite a file built up on me by now so you probably know me better than I do."

Agent Hale blushed and Miranda changed the subject.

"Do you like your meal, Mr. Hale?"

"Yes ma'am. It's really good. I guess I'm a little tired and it's affecting my appetite and please, call me Scott. "

Randy said, "Sure Scott, I understand. If you're tired, there is an extra bedroom down the hall we use for guests. You're welcome to lie down and take a nap."

"No thank you, Mrs. . . . uh, Miranda. I'll ride into town with your husband after we finish with the meal."

Logan glanced at his watch. "I was going to go over some files of a murder that was never solved. It occurred several years back. In fact, it was two murders. The guy killed two young boys and I know there isn't any connection, but I'd like to check it against your data."

Nodding his head, Scott said, "That's fine, but this guy hasn't killed, but one man that we know about and it was determined that the man walked up on the perp while he was dismembering the victim. The killer cleaved the man's skull with an axe."

A muffled cough from Miranda's side of the table caught Agent Hale's attention and he noticed the wide-eyed stare of Logan's son. He looked sheepishly at Miranda and said, "I'm sorry. That isn't exactly a good dinner topic."

Logan stood after wiping his mouth. He picked up his tea glass and refilled it.

"We can speak in the den when your finished Scott." Glancing at his son, he continued, "You need to play outside son while Agent Hale and I discuss some business."

The request didn't faze the boy as he continued to eat.

"Ok Dad."

Scott stood and followed Logan into the back room.

The room was open with a fireplace in one end that had a wood-burning insert nestled inside. Two plush recliners and a large matching sofa faced a big screen television and a large picture window that revealed the beautiful summer green of the forest and the mountain backdrop. The entire floor was carpeted except for a semi-circle in front of the stove that was carefully laid Oklahoma flagstone that offset the stone hearth and mantle.

Scott sat down in the recliner opposite of Logan.

Logan was looking out the window at the mountainside. He took a long drink of the tea.

"Do you think the guy will kill in this vicinity again, Scott?"

"Don't know. The killings seemed to be becoming more frequent as though he is dipping further and further into the cesspool of insanity. That supposition could be wrong, but the viciousness of his attacks is becoming more intense. We are authorized to hang around a few days at my discretion because he had struck in one place more than once enough to make me believe he will do it again."

Logan sat still, contemplating what he might do to find out if the killer was still in his county. All he was doing was drawing blanks. The light sound of dishes clinking in the background as Miranda cleaned up the mess from lunch was seemingly ignored as Logan sat quietly.

Suddenly, he looked over at the FBI agent. "When the bulletin went out that the woman was missing, a dog was mentioned. I think it was a French Poodle. Did your people find the remains of a poodle?"

Scott frowned. "I didn't know anything about a damned poodle!" Calmer, he added, "It might be that the dog is with the car or he might have kept it. Trouble is that there isn't any way of knowing how many people are traveling the roads with poodles in their vehicles."

"Hell, it wasn't going to help anything. I was just curious." He sipped at the tea again.

Miranda walked inside. "Do you guys mind if I sit in on the conversation?"

Logan looked at Scott and the young agent shook his head that he didn't mind. He figured Logan told his wife what he found anyway. Besides, he liked to look at a good-looking woman and wanted to see if Miranda was as sharp as she was beautiful. He was breaking a few protocols, but they were minor compared to the advantage of winning this man's trust.

The talk drifted on the subject of the killer and his methods for killing and dismembering the victims' bodies. Scott was surprised that Miranda's stomach wasn't churning at the descriptions of some of the bodies he described. She took the news as well as a veteran agent or police officer. Scott could never know of the horrors Randy had seen during the massacre in the mountains in Idaho.

"Hell Scott, you might as well take a nap. Any information that turns up will come through the wire to the police station. I could use one myself. Couldn't sleep on the plane and I didn't get any sleep last night while I was trying to arrange a flight. Nap might help me think a lot straighter."

"I shouldn't." He could see this bonding was making quite an inroad to Logan's trust and decided that it was more important to gain that trust than it was to follow normal procedures. Scott nodded in agreement. "You've talked me into it. Mind pointing out the guest room?"

Randy smiled as she said, "Follow me." She took Scott to the guest bedroom as Logan climbed the stairs to the bedroom he shared with his wife. Stripping to his underwear, he stepped into bathroom and set the temperature of the water in the shower. Removing his underwear, he showered off quickly to remove the sweat from the flight off of his body.

He had not taken time to do that before checking on the crime that had occurred.

Drying off, he wrapped the towel around his waist and then turned on the ceiling fan above his bed. He lay down on the bed as the light breeze from the fan cooled his damp skin. The towel was across his lap when his wife walked in the room.

She smiled at Logan and said, "He went to sleep when his head hit the pillow. I'm surprised you're still awake."

"Too damn geared up about this murder I guess. I'll have to lay here until I relax."

His eyes closed and he didn't see the devilish grin on Randy's face as she lay on the bed beside him. He jumped slightly as he felt her lips in his stomach and then the towel was thrown to the floor.

Randy said softly, "I think I know a way to relax you."

Logan grunted as he felt her lips kissing a hot trail down his stomach. It turned out that she was right, she did know a way to help him relax.

Scott was asleep, but his mind couldn't stop thinking about the mutilated body in the body bag or the way the slender, tanned leg had fallen from within. He slept, but there was little rest.

He could see the killer killing women just ahead of him, always slightly out of reach. The man would laugh at him as he killed the women slowly and each time Scott would finally get close, the man disappeared into a wisp of gray smoke.

Logan met Scott downstairs a little over two hours later. He was dressed in his uniform and only lacked his gunbelt from being fully equipped. The two men left together and Logan belted on his gun at the truck. The drive was twenty minutes from the Poteau courthouse.

The scenery was beautiful and Scott commented on it.

"Yeah, it is beautiful here. One of the problems we are aggressively attacking that doesn't seem that threatening is litter. If a fire gets away and burns the side of the road, the ditch sparkles with all of the different bottles that have been tossed out of cars. The plastic bottles melt into a pile of gel that remains for years. We have taken a firm stance against littering and so far, the majority of the county has been supportive of our actions."

Scott nodded his head in agreement. "I'm from the northwest and you don't see the litter up there like you do down here. I mean it isn't just Oklahoma, but Arkansas, East Texas, and Louisiana are the same damned way."

Logan nodded as he noticed Scott look at the steep hill at the edge of Poteau. A road sign named it as Cavanaugh, the world's highest hill. Scott really studied the area as they entered Poteau. The small town looked peaceful and even had a small junior college on the south side, but somewhere a killer could lurk within that disarming setting and it could be deadly for another victim.

The courthouse was a large older building that housed many of the county offices including the Sheriff's office. Logan parked the truck behind the building and then Scott joined him as he entered the building. A short flight of stairs and a room at the end of the hall marked the Sheriff's office.

They went inside and Logan saw that Ralph was out of his office. He went to his desk and perused through the folders on his desk for anything that might pertain to the case. The search was futile as he had half expected. Then he noticed a message on his desk to call the Sheriff in Haskell County. A girl was missing from Stigler, the Haskell county seat, for over forty-eight hours now.

He picked up the phone and called the number from memory. A secretary answered and Logan asked to speak to someone about the missing girl.

The woman asked to put him on hold and Logan agreed. He glanced at the FBI agent as the man used a phone on the assistant Sheriff's desk. Logan sat down in his chair as a deep voice on the other end spoke.

"Hello, this is deputy Hank Webb. Who is calling?"

"Hello deputy Webb, this is Sheriff Denton in Leflore County. I received a call from the Sheriff's office that there is a girl missing in Stigler. What is the status of that bulletin?"

"We found her already, Sheriff. She ran off with some kid from over at Porum. They found them two or three miles north of Checotah on their way to Oklahoma City. "

Logan was relieved that the girl had not fallen victim to the madman.

"Thanks a lot deputy. I was insuring that the girl had not fallen victim to the serial killer that killed the woman whose body was found here last night."

"No, thank God. We're having enough trouble over here with the feuding that is going on in the eastern part of the county. We don't need a damned serial killer stalking people over here too."

Logan thanked the man again as he hung up the phone. Unless Bill and his people in the boats scouring the river came up with something, it looked that they had shot their wad for the day.

He looked up as Scott entered the small-enclosed area that separated Logan's desk from those of his men's.

"Got an APB in Dallas for a missing woman about the same time this lady here was reported missing. She was seen leaving a nightclub with a man and no one has seen her since. She was an executive for a small computer firm in Plano. As usual, there were several different descriptions of the man. Nothing solid to go on that he's even the same guy, but I'm betting that he struck there before he did here. "

"I worked out of Ft. Worth for a while and I know there are several missing person reports filed there on a daily basis, same as Dallas. What makes you think that your man took this woman?"

The FBI agent swallowed hard and looked a little green as he answered. "They found a finger in an empty house in Denison, north of Dallas. There was a lot of blood and the finger had a ring on it. The woman's daughter and ex-husband identified it as a Christmas present they had bought for her two years ago. We believe the woman was dismembered in that house."

Logan's face was grim. "Damn!" He turned in the swivel chair and looked at the wall for a second before turning back around slowly. His face was hard and the eyes flamed with the anger he was feeling.

Scott said dejectedly, "We've found out everything we're going to find out today. I'm going to go to the motel and discuss with my people what data we have on this murder and how it correlates with the data from the previous murders. I'll get back with you in the morning."

"Need a ride?"

"No," Scott answered. "I called one of my men to pick me up. He should be here in a few minutes."

Logan held out his hand as he stood. "Thanks Scott. I'd like to catch this guy, but I also hope to God he's way to hell and gone out of my county too."

"I understand the feeling, Logan, I really do, but someone has to catch him and that means that someone is going to have to provide the bait."

The young agent walked out the door and Logan scratched at the side of his nose. He didn't want anyone in his county acting as bait. Sitting back down he looked at the paper work in front of him.

"Hell with it," he muttered as he picked up his hat and truck keys. He figured he could be more help at the river. Besides, he wanted to see if Bill had found anything though he knew the man would be contacting him the instant he did find something.

The drive to the river didn't take very long and when Logan arrived at the area that the men would have launched their boats, it was deserted except for the vehicles and boat trailers hitched behind.

He got out of his truck and walked around for a few minutes. This wasn't the first murder case he had investigated in the county, but the other one had been fairly simple. A motive had been very evident and the woman confessed to the crime when she was questioned. It had been a crime of revenge and Logan had actually felt sorry for the woman. She had murdered a man that had been beating her for years. The jury had given her ten years for manslaughter.

Logan felt like the woman should have gotten a medal, but his job was to enforce the law and apprehend criminals. He didn't make the judgements as to the punishment for the crime.

The sound of a boat came from up the river and Logan walked down to the launch ramp. Bill was in the front of the boat and leaped to the shore as the boat neared the bank. He trotted up to Logan.

"We found it Sheriff. It was against the bank less than a quarter mile down the river. The thing got caught up in a big brush pile. First place we checked. It's steep right there and we'll play hell getting the thing out of there. It may take a day or two. It's under about seven feet of water."

"Get the necessary people and equipment, Bill. I'm putting you in charge. If Ralph says anything to you tell him to talk to me. Let me know when you get it out of the water. I'll contact Agent Hale, probably swing by his motel on the way home. Take the car to the impound lot if you get it out tonight by some miracle and we'll get a crew out of Tulsa or Dallas to go through it in conjunction with the FBI. I'll be in charge of that."

"Sure thing Sheriff. Will you be at home?"

"More than likely. I'll have my pager on."

Logan turned back to his vehicle. He knew that he couldn't have left the job in the hands of a more capable individual. Bill wouldn't let Ralph run over him with the orders that Logan gave him. Ralph wouldn't push Bill knowing that he was following Logan's orders. The man simply wasn't that brave.

Bill turned back to the man that had just tied up the boat. The man asked, "The Sheriff come out to check on our progress, Bill?"

Bill nodded. "The man is very conscientious about his responsibilities and politics worries him less than any man I've ever seen. I like working for him."

Logan got home and parked the truck outside the garage. Randy had changed into a pair of cut-off blue Jean shorts and a sleeveless T-shirt for working out in the yard. A pair of sandals was on her feet and she had donned a baseball cap to shade her eyes. Logan smiled when he saw that.

It reminded him of all the times she had wore a cap when they were friends in high school. She could be as rugged as any boy that she was a friend with or as feminine as the most cultured lady. She had been a fine companion and Logan often kicked himself that he didn't see how much she loved him even way back then because now he realized he had always been in love with her. He just hadn't known it.

She stood, her arms and legs streaked with dirt from the flowerbeds. An errant weed stood little chance of surviving more than a few days in the closely scrutinized flowerbeds of Miranda Denton. She was very meticulous about the way her yard looked and Logan was proud of her for it. Sure, it meant he worked a lot of Saturdays helping her in the yard, but it was an enjoyable activity.

Walking up to her, he kissed her lightly on the lips. At five feet, eleven inches, she was tall enough that Logan didn't have to stoop much. His six feet, four inch frame wasn't that much taller than his wife's height.

"Anything new sweetheart?"

Logan nodded as he put his arm around her waist while they walked to the house. "Bill Jackson located the car in the Poteau River. He's supposed to call me when he gets it out of the river. It probably won't happen until tomorrow in the morning sometime."

He looked around the yard and asked, "Where's the kids? I can't believe they're in the house on a beautiful day like today. "

Miranda smiled. "They're not in the house. Tana wanted to go into Poteau and see some friends. Logan was supposed to go to a friend's overnight birthday party, but was going to miss it because we were going to be in Idaho. Since we got back early, he figured . . ."

" . . . . that he might as well get to go to the party," Logan finished as they neared the door.

"Logan Daniel won't be back until tomorrow and Tana said she wouldn't be back until around nine tonight. I thought we might climb into that big walk-in bathtub of ours while we have some privacy. I'll give you a massage that'll blow your mind!"

Logan opened the door for his wife and stepped in behind her, patting her firm derriere.

"That sounds like a good idea, Mrs. Denton."

Randy smiled. She knew his weaknesses.

CHAPTER TWO

Randy opened her eyes and had to wipe the sleep from them before they would focus in the pallid darkness of her bedroom. Her hand had felt the side of the bed her husband slept on and it was empty, the cover sheet cool to the touch. She sat up in bed, the sheet falling to her slender waist revealing her pert, naked breasts and flat stomach in the pale moonlight that lightly illuminated the bedroom.

A dark shadow stood in front of the big window and she quietly pulled the sheets from her legs. Retrieving a short silk robe from the armchair beside her bed, she draped it around her nakedness, leaving the front open, the string hanging down on each side. She padded softly across the room to stand behind her husband. Her arms went around his waist and she nuzzled him softly at the top of his shoulder as he looked across the backyard to the darkness that made up the mountain in the distance.

He placed his hands on her hands as they interlocked fingers across his abdomen. She could feel the skin of his buttocks against the finely muscled flesh of her flat, lower stomach that was exposed in front because of the open robe. The scent of him was a mixture of soap and a musky odor that was all his own. The odor was not at all offensive and in fact, it excited small butterflies of lust in the pit of her stomach for the man that she loved.

"I love you Logan," she said softly as she held him, the fingers of her right hand tracing small circles across the tight muscles of his stomach.

"I love you too, Randy Denton." His voice was uncharacteristically softer than normal, almost as though speaking was an afterthought.

"Thinking about the investigation?" She touched his back with her mouth again as she held him.

"No. Yes . . . . in a way I guess I am. I was thinking about James River."

Randy pulled away sharply from Logan in surprise, her voice louder than she intended as she said incredulously, "River! Why are you thinking about him?"

Logan shrugged as he turned from the window to look at the astonished features of his wife.

"I guess it has to do with the fact that he was a serial killer and the only one I've had the misfortune to know personally. I was trying to use what I know of River to figure out what this guy might do next, but they seem too different. Their MO isn't the same."

No longer disturbed by the mention of the killer that had guided them into the mountains of Idaho, Randy became intrigued by Logan's thoughts.

"In what ways?"

She watched his tall, naked body as he crossed to the armchair to sit beside the bed. There was no wasted motion, his limbs and movements graceful.

"James found his victims in secluded areas. He preferred hikers, campers, and even hitchhikers. This man is different. He seems to select his victims from public areas prior to an attack, though I honestly believe that the woman whose body we found in our county was strictly a victim of opportunity. I read some of the files that Scott gave me on previous murders that fits the same MO as this guy."

Randy noticed the papers lying on the table beside the small lamp that normally lit the area of the table for reading. She had not noticed them before and realized Logan had been awake for some time. She stopped the giggle that would have been out of place as she thought about him studying those papers so intently while sitting naked as a jaybird. The expression on Logan's face did not lend itself to humor.

"The hell of it is the murders have become more and more frequent. The age of the victims run the gamut from thirteen to thirty-seven years of age, white or black not being a factor at all. All of the ladies were pretty and so far not a single survivor of one of his attacks has escaped. The man is careful, too careful to allow any mistakes to catch him easy. At least that is true for now."

Randy knew her husband wanted this man. She asked quietly, "Is he a werewolf?"

"No. I couldn't smell the scent of a wolf on the body of the woman and it would have been there if he was a werewolf."

"You can't possibly catch every criminal in the world, sweetheart."

Logan's eyebrows came together in irritation as his wife stepped up to kneel in front of him, placing her hands on his chest and he was about to say something that he would have regretted later when she began to speak again.

"I know you want to catch this man before he kills again," she said, her voice not patronizing, but holding a note of understanding. "I know you want to stop every murder you can before it happens, but only God could do that, honey. You're beating yourself up for things that you have no control over and I hate to see you do that to yourself."

Logan ducked his head as the words of his wife penetrated the darkness of the futility he was feeling regarding the serial killer. His face had a warm smile on it when he looked her in the eyes.

"I'm lucky to have you."

She smiled back. "I know . . . . and the reverse is also true."

Her lips went to his stomach and she lightly nibbled at him, engulfing him as he moaned gutturally, Logan leaning back to enjoy what his wife was doing. The sensation was exquisite and he closed his eyes for a few minutes.

Logan stood, picked her up and carried her to the bed where he gently removed the robe from her body. His lips went to her firm breasts as they encircled the flesh of her nipples and she let out a barely audible sigh of intense pleasure. His mouth made small sucking sounds as he moved down her body to the swell of her hips and finally to the softness below.

A growl somewhere between human and something utterly unspeakable escaped his throat as he scented the secretions of her body indicating sexual arousal. She smelled inflamed with sexual desire and he shivered as he nuzzled her softness, lapping at the heat of her passion.

Their lovemaking was a combination of fire and ice. They had been together for several years now and they knew each other well, knew what the other preferred and what heightened their passion when making love.

The distant sounds of the late night were soon joined harmoniously by the faint sounds of two lovers enjoying each other.

He looked at the gallows to the side of the courthouse. He had already read the story of Rufus Buck and several others that had died on the gallows of "Hanging Judge" Isaac Parker of Ft. Smith and Indian Territory. It had been interesting. Justice was swift back then and while man had progressed so much in the last one hundred and twenty years, justice, sadly, had not.

The exhibits at the old Fort Museum had been interesting as well. Several women in summer short sets had been touring at the same time that he had, but the hunger had abated for a while. He was attracted to some of the women that he saw inside of the museum, but didn't feel the need to watch them die or see them grovel in fear as he held their life in his hands.

The last woman he had killed had been different. He had never bitten a woman when he molested her, never sank his teeth into their flesh, but an overpowering urge while he was on top of her had caused him to bite her on the shoulder. The salty taste of her warm blood mixed with the pure terror in her eyes had put him on a power high unlike anything he had ever experienced. It had possessed him to bite her all over, each time taking the time to taste the blood as it dripped from the wounds. The high had lasted for three days before he had came down from it.

The woman at the park had been one of the prettiest of his victims. Her smooth, unblemished skin attested to her purity and he had delighted in her death. She had been a sweet and pure sacrifice for the hunger that lived inside of him. That was why the hunger was not calling as quickly as it had done with the woman it had consumed in Texas.

The gun inside his belt was well hidden by the tail of the long shirt, but he was often reminded of it as he moved through the innocent maze of humanity. The innocent lambs were not aware of the great tiger in their midst.

His eyes touched the smooth legs of a girl that was in her early teens. The tight shorts hinted at the sweetness of the forbidden area between her legs and for the first time in over a week he felt the hunger stir. Not much, just enough to let him know that it was there, inside of him, watching everything that he was seeing, aware of everything he was doing. It let him know that it liked the girl too. Young girls seemed to be the favorite choice of the hunger.

The girl wore a ponytail and a white and purple shirt that matched the white shorts. Her breasts were budding nicely for her age and she would be a doll when she got more mature. She moved to the side and he found it extremely hard to remove his eyes from her pert, young buttocks. His tongue touched his lips and nervously, he moved on to where he could no longer see her.

His right hand went to his pocket and he felt the knife inside as he came to a halt. A woman in front of him, holding a baby, was stopped while viewing the contents of a display case. She was short, not more than five feet tall, but well proportioned. The loose shorts swelled at hips that were deliciously female and his breathing quickened as the hunger stirred again.

He watched, unable to remove his eyes as the child the woman was holding dropped its pacifier to the ground. The man almost gasped as he detected the sheen of white satin panties as the woman's shorts billowed at the legs when she bent to the floor to retrieve the baby's pacifier. The hunger throbbed once harder and he felt a sexual stirring begin as the power inside him started to slowly increase in intensity with each soul-wrenching pulse. It was like it was telling him that together they were invincible.

He hurried out of the building to the warm, humid air outside. The light breeze caressed his face as the throbbing dissipated with each step he took back to where he had parked the car. The Corsica's keys were deep inside his pocket and he had to dig for them for a few seconds.

Opening the door, he quickly started the engine and felt the coolness of the air conditioner blower as it washed across his face. The hunger was silent and the man felt like he would be able to breathe again. He put the car in gear and pulled out on the road. He had intended to stop at the large mall in the city before driving back to the station, but settled on going back to the station and then to the motel. He was sure it would be full of women shopping and they would be wearing the summer clothing like the women at the museum had been wearing and there would be more of them. It wouldn't be a good thing to take any more chances of arousing the hunger so soon.

Miranda had started getting ready for town before Logan had left for work and her lips still tingled with the goodbye kiss he had given her only minutes past while she stood in front of their bathroom mirror clad only in her underwear. She had finished with what little make-up she wore and was ready to put her clothes on.

A knock on the door caused her to slip on a nightrobe from her quilt rack that usually served as a clothes rack. This nightrobe, in contrast to the one she had wore with Logan the previous night, was full length and of a flannel material. It was made for comfort, not for seduction.

She said, as she cinched the robe around her, "Come in."

Tana opened the door, the hinges creaking slightly in protest and Randy saw that she was already ready to go to town. Tana's muscular legs were tanned a deep bronze and the short set Logan's mother had bought for her was beautiful in the summer pastels that covered the cloth. The girl's body was already more mature than many women five years older than her. Her long, silky hair flowed across her shoulders in a shimmering array of auburn beauty and a hair clasp at the back that matched the shorts set off her hair quite well. The skin of her face was unblemished and Tana had been one those few teenagers that had been blessed by not having any type of acne at all.

"You must be feeling better this morning."

"I am. I guess it was the two day creeping croop and not anything serious."

Randy laughed lightly at the creeping croop remark. Tana had gotten that from her mother. Randy's mother had come to think of Tana as her grandchild too. Creeping croop denoted colds while creeping crud was what any unidentified rash was named.

"Well, I'm glad you're feeling better." She turned around to pick up her jeans from the bed when she realized Tana was still standing there as if she had something else to say.

"Is something wrong, sweetheart?"

Tana's lips tightened a little in apprehension as she moved to sit on the end of Randy's bed. That whatever she was going to say was going to make her uncomfortable was easy to see. Randy slipped the jeans on beneath the nightrobe, removing it to slip on her shirt. She was giving Tana time to get up her courage.

"Tana, I've told you that you can come to me for anything, anything at all."

"I know Mom, but this is different. I don't know how to start it."

Randy moved to sit beside her daughter. "Just say it."

Breaking the final restraint, Tana asked hesitantly, nervously, "How old were you when you made love for the first time?"

Randy took a deep breath before answering. She wasn't sure she was ready for this type of conversation. "It was about a month or two before I became engaged to Mike. I was twenty-three, almost twenty-four years old. That seems old, but I didn't find anybody that I really loved and that loved me back until then."

Tana's face was clearly puzzled. "You mean you and Dad didn't ever in high . . . . ?"

"No. No, your Dad and I were best friends, but our relationship didn't take that route. I loved your Dad very, very much and honestly, I would have made love with him if I had thought he felt the same way, but he never showed that he did. Not then."

Miranda looked at Logan and Sandy's daughter, her daughter by choice. "Why are you asking these questions, sweetheart?"

Tana started to shrug her shoulders and then stopped. She looked Randy in the eye and Randy's heart soared at the courage in this young girl's heart and the trust she had in it for her stepmother.

"Tim Kresser, my boyfriend has been pushing me to go all the way with him. He tries to touch me . . . places . . . and I tell him I'm not ready for

that yet. He always stops when I tell him to stop, but he always tries too."
She looked at Randy's hands in her lap.

"I let him touch me through my clothing some the last time we went out
and I made him stop when I thought we had went far enough. I asked him
to stop and he does stop, but he said he loves me so much that he is ready
to take the next step. Randy, I'm not sure I'm ready for that! I can't take a
step that might leave me pregnant at eighteen -- that would mean I had to
raise a baby this early in life -- and I don't think he understands that!"

Tears showed in the girl's eyes and Randy wiped them away gently with
her fingertips.

"The first time is special, Tana. I . . ."

Tana looked sick as she peered at the floor. "That is the part that really
bothers me, Randy. I'm not a virgin anymore. I let Steve Becker have sex
with me last year before school was out when Tim and I broke up for a
while."

Surprised, Randy said, "Steve Becker?! Wasn't he the boy that took
you to the prom in Spiro?"

"Yes," she said sadly. "I only dated him for a little over a month and
I didn't plan for anything to happen. I let him the night of his prom.
Someone had brought some wine and we went out to the lake afterwards.
I had never drank before and I . . . I made a huge mistake . . . I think part
of me was so mad at Tim and part of me was just confused . . . . . I knew
I didn't really love Steve. For two months afterwards I was scared to death
I was pregnant! I can't handle that thought again, Randy, even though I
do really love Tim."

"Getting pregnant is a very real danger," Randy said, searching for more
words that didn't want to come. She felt anger at the boy from Spiro, but
in Oklahoma the legal age of consent was 16 years old and the boy had
only been two years older than Tana.

"I don't want to lose him Randy. I really care about him. He cares
about me too."

Randy sat quietly for a few minutes holding the sobbing girl before she
then said in a hushed tone of voice, "Tana, you don't have to do anything
that you don't want to do. I can tell you not to have sex, but I can't keep
you from it. You are eighteen and practically an adult."

Tana watched as Randy looked at the ceiling for a moment and tears
were rolling down her cheeks as well.

"If the boy really loves you, then he will stop when you ask him to stop.
He will respect your feelings. It's always easy for a parent to say that if the
boy doesn't want to wait then he isn't worth having, but that doesn't fill
the void in your heart."

By the look on Tana's face, Randy could tell that she was slightly confused.

"I'm sorry Tana. I was rambling more than I should, but this is so hard to do because I love you so very much. It's like when I look at your blond hair sometimes and wonder where you got blond hair. There isn't much of it in your father's family or any in mine. Then I remember that you weren't actually born to me, I'm just lucky enough to have you, spend all this time with you.

"What I'm trying to say is simple. Don't allow the boy to manipulate your feelings and get you to do something that you feel is wrong. If you feel it's wrong, then it probably is. If he loves you as much as you love him, then holding you and kissing you will be more than enough. If he loves you, then he will be willing to wait until you're ready for the next step." She smiled as she took Tana's hands in her own. "Don't you be in a hurry to rush that next step either. It is a wonderful thing to share with someone you love."

"I'm not in a hurry," Tana said. " It's just when you are kind of pretty, a lot of the boys hit on you for that reason only."

Randy looked at Tana and admonished her jokingly, "Kind of pretty!! You're beautiful. You look like the best parts of your mother and father and they are both very good looking people."

The teenager felt relieved talking to Randy and she was surprised when the older woman took a firm voice. "Tana. You know how to protect yourself don't you?"

"I take pills to regulate my . . ."

"Not just birth control. You need to protect yourself from diseases. Did Steve and you use a condom?"

"No," Tana admitted, her eyes wrinkling in thought. She had not considered everything before she slept with him.

Randy sighed sadly. "I don't condone what you done, but I don't want you getting yourself hurt or sick with something that can't be cured. What do you know about Steve Becker?"

He claimed to have slept with several girls before sleeping with Tana, but that admission made her sick to her stomach. She shrugged her shoulders unconvincingly. "Not that much," she stated.

"Tim?"

Tana said, "He had one steady girl friend since he was in the eighth grade. He may have been with her, but that is it. He is a nice boy, Randy."

Randy pressed her lips together tightly. "I know he is, baby." Her green eyes were looking into Tana's eyes and she could see her husband in

the girl. "I know you are not promiscuous and what happened with Steve
Becker . . .

"Was a mistake," Tana said, finishing the statement for her.

Randy smiled weakly as she realized Tana had learned from her mistake. It would be nice if all kids learned from their mistakes. "Your daddy
and I would die if something happened to you. Make the adult decisions
like an adult, sweetheart. Consider what could happen and how it affects
everyone."

Tana smiled as she hugged Randy. Tears still glistened in her eyes. "I
love you Mom . . . and even if you aren't my mom biologically, you have
been more of a real mother to me than anyone else could be."

"I love you too Tana and thanks."

Randy felt the tears start again as she held her daughter. They cried
for a while and then laughed at each other for crying so much. Then they
repaired their make-up and went to town.

Logan was standing on the bank of the Poteau River when the car was
pulled out. Bill stood beside him, a little exasperated that it had taken two
days to get the equipment needed to break up the brush to where the car
could be retrieved. Scott had not arrived yet. He had spent the previous
day in Ft. Smith checking some files on a murder in the Jonesboro area
that might have been related. It had turned out to be an entirely different
style of murder and the day had been wasted.

The two men watched as the rental car pulled up and the tall detective
stepped out after parking beside Logan's truck. He had traded his suit
for an oversize short sleeve shirt and light slacks. His gun was in sight on
his belt, though it would have been easy to hide if the man had wanted to
do so.

Standing beside Logan, he asked, "Where did you get the team to go
over the car?"

Bill answered before Logan could speak up. "We got them out of Tulsa.
The Sheriff here actually intended to use some guys out of Dallas he was
acquainted with, but they were already tied up with another investigation
down there. I've worked with these guys out of Tulsa. They're good."

Scott nodded, his hand fumbling with the knife in his pocket. He
didn't say anything. He had already informed the Sheriff that he had
a team coming in to go over the car in conjunction with this team. The
Sheriff had readily agreed to the joint effort.

The large crane rumbled as it backed up, the massive diesel engine
revving up as it placed the car on the cleared bank. Yellow mud from the
silt the river had picked up and deposited inside, stained the interior that

was visible through the windows. Water ran from the cracks in the doors. Logan walked to the car as the other two men fell in beside him. The crane had been shut off and the silence was unnerving after the deafening roar of the large piece of machinery while it was being used.

Scott grunted as he saw that the keys were in the ignition and in the run position. Opening the door, trapped water flooded out of the opening. No fish had been trapped in the sealed confines of the car. The windows had been surprisingly intact, though one was partially down.

He retrieved the keys and motioned towards the storage compartment of the vehicle. Logan nodded and the two county officers watched as the FBI agent inserted the key in the lock and turned it until it released with an audible click. The lid came up and Logan grimaced at the sight inside.

"Well, now we know what happened to the dog," Bill said wryly as he viewed the bloated remains scattered in the car's trunk.

Logan shook his head and walked away. The sight of the dismembered dog was almost too much to take after having seen the remains of the woman only a few days earlier.

The sound of the lid closing didn't even cause Logan to falter in his steps. It hadn't happened the other day, but suddenly all the memories of the disfigured and mutilated bodies of his friends that died in the massacre so many years ago flooded him in waves. Jerica, Kent . . . . the others that had died so senselessly.

Perhaps that was what tied these murders together so much in his mind. The senselessness of it all was so similar.

Bill touched Logan lightly on the shoulder. "You alright Sheriff?"

"Yeah Bill. I'm all right. Just thinking is all."

Bill nodded his head, not quite understanding, but not disposed to push the issue. No one on the force had ever questioned Logan about what happened up north, but they all knew it haunted him sometimes. Bill was sure that something about the massacre had just slapped Logan in the face.

"Those boys from Tulsa have rented an old body shop on the east side of town to check out the car. It's the one that used to be Powell's. I'm going to stay with them until they're finished. I'll get a hold of ya' if they find something important."

"Good." Logan glanced at the FBI agent as he approached.

"I got the data from the lab work on the woman's remains. It's in a folder in the car. I wanted to hand deliver it to you personally."

"Appreciate it." He stood while the agent opened the door of the rental car and handed him a manila folder from the back seat. Logan took it and put it in his truck without even glancing at it. He wanted to study it before he started comparing insights with Agent Hale.

"You going back to the office, Logan?"

"No, I'm going to take a little drive through the Winding Stairs. It helps me to think."

Scott watched as the four wheel drive pick-up pulled on the highway. He nodded at Bill and opened the door of the Corsica and got inside. The air-conditioner blew cool air in his face as the car started. He was two miles down the road before he thought about the fact that he had not even asked what was the Winding Stairs.

Logan drove south and decided he would take a run down around Page and Big Cedar instead. He had seen an albino hawk on the stretch of highway between the two small communities a few weeks before and hoped to see it again.

He drove a few miles an hour less than the speed limit. No white hawk showed up, but he did see a large Eastern gobbler cross the road near Pipe Springs. He pulled into the small rest stop and got out. A rock piling mortared into place with a pipe that had a continuous flow of water was what gave the place its name. The parking lot was empty.

Cupping his hands under the pipe, he allowed it to fill and then washed his face off. For some reason the mutilated dog had bothered him more than the sight of the woman. It wasn't right probably, but the willful destruction of an animal that was incapable of divulging the man's identity proved that the man took immense pleasure from the pain and suffering he was inflicting upon his victims. Wanton cruelty. Maybe that was the essence that made the difference this time.

How long had he kept the woman alive? Torturing her, raping her and telling her all along that he was going to let her go? Or worse, telling her he was going to kill her?

The feeling Logan was having was not the kind of feelings that a county Sheriff was supposed to have. He didn't want to apprehend the man. He wanted to kill him. Logan knew he could not allow that feeling to influence the way he would conduct this case. With a chuckle he knew that his friend, Loren Chadley, would not hesitate in shooting the killer when and where he found him. Loren would have made a great avenging angel, but he was way too sudden for the legalities facing a lawman these days.

Climbing back in the vehicle, he turned north and started back. At the crossroads in Page, he got behind an old International pick-up. Two little dirty-faced kids rode in the back and though Logan didn't like it, he wasn't going to stop them for it. People in this part of the country had been allowing kids to ride in the back of pick-up trucks forever.

Logan couldn't believe his eyes when the man pitched a pop bottle and a candy wrapper out of his window. He turned on his light and flipped the switch to the siren for a few seconds. He could see the man looking at him through his rear view mirror and he seemed to be cussing pretty hotly as the truck slowed.

The truck came to a halt with two tires on the paved shoulder and two tires in the grass. The man got out of his vehicle to meet Logan at the back of his truck. The man was big, he outweighed Logan by at least fifty pounds. Logan hadn't even taken the precaution of removing the strap from his pistol.

"Hallo, off'cer. Can I help you with sumpin'?"

Logan looked at the big man in his dirty overalls and unshaven face. The smell of old whiskey and body odor assailed his highly sensitive nose. Glancing at the two children, he saw that they didn't look like they had eaten anything substantial in a while. A woman too young to be the mother for the kids in the back held a baby while she looked anxiously through the back window. If she had fixed herself up some, she would have been cute.

"Yes sir you can. You tossed out a pop bottle and a candy wrapper of some kind less than a quarter mile back down the road."

The man's expression was one of disbelief. "Why those must have flew out without me a knowin it. You know how things can fly out an open window of a truck when all that air gets to whirlin' around."

Logan barely contained the look of irritation. The feeling did not stem from the fact that the man was a jerk, but that Logan could tell the man was lying to him. He was putting on a dumb local yokel act to try to get out of a ticket.

"It's called littering. I would like to see your driver's license. "

The man's eyes narrowed. "What are you botherin me for? I can't help it things fly out on their own."

Logan said, "Either you can go back and pick up that trash while I watch you do it, drive to Page and dispose of it in a garbage can, or I will write you a ticket. The tickets that I've been writing for littering has ranged from seventy-five to one-thousand dollars for littering or dumping."

The man snorted in anger. "I ain't pickin' up that fuckin' bottle! There ain't no law says I got to do it! You lawboys let the power go to your head!"

"You can always go to jail," Logan commented softly.

He looked at Logan, a snarl on his face as he noticed the strap on the holstered pistol. "Ya' high and mighty lawboys thinks ya' can push us regular folks around, but we ain't goin' to put up with your bullshit! We got our rights!"

Logan wrote the ticket out and the man watched him intently before threatening him.

"Lawboy, if you tries to give me that ticket, I'm going to stick it as far up your ass as it'll go!"

Logan continued to write as the man stepped forward and swiped the book out of his hands. Logan said in a voice as cold as the Antarctic winds, "You have just assaulted a police officer. You take the ticket and I'll forget about it. You push me any further and I'll kick your ass and lock you up until the dogwoods bloom!"

"Fuck you!" The man lunged at Logan and the officer executed a near perfect judo move known as the te-guruma or handwheel throw.

Logan dropped his center of gravity by spreading and bending his legs in one fluid-like motion. He grabbed the man by his front bib with his right hand and the top of the man's thigh with his left and lifted him up by straightening his legs. He pulled the man downward with his right hand and up-ended him with the left. As the man fell, Logan pulled up sharply with his right hand and dumped the man flat on his back, the man's air leaving his lungs with a whooshing noise.

Dropping across the man, Logan punched him hard to the jaw to stun him, then hooked an arm under the man's shoulder and flipped him to his stomach. The cuffs were on the man in seconds.

He was helping the man to his feet when the car pulled up behind them. It was one of his deputies. The young man sauntered up to Logan casually, eyeing the man that the Sheriff had apprehended. There was a glint of humor in the man's eyes.

"Problems Sheriff?"

"Nothing I can't handle, Jim. Take him to Poteau and I'll be there later to file the charges. Read him his rights."

The redneck said, his face livid with rage, "You cain't hide from me, boy. I'll catch you out without that badge and beat your ass! You done fucked up like a motherfu . . . !"

Logan suddenly grabbed the man by the shirtfront, tolerating the man's putrid breath, Logan's lips curled in a snarl. "Come looking for me! If you want me, I'll make goddamned sure you are able to find me!"

The man swallowed hard. He had detected a savage wildness in the gray eyes of the Sheriff. It had not been insanity, it had far surpassed crazy. It was something feral, something bestial hidden in the thin cloak of humanity. He shut his mouth up, his face taut in fear while the deputy escorted him to his vehicle.

Walking to the cab of the truck, dusting the knees of his pants off with his hands, Logan was polite when he faced the young woman in the truck.

"Ma'am, we have to take your husband to Poteau. Can you drive your truck home?"

She nodded and Logan was perplexed as she seemed to be in fear of him. Her baby was held tight and Logan noticed a bruise on the girl's arm. He reached in the truck and pulled her arm to him. A dark purple bruise covered the inside of her arm. He noticed the remnants of a black eye on her face.

His voice was soft. "Did he do this to you Ma'am?"

Her eyes were wet and she shook her head in the negative. He nodded his head, slightly disappointed at her obvious attempt to cover for a man that did not deserve it. He would never understand how these pretty, young girls could mix themselves up with such ignorant scum like the type of man he had just arrested.

He rubbed his forehead, wiping sweat from his brow while he walked to his truck. The woman was holding the baby and walking around the truck to the driver's side. The two small children in the back got in the front. Logan saw her hand the baby to one of the kids and then, with a puff of blue smoke, they drove the old truck down the highway.

Legally, he was supposed to ticket them for not putting the baby in a car seat, but he knew that the ticket would only be taking food out of their mouths. That wasn't the reason he took this job and had no intentions of stopping the woman again.

Logan was ready to go home, but he still had to take care of some paperwork at the office. He started his truck and turned it around. He got a call over the radio.

"There's a fight in Billy's Bar outside of Heavener, Sheriff."

Before he could respond to the call, Bill came over the police radio. "I'm in the immediate vicinity, Sheriff. I'll take care of it."

Logan acknowledged the call and heard that the city police in Heavener were going to provide back-up. He smiled. Those boys in Heavener were good cops. Billy's Bar wasn't in their actual jurisdiction, but they had helped out the county in several fracases on the premises.

The drive back to the courthouse was quiet. He got out in the parking lot and walked into the building. He nodded at several county employees as he went through the building.

Sitting down at his desk, he shuffled through the stacks of papers with a bored expression on his face. He hated paper work.

A slip of paper posted to his desk informed him that his wife had called to inform him that they would have guests this weekend. He smiled warmly when he saw that Loren and Milly Chadley were driving in for a visit with them. He had to work some this weekend, but Loren would be all for riding around on patrol with him.

Opening the folder that contained the dead woman's lab report, he paged through it. The typical things were there, nothing that gave him any new clues. The bite marks were mentioned and the notes "savage" and "ripping" were penned in near some arrows on a couple pictures of the victim where the bite marks were easily visible.

Tossing the report in the basket with the other papers, he snorted in disgust.

"Looks like you've had a heck of a day," a soft feminine voice drawled from his office door.

He looked up, a smile on his face. The speaker was Tina Nethers, the county clerk's assistant. She was tall, blond and around twenty-seven years old. The smile on her face was genuine, her personality bubbly, her skin pale, smooth and soft. Well, it looked soft anyway; Logan had no real way of knowing as he hadn't actually touched her.

"It hasn't been great," he replied, setting the papers down on his desk, swiveling around in his chair. "Had a hard day today, Tina?"

She walked into his office, her womanly hips swishing provocatively and Logan was positive it wasn't an accident. The woman found him very attractive and he could scent her arousal when she stayed near him for any length of time. There were times that being a werewolf with the senses of an animal was quite an advantage.

Sitting down in a chair in front of his desk, she leaned back, her pert breasts pushing against the thin fabric of her blouse. Tina was a beautiful woman, but she couldn't even begin to match Randy.

"We've had a few problems, but nothing serious. I heard they pulled the woman's car out of the river today. Find anything?"

Logan chuckled. She always came in here to spar back and forth with him, attempting to find out what information she could get from him. She didn't go to the press with it or even tell her friends in the courthouse. Dwelling inside of her was a deep need to satisfy her own curiosity and Logan believed that this is what compelled her to approach him in these little fact-finding forays.

"You know I can't tell you anything, Tina. We're working with the FBI on this one and they would yank this entire investigation right out from under me if I allowed information out about what we found." Leaning forward with a knowing smile. "It wouldn't take them long to figure out where Jay got his 'unrevealed' information at either."

Blushing slightly, Tina said, "You don't think I would tell him do you?"

"Tell your own brother?!" He laughed as though he did not doubt for a moment that she would go running to her brother with the information.

"I haven't ever told Jay anything!" Tina insisted and then her lips tightened when she saw that Logan was having some fun with her.

"You asshole!" she muttered, joining in his humor at her cost with a smile of her own.

Seriously, Logan said, "Really Tina, we haven't found out much of anything at all. The press knows just about everything we know. They've reported it and you've seen it on TV. Hell, you may know more than me."

"Yeah right!" she said disbelievingly. Her eyes grew sultry and she leaned against his desk. "You know, you and I could go back to my place, run a hot tub of bath water in my big garden tub, get in together, drink a few beers and discuss what has been going on at work." Her prominent breasts bulged her blouse nicely and Logan could not help noticing and she could see that he was noticing.

Logan smiled. This wasn't the first time she had propositioned him this way. He had always believed that she would be startled to death if he had actually accepted, but there was enough fire in her eyes to keep him from calling her bluff.

"Could you, me and Randy fit in it?"

Sighing sadly, Tina said, "That's just like you. Always wanting to bring your wife to our private parties." She stood, walking away like a scolded child.

Logan watched her as she stopped at the door, turning to look at him over her shoulder. Her face suddenly grew serious and she turned fully around. "Be careful, Logan. That man might still be around."

Eyes narrowing, Logan asked, "Why do you say that?"

Her face grew dark as though she was brooding before she finally spoke. "You know how a mountain lion travels across a lot of territory during its range, hunting for food, prey. When he finds a place that has an abundance of game, he stops for a few days, maybe a couple of weeks to feed on the bountiful plate set before him." She looked directly as Logan. "We have a good police force here, but we are rural, the law often far away. He may be like the mountain lion, Logan. He may have found a place where the hunting is easy."

"No one is missing in this area," Logan informed her.

"Not yet," Tina said, swallowing hard.　She turned and walked out, leaving a very thoughtful Logan Denton sitting in his chair behind the oak desk.

Watching her disappear down the hallway, he hoped that she was wrong, but for some reason that shot fear throughout his body, he did not believe it.

The cold beer tasted great as it went down his throat.　Logan leaned back in the wooden chair, watching the other people in the small country bar.　A couple of men were at the bar, minding their own business as they engaged in private conversation while sipping at their suds.　An occasional glance by them let Logan know that they knew who he was and had commented on it to one another.

He wasn't wearing a uniform.　Blue jeans and a green pocket T-shirt was what he had taken with him to change into after getting a shower at the court house.　He often used the shower in the county lock-up for that purpose when he had worked over late.

His gun and belt were in his truck and he was content to sit, drink quietly while waiting for Bill to show up.　Bill would have the latest on what the labs had came up with in the investigation.

The murky light of the bar made it hard to distinguish features across the room, but he had not seen anyone he knew.　There were better bars to visit, but this one was seedy enough that the more prominent citizens did not have to see their duly-elected sheriff relieve a little tension of the day, nor was its denizens brazen enough to try goading him into a fight.

The door opened and Logan was pleased to see Bill make his way across the wooden floor, pulling a chair from the table and sitting down.　Holding a single finger up, he nodded at the man at the bar.　The man was soon at the table with bottle of Budweiser.　Bill took it from him thankfully.

Logan let Bill take two good swallows before speaking.　"What did we get today?"

"Doodly-shit," Bill replied caustically.　"The water and mud screwed up anything we could get out of the car.　The only thing they told us was that the dog was killed with a large knife, like that big Buck you carry during deer season.　He's used that before as well as an axe.　First time he's bitten his victims though."

Logan grunted, sipping his beer quietly, his mind going over the scene of the crime.　He hadn't killed her there, probably hadn't killed her at the gravesite either.　Exactly where in the hell he had killed her would be something that might give them a better idea as to how the murderer operated

"Something else," Bill added almost as an afterthought, "The federal boys was blaming someone for screwing up the bite marks. Saliva traces weren't exactly matching with what they believed was saliva from the perp off of other victims."

"What do you mean not match?" Logan asked curiously. "They didn't have that in the report given to me."

"No, I heard it from those boys working with Agent Hale. I'm no forensic specialist, Sheriff, but they can get a lot of info out of very little evidence anymore. This DNA business is a bunch of mumbo-jumbo to me, but I know enough to know they can tell a lot with just traces of evidence. Something in the lab work simply didn't match. They wouldn't go into specifics when I asked."

"So much for open relations," Logan snarled, finishing the beer and placing the bottle down solidly on the table.

"Heard on the news out of Ft. Smith that the weather is supposed to turn nasty. They are predicting up to two inches of rain."

"Slow or fast?" Logan asked.

"Calling for thundershowers Saturday and Saturday night. Could be either or not at all. You know what weather is like in Oklahoma."

Logan nodded as if to let him know that he didn't have to remind him.

"Heard you had to get rough with one of those mountain boys today, Logan," Bill commented without really asking a question.

"He tried taking a swing at me. I was in the mood for it and barely stopped myself from working the son-of-a-bitch over." Remembering the bruises on the woman in the truck, he added, "I should have slapped him around some more."

"Not taking your frustrations out on other things are you?"

Logan looked up from his beer. "If I had Bill, he would have needed a trip to the hospital, not the jail."

"You know that not all of those folks back there in those mountains are civilized yet. Watch your back on the dirt roads. They may try getting a little of their own back."

"That would be a mistake," Logan said ominously.

Bill didn't doubt him one bit.

"How many you take in over at Billy's?"

"When we got there, Billy's bouncers had already tossed them out. They took off. One of the waitresses, a new girl, jumped the gun on calling it in to the station. Billy was damned apologetic."

"I'll bet he was," Logan commented with a knowing grin. "I told him that the first time we showed up at his place, especially if we broke up a fight, and he didn't press charges would be the last."

Tipping his hat back, Bill leaned back in the chair, beer in his left hand. "Sheriff, I think we've done all we can do to solve this murder. Hell, the FBI has been to every one of this guy's known sites and they still haven't caught him. We don't have the resources or the evidence to justify a lengthy investigation."

"And if he strikes in our county again, Bill? What then? What do we do when some sixteen-year-old kid doesn't come home from basketball practice or band practice? What do I tell people then? That we spent two hard days on it and came up empty? I don't think they would be impressed."

"Tell them that we're doing our best!" Bill shrugged his shoulders. "Ain't a damned one of them that could do any better, Logan." Bill felt relaxed and Logan was listening so he kept talking. "Most of our murders in this county has been feuds, family squabbles, women trouble, the usual crap. Every once in a while someone is killed over drugs, but not very often. People expect us to keep the rowdies under control, the pot growers from getting out of hand and making it safe for folks to go about their business."

He repositioned his feet, leaning his forearms against the table as he spoke. "This serial killin' is a new thing and has folks shook up. You weren't in this part of the country when they caught that crazy bastard that was killing those boys and dumping their bodies in a pond between Cameron and Pocola. It made folks reevaluate the situation for a month or two then they went on about their business. A month ago you could have asked a dozen people in Poteau if they felt endangered by a serial killer and they would have most likely laughed at you outright. We just ain't set up to investigate those kinds of killings. This man is a psychopath and we have as much hope of finding him as I would of being elected president."

"I'd vote for you," Logan stated with a straight face.

"Yeah, but you and my wife wouldn't be enough to get me in the White House," Bill retorted jokingly.

"After that scolding she gave you for ruining that pair of jeans the last time we went frog gigging, I bet she won't vote for you either."

Bill said, suddenly serious, "You and Miranda need to come over and we'll cook up those legs. We been waiting for a good time. How about this weekend?"

Logan looked perplexed. "We'd like to Bill, but we have some friends visiting this weekend. We'll be tied up with them all weekend I imagine. Besides, I work Saturday night."

"That friend of yours from out west?"

"Yeah, Loren Chadley. We went to high school together."

You also spent some time together on some mountains in Idaho, Bill thought, but did not say. He and Logan were good friends, but Logan never talked about that trip to the mountains or what happened up there. A lot of people had died, a lot of Logan's friends.

Oh well. Friends didn't push friends into explanations about themselves, or they didn't in Bill's book.

Logan stood. "You're right about this case, Bill. Randy tried to tell me the same thing last night, but I didn't want to listen."

"She's right," Bill said with a wave of his hand. "If you was smart, you'd listen to that woman. She's a lot more intelligent than you."

"Don't take much," Logan remarked with a grin, shaking Bill's hand before leaving. Bill remained in his seat. He would drink another beer or two and then he would go home. Logan hoped this weekend would be slow.

The night was dark, clouds gathering overhead and the great beast shook its head as it ambled down the mountain trail. It paused, sniffing where a black bear had passed through less than an hour past. The bear was a big one for Oklahoma, weighing over five hundred pounds. The beast went on. Here, Logan was king.

Maybe in the jungles of Africa or in the wilds of Asia there were animals that could match his strength. He had often wondered how his great strength would match up against the king of beasts. He found humor in the thought. He could see himself booking safari for one werewolf with luggage.

This helped to relax him more than anything he could do at home. The scents intermingling with each other as they wafted through the air, crossing the ridges, angling around the trees.

He slowed, sniffing of the air. A sound ahead let him know the approximate position of the deer. A wild impulse pushed him to kill it, to eat its warm flesh.

Crouching, he changed into the form of the wolf, slinking along the forest floor quietly as he stalked his prey. The deer was feeding on post oak acorns that were scattered along this lower bench. It was unaware of the danger that lurked.

The beast could see it, head down as it fed. Lying on his belly, he eased forward, pulling himself forward with his paws. When he got within thirty feet of the animal he bunched his muscles and sprang, running at the deer as it threw its head up, then ran. Its reaction was too late as the werewolf severed its hamstrings, the deer bleating its terror. A quick bite to the back of its neck silenced it forever and Logan began feeding upon the deer.

As a human, the raw flesh of a kill such as this would have sickened him to think he had to eat it. As a wolf, it was the sweetest peach, the filet mignon of beef. No human could understand and Logan gorged himself on the kill, eating far more in his wolf state than he could have eaten as a man.

After he had eaten, he went to a stream, leaping into the cool water and swimming around to wash the blood off his pelt. Climbing out, he padded home, changing into his human form before he reached the house. Going to the shower room in the storehouse, Logan washed himself off. He had a fear of walking into the house with blood all over him and scaring the hell out of his kids.

Randy rarely changed into a wolf though she could. The years Logan had spent as a werewolf in Idaho had left him with a need to roam free with the wildness within him in charge. A few times each month he hunted like this and though he did not always take an animal, he came home feeling refreshed. Dressed, he went to the house, walking up the stairs quietly. He could hear Randy breathing when he went inside. Without awaking her, he undressed, lying down to sleep. He rested as well as he had in days.

Friday was clear, the morning muggy and humid as Logan worked out on the weights in the shop. The air conditioner had the temperature in the house comfortable. He was taking today off, though he wore his pager on his shorts.

The day off was a facade. He knew that he would get dressed later and check on the investigation. Bill and Randy were right. He should let the FBI handle this one, but it wasn't like him to give up. More than likely though, the man was long gone.

More than likely.

The analogy about the mountain lion kept coming to mind and he smiled while thinking about Tina. She was a fine looking woman. If he was a little less loyal, he thought she would tear him up. Hearing Randy moving in the house, he grunted humorously. Randy would tear him up literally for even thinking thoughts like that.

No, Randy wasn't one of those jealous women that kept a short leash on their man. She trusted Logan and he would never do anything to betray that trust. Not to mention that he loved her. Still, he was a man and men appreciate beautiful women whether they meet on the street or work together in the office. He would not apologize for being the person that came natural.

He had just finished doing curls and set the bench up to do an incline military press. He worked the weights smoothly up and down while counting his reps. The door slammed and he finished up as he heard foot steps nearing the shop. The scent was his daughter and he set the barbell on the stands before she walked inside.

Tana came inside the shop, her hair back off her head in a ponytail. She was wearing a pair of gray gym shorts over spandex biker shorts and a tank top. She was well-tanned and he could see bikini straps partially hidden beneath the straps of the tank top.

"Your skin is going to be dried up and leathery from the sun," he growled at her, leaning against the incline as he took a break. Sweat was running down his face and arms.

"Like your skin, Dad?" she asked innocently.

"That didn't win you any brownie points," he informed her, standing up from the bench and wiping his perspiring forehead off with a towel.

Tana grinned, turning on the treadmill, setting it for six miles an hour and began to jog. She ran on the treadmill almost every morning. Logan looked at his teenage daughter proudly. She was almost a full-grown woman and it bothered him at times. He missed holding her, comforting her when she was scared of the thunder and being the hero that she could always depend upon.

That was what sucked about growing older. Just when you were sure you knew your kids, they had matured some more and it all started over again. He knew she was wanting to ask him something, could tell it when she came in the door, but she had to work herself up to it.

Using the leg machine, he worked his legs strenuously, grunting as they flexed, muscles rippling. He used a lot of weight when he worked out. Logan had finished doing his sit-ups when he heard the treadmill slowing down and Tana stepping off of it.

"Dad," she began wistfully. "I wondered if you cared if I went out with Tim on Saturday night?"

"What are you doing tonight?" he asked. She was eighteen, but she would be in college before he let her go anywhere without informing him of her destination.

"Jennie Tolbert and I are going to go to the mall in Ft. Smith to get a new outfit. Mom said I could get one and Jennie has all of her birthday money left." She was looking at him hopefully and he melted.

"Okay, but you drive my truck. I feel better when you drive in Ft. Smith in a truck for some reason," he said.

Hugging him, ignoring the sweat from his arms, she said, "Thanks Dad! I'll be extra careful!"

He shook his head, watching her run out the door, headed for the house. Undoubtedly, Randy had hatched the idea of cornering him in the shop. What could a man do when two women ganged up on him? He would be glad when Logan Jr. got older and sided with him. The boy still sided with his mother and Logan usually found himself cornered on three sides.

It wasn't a bad place to be. He dearly loved his family and would not trade them for anything.

He showered in the storehouse, grimacing at the wad of dark hair on the drain. Picking it up, he dropped the hair in the trashcan near the door. Those black hairs would cause a forensic scientist to go nuts. They were not quite human, not quite wolf.

The call of the wolf was powerful and he could feel the wild animal living within his body, the primal beat of its heart in his chest. He had awoke in the night, halfway caught between the change, stirred by the sharp yapping of the prairie wolves that skirted his house and yard like it reeked with poison.

They knew. Most animals knew by his scent that he was different. Cats hated him, but that was okay too. He wasn't overly fond of cats. Big dogs would act vicious at times, but most dogs grew accustomed to him rather quickly, though their eyes never left him for long periods of time. Cattle did not sense the difference in him and other men at all. They were stupid beasts.

Drying off with a towel, he opened a drawer that he always stored at least three extra pairs of under-shorts, a pair of gym shorts and a tank top. He would wear them to cross the yard, even during the cold of winter.

Carrying his clothes into the house, he trotted up the stairs and put them in the dirty clothes hamper. The shorts and tank top were placed on the floor beside his dresser and then he dressed in jeans and a dark green pocket T-shirt.

"You going in to work?" the soft voice asked.

Surprised, Logan turned to his wife and nodded his head. "Yes, I'm going to see Bill and find out if he knows anything new."

Walking into the room, she looked at him coyly. "You know there is a wonderful invention called a telephone that will let you call and talk directly to whoever you are needing to talk to."

"I know," he replied lamely, looking at the floor. "Just let me go in for a couple hours and I promise I will be back before Loren and Milly arrive this evening."

Putting her arms around his waist, she asked, "Are you positive?" Her eyes delved into his and he kissed her lightly on the lips.

"I promise."

"Do you want me to put something special out for supper?"

"I thought I'd put out those elk steaks that Vitoro gave us if you'll cook some fried potatoes with fresh onions and a big dish of your famous squash casserole."

Arching an eyebrow, she said, "As long as there is nothing special."

"That comes after the meal and Loren and Milly aren't getting any of it."

"You're awful!" she protested, but Logan could see in her eyes that she enjoyed the teasing.

Kissing her a second time, he removed a revolver in a leather holster from the top dresser drawer. Sliding it on the belt of his jeans, he released the strap and opened the cylinder to check the loads. The gun was a Smith & Wesson Model 57 in .41 Magnum. He owned a dozen different pistols and loved to shoot.

"I'll put the steaks out to thaw," Randy said, Logan nodding his head in understanding. "You be careful."

"I'm always careful," he replied, walking down the hall to the stairs, descending them to the small closet beside the front door. Retrieving a pair of hi-top running shoes, he slipped them on.

Randy watched him leave, smiling prettily while watching her husband go out to face the criminals that lurked in the world. The smile faded away when she thought about Logan's own inner demons pushing him to search for an answer to something that might be out of his hands.

His motorcycle started and she heard him rev the engine before pulling the bike out of the garage, the motor audible until he reached the highway. Sighing, she looked at the house. It was clean, but she wanted to dust again before Loren and Milly arrived. She was sure she would find a dozen other things that needed to be done too.

"Dad leave?" Tana asked, peering down the stairwell, her hair in curlers, and a cotton robe around her. She had been in the shower a few minutes earlier.

"Yes. I guess you plan on picking up Jennie early?"

Shrugging her shoulders, Tana said positively, "There are a lot of stores in Ft. Smith calling our names. I'd hate to run out of time."

"Be home by ten. I know you like to shop until the stores close and that's fine, but I want you to come home right after," Miranda stated, knowing that Logan had probably told her something similar.

"I'm going to try to be home earlier than that, Mom. I'd like to visit with Loren and Milly some myself." She disappeared down the hallway and Miranda heard the bathroom door close. She had work to do and it looked like she would be doing it herself. She put out the elk steaks, setting them in the sink to thaw. Getting the spices and the large bottle of Worcestershire sauce, she began preparing the marinade for the elk. Logan's recipe was a secret, but one he had shared with her. The elk would be delicious and she was already looking forward to it.

He tossed on the bed fitfully. Clutching his face, he felt like tearing the flesh from his features. The bones of his face creaked as he flipped over to his stomach, screaming into his pillow, the muted sounds barely reaching his own ears. He shook, fingers moving from his face to the pillow, leaving livid welts that were white in the center and circled by red. The muscles of his arms stood out as his entire body was racked with intense spasms.

Crying, he dug his nails into the pillow, ripping at the covering, feeling it come apart in his hands. It gave him pleasure and he raised up, a maniacal expression of savage hatred covering his face. He beat the pillow like it was an animate object that he feared, an animal that must be killed for survival.

Casting the pillow away from himself, he rolled to his feet. The backs of his hands seemed to ripple, the hair growing coarse and dark. Shaking his head in the dim light that managed to steal into the room around the blind, he studied his hands a second time. They looked normal.

The irony of that thought caused a grim humor to well up in him like a virulent gas waiting to explode in a plume of voracious flames.

These hands had killed people. These hands had welded the ax or saw that dismembered some of those victims. These hands were mere pawns of the hunger that dwelt within him.

The hunger waited.

It gnawed at his inner stomach, threatening to devour his entrails from within his own body. Never had it been this strong! It was causing him to thrash uncontrollably. It had always dictated his actions, but it never caused his body to behave so erratically.

He moved towards the shower, stumbling like a drunken man into the small table beside his bed, scattering the contents across the floor. A guttural snarl escaped his throat and he felt his breathing calm as he fumbled for the light switch.

Turning on the light, he lurched towards the tub, shoving the curtain out of the way while turning on the water. The shower selector was on and the water hit him across the back of the head, cold at first and then warming as his breathing returned to normal. His legs felt sluggish, like they were dead appendages that he was being forced to carry. A life form with parasitic extensions that moved when he willed it. With a grunt, he managed to climb into the shower, allowing the stream of water to flow over his shoulder and down his back.

With a harsh chuckle, he realized that he was still wearing his underwear and they were soaked. The water had forced his mind to focus on himself and the reality of where he was.

After several long minutes, he picked up the bar of soap, bathing with it while listening to the rhythm of his own breathing. Rinsing the soap from his body, he retrieved the towel from the towel bar, drying his hair and upper body before wrapping it around his waist. Stepping out the door, he cursed as he stepped on something in the floor.

Leaning over, he picked up the gun and the badge, laying it on the nightstand as he went to pick out some clothes from the closet.

The day passed quickly and Logan had found that little had changed in the investigation since the day before. Bill was working harder than any man should expect. Not wanting to get in his way, Logan left, riding his motorcycle out of town.

He took a ride in the northeast section of the county, riding the back roads near the Haskell county line. Taking a circle through Bokoshe, down the county road by Twi-Light Station and on through Cowlington, he hit Highway 9 and followed it to Sunset Corner where he decided to cruise on in to Spiro for a burger and milk shake.

The day was beautiful and something about riding the big Harley helped him to relax. He didn't stop when he cruised through Poteau, taking the bypass rather than driving through the middle of town and got home close to the time he had given Randy earlier. His truck was nearing the end of the driveway as he slowed beside it.

"Hey Dad! I'm going to pick up Jennie!"

"You got enough money?" he asked, reaching for his wallet as he spoke.

"Teenagers never have enough money," she responded cheerily. Logan nodded his agreement, thinking that neither did the parents of teenagers.

Handing her a twenty and a ten, he couldn't help noticing how pretty she looked. So much like her mother, yet she had his temperament.

"Will that be enough money to put some gas in the truck and feed you?"

"More than enough! I'll be careful," she cried out, the window rolling up as she pressed the electronic switch on her door. Logan motioned for her to roll it back down.

"The Colt .22 is under the seat. It has a full clip in it and the extra one is in the door pocket. If you break down, the radio should be set up to the one in the house. Give me a buzz," he informed her.

"And I'll call Mom if I break a nail. I have my cell phone, Dad," she chided with an impatient shake of her head.

"Then get out of here smart-butt," Logan said, watching her roll up the window as she pulled up, stopping to look both ways before getting on the highway.

He lifted his foot and gave his bike some gas, motoring toward the house slowly. The Colt was her pistol and it was an excellent pistol. Smaller than most .22 automatics, it fit her hand well and she could shoot like an expert with it.

Some parents would disagree with the training he had given his daughter as well as the fact that he trusted a eighteen-year old to have the judgement needed to be responsible with a firearm. He did trust her and one thing was for certain: He would rather have some upset parents as his daughter's corpse in a plastic trash sack like that poor woman from Tulsa. Maybe if she had been armed . . .

It did no good to plot out all the "if's". You could justify Hitler's existence with enough "if's".

The elk steaks sizzled when they hit the grill and the sweet aroma of the marinade made Logan's mouth water.

"Those smell good, Dad!" Logan Jr. commented, leaning forward to sniff of the smoke that came from the grill.

"You're going to burn your nostrils, son," Logan warned with a chuckle.

"Naw, I ain't gettin' that close," the boy assured him, disappearing in the house.

The sound of gravel crunching caused Logan to turn his head and he whooped loudly. Randy came outside, wiping her hands with a dishtowel.

"They're here," Logan called, a big grin on his face. He could see Loren's dark face behind the wheel of the Blazer and Milly's face on the other side.

"I have just about everything ready in the house. You want to eat inside or out?"

Swatting a mosquito on his arm, he gave her a look that clearly communicated his choice.

"I'll put out the place mats on the table," Randy said, walking out to meet Loren and Milly as they climbed out of the utility vehicle.

"Looks like we got here in time," Loren said amiably, striding forward slowly as his wife took the lead. Their daughters darted around each side of Loren's legs and Logan felt warmth in his chest at the sight of Loren with his family.

Randy hugged Milly and then Loren. "I think I like this better than the steak," he said jokingly. He and Randy were good friends and had been friends as long as he and Logan had been friends.

Milly gave Logan a hug and warm peck on the cheek, though he had to bend down for her to reach him. He smiled warmly and then gripped Loren's outstretched hand. There was a little gray among the dark hair at his temples, but he looked the same. Indomitable and strong, he seemed to have found peace with the blackness that dwelt inside of him and the way he looked at his family was explanation enough.

Lacy Dawn and Shasta Marie were his daughters' names and they were pretty girls. The younger girl was dark like her father, but the older one was the mirror image of her mother. Milly Chadley was a beautiful woman.

Milly was two inches over five feet and she was built well for her size. Her hips might have been a little wider, her face a touch rounder, but she looked very good. There wasn't any gray in her hair and she did not look like a woman that was nearly forty years old.

"Have a good drive?" Logan asked, directing Loren to follow him to the grill. Logan Jr. came outside, joining the two girls, leading them around the house to the wood playset behind the house. The sounds of kids screaming in fun was added to the crickets' song as the evening drew to a close.

"Pretty good," Loren replied, opening the red cooler behind the grill and picking up a beer. Popping the top, he dropped the lid back in the cooler. "Thank God for hand-held computer games! They kept the girls from fighting and raising hell through the whole drive."

Logan chuckled, flipping the steaks over before pouring a splash of beer on them and swabbing them with his marinade.

"That sure smells good," Loren commented again. "Vitoro give you that package of steaks?"

"Yeah. Said for me to talk you into going up there and trying for a couple of trophies ourselves." Keeping his eyes on the steaks, he said, "Told him that I didn't think we would care to hunt in that area."

Grunting without humor, Loren said, his voice strangely melancholy, "Too many memories. Too many of them are bad memories. But, I like that old man. Just don't care to bring back the memories of good friends dying."

"That's what I thought. But, we could take a hunt in Colorado next year."

"I'd like that. Been a long time since we did any big game hunting together," Loren said longingly. Changing the subject, he commented, "Hear you have a big investigation going on over that guy that's been killing all of those girls across the south."

"That's about it too. All we have been doing is investigating. Nobody - and that includes the feds - have any idea who this guy is."

Looking around, Loren asked, "Where's Tana? The last time I saw her, she looked like Sandy Trent made over."

Nodding his head in agreement, Logan verified his comment with one of his own. "Only taller and darker. She is growing up. She's already more pretty than her mother and I'm afraid that I'm going to have to fight off the boys like houseflies over the honey pot."

Sipping his beer, Loren said, slapping Logan on the back as he spoke, "At least it'll be a few years before I'll go through something like that!" Looking at Logan, Loren took a drink of beer, but Logan could tell that he wanted to speak.

"What?"

Gesturing with his beer bottle, he said, "You. It amazes me that you don't look like you've aged a day since we left you in those mountains. Maybe being one of those things ain't so bad after-all."

Several years in the past, Logan had offered to give Loren the gift of lycanthropy -- or, the curse depending upon how one looked at it. "You thinkin' of changing your mind?"

"No," Loren said with a calm finality. "Not at all. It isn't really immortality. I've talked to Vitoro a few times since then, mostly when he was helping us sell that land of Milly's. Like all things, a werewolf eventually dies too." Taking a measured breath, he continued expressing his thoughts, "I've changed, Logan. My temper ain't so bad. The nightmares are different and they don't come as often as they did in the past. Milly growed up in the church and she got me to goin' with her after Lacy was born. I listened to what the preacher said and did some reading myself. Man ain't supposed to live forever. At least I ain't. I've got a good family, a beautiful woman that loves me and a strong body that doesn't fold up to hard, honest labor. I reckon I couldn't ask God for more."

"If you were on a rafting trip in the West and you found out the guide was James River's evil twin?"

"I'd shoot the son-of-a-bitch between the eyes and kick his bloody carcass in the river to feed the fish!" he snarled with a grin that was half-savage and half-friendly and one hundred percent honest.

Logan chuckled as he pulled the steaks off the grill. Loren hadn't changed that much.

The sky had grown cloudy, thunderheads gathering in huge clumps high above the earth and there was a scent of rain in the air. It was really dark and back to the west and the south, flashes of lightning could be seen in the sky.

Tana didn't know that Jennie had told Tim and Greg that they were going to Ft. Smith. The boys had met them at the mall and went to the stores with them. The girls had bought a dress apiece and Jennie had bought a pair of tan flats to go with one of her summer dresses. Tana had purchased a pair of forest green shorts and a light T-shirt to match along with the dress she had bought.

The boys had taken them to a steak house on Towson to eat and Greg suggested they take a side trip to the lake at Short Mountain Cove. Tana and Jennie had been hesitant, but the boys were playfully teasing them about being mama's girls and they agreed. Greg had driven his Camaro and Jennie got in the car with him. Tim slid into the passenger seat of the four-wheel drive, kissing Tana's cheek as she started the truck.

Tana had never drove to Short Mountain Cove and she had to follow Greg. They turned into the cove, taking the first split to the right to pull around to the camping spots in that area. The lights from the lock and dam across the Arkansas River were visible across the lake, Short Mountain looming ominously to the right of the lights.

They had been parked for almost half an hour, Tana holding Tim as they kissed, their lips pressed tightly together. Tim had one hand on her leg, the other on her side, rubbing up and down her back while they kissed.

The night was cooler than it had been the previous evening, but it was humid and they were sweating some from the heat of the night and the closeness of their bodies. Tana wore a pair of tan shorts and a white blouse with a tan tank-style T-shirt beneath. A pair of sandals was on her feet and she did not complain when Tim's hand moved up and down the top of her bare leg.

"Can I take off your blouse? Just so we won't get it stained with sweat," Tim suggested, adding the explanation hurriedly. His hands had been all over her breasts and the hard buttons beneath her shirt had made him curious how they would feel with another layer of fabric missing.

Tana nodded her head, her bosom rising and falling heavily from the impassioned kissing they had been enjoying as she unbuttoned the blouse. She folded her blouse and lay it on the dash. Tim put his arms around her waist and pulled her near him, slipping his hands inside her shirt to caress her back. Their lips were together, the tips of their tongues dancing with each other.

She felt warm inside and Tim's hands were moving up her back, roaming up and down - strong, sensitive fingers that traced her spine. His forearms were lifting her shirt up, the hem right below her bosom, but she didn't notice it or care if she did. Tim was pulling her tighter, seeking to draw her even closer to him.

His hands stopped at the back of her bra and she could feel him fumbling with it. Her heart was hammering in her chest, thumping like the background beat of a bass drum. She touched his chest, letting her hands slide to his waist, tentatively touching his bare back and ribs as her hands went beneath his shirt.

Tim sighed, barely suppressing the shudder that tried to go through him. He was growing frustrated with her bra! He couldn't find the catch. Not that he was experienced at that anyway, but he did know how to unhook one. He had practiced on a bra he had stolen from his older sister's lingerie drawer. He let his hands drift to her side, then he held her firm breasts in his hands, the heat permeating through the cloth. The tip of his finger touched something between them and he almost choked with the thrill at having found the catch at last!

Unhooking the catch, he felt her bra spring open and he eagerly swept the cups out of the way, delighting in the warm flesh of her bosom, the hardness pressing his palms. He was breathing hard and slowed long enough to take off his own shirt, laying it on the other side of her.

Tana felt like this was wrong! It was not what she should be doing, but she couldn't deny the passion that swelled her heart, inflaming her inside to respond to Tim's velvet-like caresses. She watched him lift her shirt over the peaks of her breasts and sighed sharply when his mouth made contact with her flesh, his lips encircling her taut nipples hungrily, moving from one to the other every few seconds. Moaning softly, she felt his hand touching her flat stomach, easing up her chest to touch her, then falling back to the snap of her shorts. His fingers found the snap and it opened much easier, the zipper making hardly any noise at all as it moved down.

Tana started to protest, but her heart was racing, her mind clouded by the desire of her nubile young body. She felt his hands move across the waistband of her panties, slipping inside along the skin of her hip and ease downward.

Was this what she wanted? She loved Tim very much and Tana admitted that she wanted to do this too, to be with Tim the way he wanted her to be. His lips were hungrily kissing hers and she felt him tense when her hands move to the top of his hands, holding them. He seemed to have been halfway expecting it.

"Tim, I . . . "

Tim interrupted. "I'm sorry Tana. I know you aren't ready . . ."

Tana put her hand on his lips and he hushed. She seemed a little unsure of herself and her voice was a little shaky too. "I am ready, Tim, but not here. Not rushed with our friends parked next to us in another vehicle."

Tim seemed surprised. "Where?"

Shrugging her shoulders, Tana said, "Somewhere we can be alone. I want it to be where we can take our time."

"I love you, Tana," Tim said, "and I want this to be as special as you are to me. Do you want to get a motel room?"

Tana grunted. "In Poteau? Someone who knew us would see us. Same if we went to Wilburton."

"Ft. Smith isn't out of the question," Tim said, thinking that he would drive just about anywhere in the USA if it meant finally being with Tana.

Tana shook her head. "No, I don't mind being in a vehicle with you Tim. I just want it to be alone where our friends can't pop up in a window to cheer us on."

They both laughed, Tim glancing at the vehicle with the steamed up windows next to them. He really loved Tana and he could feel that warmth in his heart that came from just sitting next to her. "That ain't asking too much, Tana. "

The sharp knock on the window made them both jump in surprise, Tana pulling her shirt down to cover herself, hiding behind Tim as she hastily fastened her shorts. Jennie was grinning sheepishly as Tim rolled down the window.

"What do you want?!" he asked harshly, fighting to catch his breath and to keep his disappointment from overwhelming him. He wanted to talk to her longer.

"We promised my Mom we would be back between nine and ten tonight. We're going to have to hurry to make it by nine-thirty," Jennie explained.

"Hell, we can stay another half hour," Tim pleaded, unable to keep the tone of frustration out of his voice.

Tana looked at her watch, unable to see it in the dim light. Turning the key on the truck, she saw that it was later than she had first thought.

"We do need to go," she said, swallowing to catch her own breath.

Tim sighed disappointedly. "Okay. I guess I better ride with Greg then. I wanted to talk some more with you." Getting his shirt, he leaned forward, kissing Tana on the lips before he climbed out of the truck. Jennie walked around and Tana quickly clipped her bra together. The other girl slid into the truck, waving at Greg who waved back.

"What time can I pick you up tomorrow?" Tim asked, wishing that he could skip all day tomorrow for the night that followed.

"Around six, I guess. Dad said I can stay out to midnight," she said, smiling at him as he put his shirt on. She started the truck and backed up, seeing that her boyfriend was standing in the road, watching her leave.

"How did you do?" Greg asked snidely, an interested look on his face.

"We kissed. That's all," Tim replied, unwilling to discuss what went on between Tana and him.

"Riiigghhht," Greg said, starting the Camaro. "That's why you had your shirt off."

Tim didn't reply as they left the Cove area. He didn't want to make the direction their relationship was going public, but he was wistful for a just a little more time tonight. He wanted to be with Tana. He wanted to actually make love to her, his teenage hormones ached for it, but he did have tomorrow night to look forward to and he was planning something special in his mind already.

He loved her. That was hard to admit and he knew that his friends would make fun of him if he told them how he felt. Tana was one of the prettiest girls in school if not the prettiest. The words she spoke tonight electrified him!

A sudden pang of fear struck him! Suppose he had not said enough to her about the way he felt. What if she had been expecting more?

Closing his eyes, he hoped it wasn't so. He'd know tomorrow for sure.

"You and Tim were getting pretty hot," Jennie commented as they drove through Panama.

"More so than usual. I let him take off my bra," Tana admitted nervously. "I've never let him do that before. I've never let anyone do that!"

"You let Steve Becker do more than that," she accused with a knowing glint in her eyes.

Tana blushed shamefully. She hated it when Jennie brought up Steve Becker. Tana knew she had made a mistake with him and she didn't need it slapping her in the face all the time. Still, Jennie was right. She had let Steve make love to her. "I told him I was ready to go all the way soon," she said, blushing again, hoping her friend did not make fun if her.

"Wow!! What did he say?" she asked, a smile on her face.

"That he loved me," Tana answered thoughtfully, grinning despite herself as Jennie chortled.

"I knew he did!!! At least I knew he was in love with your body!" Jennie exclaimed excitedly, happy for her friend, knowing she loved Tim very much..

"I am sure he is in love with me, although I know it might have something to do with my body," Tana admitted, not wanting to give Jennie more ammunition to tease her with tonight, but Jennie was chuckling happily, a satisfied laugh as she looked at the road disappearing beneath the truck.

"What are you laughing about?"

"You! When are you putting out?"

"I don't know," Tana said weakly. "We didn't discuss it. I don't think about sex that much."

"I do sometimes," Jennie admitted, her sexuality a flamboyant part of her personality at times and it made Tana uncomfortable. Laughing again, she blurted, "Your Dad would crap a round pile of doggy biscuits if he knew Tim was in the process of stripping your clothes off in his truck tonight and you practically promised to let him sleep with you!"

Raising her eyebrows worriedly, Tana said, her voice trembling, "Yeah, I guess he would."

Touching Tana's arm, Jennie encouraged her. "Don't sweat it, Tana. He won't find out and besides, he was just like Tim when he was a boy. Eager to be a man and to prove it!" Then she was laughing some more.

Tana joined her, but she did not think much of what Jennie had said was funny. She believed she was in love with Tim, and he was in love with her; that she wasn't some conquest to test his manhood. Tim wasn't like Steve Becker. It had taken less than four days for the rumors about Steve making love to her twice at this same Cove to reach her school. She had denied the rumors even as the scathingly correctness of the story upset her. She disliked Steve, though he did try to apologize later. She doubted if that had been sincere either.

After taking Jennie home, she stopped along the road, slipping on her blouse and straightening it up. Making sure she had not missed a button, she checked her hair, fixing it where it had been flattened somewhat before driving home.

Things had gotten out of hand tonight. She swallowed nervously at the thought of what she and Tim had almost done. What they might have done. What they planned to do. Nothing like this had ever happened before with Tim and she hoped she had not betrayed Randy's trust?

No. She didn't think so, but she was confused. Going to Randy again didn't seem like the answer. Her real mother might have an answer, but it probably wouldn't be something that she wanted to hear. Sandy blamed her dad for everything.

It was a few minutes to ten when she entered the house, finding Loren and Milly sitting with her parents in the den. Her Dad and Loren were sipping bourbon and Coke; Milly and Randy drinking a frozen strawberry daiquiri.

"Hello Tana," Milly greeted her warmly, rising from the chair to give her a hug. "What kind of goodies did you get at the mall?"

Tana showed her the things she had bought, giving a short summary of her day, sans the parking adventure at Short Mountain Cove. They visited until after midnight, Tana joining in with the talking when she had something to add or tell them.

She had always liked Loren. Quiet and amiable, she had never seen the dark temper her father had warned her laid hidden below the surface of Loren's emotions. In some ways, she thought of him as an uncle. Her brother and the girls had gone to bed early, tired from playing so hard. They had not actually been ready for bed, but coaxing on Randy and Milly's part had helped.

Loren stood, looking out the picture window, his face pleasant as a streak of lightning ran along the Oklahoma mountain ridges. It looked wild outside and that sparked an interest in him that lay mostly dormant.

"What do they call these mountains?" Loren inquired, taking a sip of his drink.

"They are all part of the Kiamichi Mountain range, but those are known as the Winding Stairs. The small mountain between the larger one and us is known as Bear Mountain locally. There are a few on it," Logan informed him. Milly had been listening aptly.

"I don't think I care to run into any bears," she said with a shudder that did not seem feigned.

"They're small ones," Randy said.

Grunting as though it didn't matter, Milly didn't offer another comment, allowing her first opinion to stand.

"You going to have time to do a little fishing in the morning?" Loren asked. "I brought my fishing rod and tackle box in the truck."

"I reckon I do," Logan said, shaking his head. "You want to lake fish or pond fish?"

"Don't matter. Don't want to keep any unless it's a trophy. Pond fishing will be fine."

"Loren has been fishing more and more every year we've been married," Milly confided to Randy in a whisper.

"No need to whisper, woman," Loren said with a gruff drawl. "You go with me most of the time."

Milly chuckled softly. "We fished a few couples' tournaments on the lakes. They were fun."

"I like to canoe, but we haven't gotten to go this year. The creeks are down around here and it is a couple hours to float the Illinois. We would put in near Gore." Logan sounded like he was making a suggestion.

"The girls are too small anyway," Milly said, though she did like the thought of a float trip. She had gone down the Illinois once when she was a freshman. It wasn't a fast moving river.

The banter was friendly and they talked late into the night, Tana finally going to bed a half-hour after midnight. She excused herself, giving her Dad and Mom a hug, as well as Loren and Milly.

After she left, Loren said, "She is an adult, Logan."

"She thinks so," Randy commented before Logan could reply. She really felt as though Tana was her daughter too. "I rely on her a lot and she very rarely lets me down."

"Second that here," Logan said, proud of his teenage daughter."

"She's beautiful," Milly said, wistfully remembering her own teenage years. "I wish I was that tall."

"Me too," Loren said with a taunting grin that drew a thrown pillow. It hit him in the face and everyone laughed, Loren included as his face turned red with humor. Milly always had been feisty.

Finally, they went to bed, the women first and later, Loren and Logan after discussing the ponds they would hit, the latest bass plug and how effective it was this time of the year. Nobody wasted any time counting sheep when their heads hit the pillows.

The man in the Roper had made her mad and Tina Nethers walked impatiently to her car, an irritated expression on her face. He had no right to keep patting her rear every time she danced by him. Then his gall really made her angry! He had tried to talk her into going home with him! He even got indignant when she refused him!

The Roper was a huge barn-looking building that served as a country dance club. It was a bring-your-own-bottle affair that always had enough people in it during the weeknights that it was packed solid on the weekends. It was big and the atmosphere was usually sociable. Every once in a while though, one of the local rednecks got too frisky for his own good. That man had no idea how close he came to being kicked where it really hurt!

Her car was a white Chevy Lumina and she had bought it new in Poteau. It was the first new car she had ever owned and she really liked it.

There had been several cars around it when she parked earlier tonight, but now it was by itself, hiding in the shadows of a tree that blocked the nearest light. Fumbling in her purse for her car keys, she grunted in exasperation when they fell to the gravel. Kneeling to searching for them, she saw a shadow cross above her and she glanced up with a short, startled gasp.

A man stood beside her car, a solitary figure that had appeared from no where. He watched her, a look of curiosity on the lower half of his face, the only part she could see for the same shadows that hid her car.

"Hello," she said, finding her keys and standing. "I'm not drunk, I just had my mind somewhere else."

The man was quiet, unmoving and Tina felt spooked. There was a can of pepper spray inside her purse and she reached inside, cursing to herself when she felt her billfold and address book on top. It was covered beneath the rest of her stuff in the purse.

"Look, I forgot something inside," she said, thinking fast, half-turning towards the building when the man stepped forward. She stopped, recognizing him. "I know you. You're one of the FBI agents that has been working with Logan."

The man drew up sharply, the intent expression on his face turning stoic, then friendly with falseness to it that was almost petrifying. "I'm sorry, I don't know you," he said, his voice gravelly like he did not speak much.

"I work in the courthouse. We see you guys pass by going back and forth to the Sheriff's office. You've been working with Bill probably more than you've been working with Logan." Tina had relaxed, visibly relieved that it was one of the federal agents and not some kook trying to pick off a woman coming out of the club.

Nodding his head, he said, "That's true."

Pointing back at the club, she said, "I don't really have anything in there. You were kinda' scaring me, standing there all quiet."

"Throat's sore. Sorry," he replied, no emotion in his voice to verify his comment.

"No, it's me," she insisted, walking towards him, putting her hand on his shoulder as she chuckled. "There was some asshole in there coping a feel of my butt every time he walked by, then he decided that he wanted me to go home with him. I had to leave or gag."

He was smiling, but it didn't actually look friendly. Placing his hand on her arm, he looked into her eyes. Tina thought the man was handsome. No supermodel or anything like that, but a good-looking man.

"I'll walk you to your car," he said in a tone that did not allow argument, putting his right hand gently on her back, walking behind her. His left hand hung by the index finger in the belt loop at the back of his pants.

"Were you inside earlier?" she asked, positive she hadn't seen him.

"Couldn't sleep. Thought I would stop here for a beer before it closed," he replied. Tina nodded her understanding as she allowed him to guide her towards her car.

The man felt a wicked thrill go through him and he felt the hidden blade in the back of his pants. The handle was rigid and he could grasp it easily enough.

The door opened on The Roper and four men came out, laughing and carrying on with each other. They started across the parking lot towards their truck and it was parked a few yards farther away than Tina's Lumina.

The man moved his hand from his back, stepping back as Tina opened her door. She smiled sweetly at him as she got inside. "Thanks. I really appreciate it."

"No problem," he replied, that false smile on his face again.

She shut the door, starting her car and driving away. The FBI agent had turned towards the darker shadows further down the building, disappearing. He was cute in a way. No Logan Denton, but she was going to have to quit pining away after him anyhow. She wasn't into one-night stands, but that man had been a temptation. Two miles down the road she felt embarrassed. She hadn't even asked him his name.

The rain had slowed to a light sprinkle and Loren had brought his raincoat. They stood at the bank of the pond, casting around some stumps in the shallow end. They had caught a few small bass, but nothing of any size.

"I like the smell of the morning after a rain," Loren commented, spitting a stream of tobacco into the water, wiping his lower lip with the back of his hand.

"Lots of people like a sunny day, but a good rain after a drought is like a rebirth. It washes away the dust and film of life past and cleanses the earth."

"You are the same guy that bitched about it raining when we wanted to hunt as a teenager aren't you?" Loren asked, chiding his friend.

"Yes, I'm that guy," Logan agreed with a chuckle. "I do wish it was better weather this week-end. We could go up in the mountains and drive around."

"You gotta work tonight?"

"From about six in the evening to two or three in the morning. You wanting to ride around with me?"

"Of course," Loren grunted. "How long do you think I could take being cooped up in the house with a bunch of women and kids?"

"Longer than you'd admit," Logan teased snidely.

"You thought I was crazy for marrying her didn't you?"

"Never said that. Glad I didn't because I would have been wrong." Logan felt a bass hit his salt-craw, letting it take the plastic bait for a few moments before jerking.

The line arced as the bass headed for deeper water. Logan fought it, working it closer to the bank.

"Is it a good one?" Loren asked, casting while watching Logan work the fish.

"I'd guess a couple pounds," Logan answered, bringing the fish away from a bunch of brush, working it close to the bank before bringing it up to where they could see it. The bass would go around three pounds.

"That is a nice one," Loren commented, working his plug next to some lily pads.

Taking the hook out of the bass' mouth, Logan put the fish in the water, watching it swim away.

"You got to promise me that you won't try to help me if I get an emergency call tonight," Logan said, tossing the shredded salt-craw into the pond, the remains sinking slowly to the bottom.

Scowling, Loren agreed. Logan could not keep the amused grin from his face. His friend had faced as many or more dangerous situations than Logan had ever had the misfortune to experience. The problem was that Loren had no mercy in him at times and Logan was bound by the position he was in to bring in even a dangerous criminal alive when possible. Loren had just as soon save the taxpayers some money.

CHAPTER THREE

Tana looked at Randy sleepily. Her words had seemed garbled. "What did you say, Mom?"

"I wanted to know if you were interested in going to Ft. Smith with us this morning? Or are you all shopped out?"

"Do I have to keep the kids if I don't go?" she inquired somewhat anxiously. She didn't feel like babysitting.

With a chuckle, Randy said, "That's a good idea! But, no. Milly wants to get some things for Lacy and they are going with us."

"I'm staying," Tana answered, lying back on her pillow, turning on her side while burying her head.

Randy shut her door and met Milly in the den. Everyone was ready and she had not expected Tana to want to go. They got in Milly's Blazer, the kids in the back. They were under control right now, but Randy knew they would be going wild before the day was over.

The numerals on the clock showed that she had slept through the morning. It was a couple minutes after twelve and Tana rose from her bed, walking sluggishly to the bathroom. She had lain awake for a while last night thinking about what had happened. It was hard to forget the icy streaks of pleasure that rocketed through her when Tim had been with her.

He was supposed to pick her up at six today. They were going to an early movie, then out to eat. After supper, they were going to a teenage dance club called Keller's Hideout. It was in Poteau and her dad approved of the place whole-heartedly. No one over twenty was admitted and they had two guys to assist any troublemaker out the door. The proprietor had no qualms in calling Logan or his deputies to get further assistance if it was needed.

No one was home and she grumbled to herself when she realized that she had not brought any clothes with her to the bathroom. After using the bathroom, she went to her room, getting clean underwear, a pair of cotton, gray shorts and a T-shirt with Nirvanna across the front. They were her bumming around clothes.

She washed her long hair, wringing it out with her hands. She was going to let it air-dry for a while before blow drying it.

Dressed and sitting on the edge of her bed, she turned on her CD player. It was a four-disc unit and she filled it with Aerosmith, Van Halen, Depreche Mode and Pearl Jam.

What was Tim thinking about? Was he eager to see her again? If so, was it because he hoped to finish what they had started last night? They had been going out for ten months now with only one break up for a month after he got very drunk one night at a party, nearly wrecking the car with her inside. Steve Becker happened that month and later, they got back together with Tim promising never to drink. They had been together ever since and Tim was ready for their relationship to take the next step. That was along time and they were respectful of each other, but she could sense the urgency in him sometimes. She couldn't deny the feelings within herself either. That was why she partially gave into temptation last night.

Why was it so hard to be a teenager? Was it because you had two constant pressures on each side of you? The pressure of your parents to do one thing and the pressure of your friends to do another. Then, there was herself and the heat of her own young, inner passions. So maybe it was a three-way deal with everyone having good points and bad points.

Regardless, she was confused and that didn't help things. Her tummy rumbled and she got up, going to the kitchen and preparing a sandwich out of turkey and wheat bread. A dab of mustard and some lettuce were the only condiments. A can of diet soda in one hand, sandwich in the other, she went back upstairs. She was at the top of the stairs when her dad and Loren pulled in the driveway.

The two men were chuckling at each other when they came in the house. Her dad had just made a vulgar comment that had Loren laughing raucously. It obviously wasn't intended to carry with him into the house. Logan was soaked and Loren was wet from the rain.

"Did you fall in, Dad?" Tana asked, her sandwich halfway to her mouth.

"And sunk like a damned rock!" Loren chortled, his dark face split with a shining grin of humor. "The bank was muddy and his feet shot out from under him like rocket. Gravity and a big ass did the rest."

Tana laughed at the sheepish look on her dad's face. He looked like a boy with an expression of having been caught doing something silly.

"The bank was slick," Logan commented, unable to keep a straight face.

"How did you get wet all the way to your shoulders?" she asked, seeing muddy streaks along his jeans after he peeled the rain slicker off.

"It was deep where he went off. I don't know if it was a beaver channel where they dug out the mud to make a hole in the bank or if it is just deep," Loren answered for Logan. "That was worth the entire trip."

"Glad you could be entertained," Logan growled good-naturedly.

"Did you catch any fish?" she inquired, feeling that she had teased her dad enough.

"A few. I caught one that weighed about three pounds. Loren had one that would have went five or six, but he claims that he thinks it was a catfish."

"Didn't fight like a bass and the line was a little slimy along the end. It got caught up in some bottom brush and broke the line. The slime could have been from whatever he wrapped the line in or around, but I'm pretty sure it was a catfish," Loren maintained.

"Are you just getting up?" Logan asked, stripping his muddy shirt off and laying it on his slicker.

Glancing at the miniature Grandfather clock down the hall, she said, "I've been up about an hour."

Logan glanced at Loren, his hair wet and clumped from the water. "Go ahead and use the bathroom you used last night. I'm going to get a hot shower, get some of this mud off of me."

"Sounds good," Loren replied, having stripped off his rain slicker and pulled off his boots. Logan was in his sock feet and headed up the stairs.

Tana disappeared into her room, turning down her CD system before her dad asked her to turn it down. He passed her door and she could hear the door to his room shut.

She couldn't believe he had fallen in the pond! Mom would get a kick out of that. As far as that went, so would Milly. Mr. Balance-and-Agility going ass-end over tea kettle into the pond! She laughed, falling back on her bed as she thought about how it must have looked.

Logan grunted sleepily as he fumbled with the alarm clock, groggily slapping at the button to silence the alarm. He finally connected and lay still for a few moments. It was time to go on patrol and he could hear the pattering of rain outside. He flipped the covers off his body and stood, stretching his muscles.

It didn't sound like the kids were here so Milly and Randy weren't back yet. He was going to work casual tonight. Blue jeans and one of the blue shirts with the insignia of the sheriff's department lay on the quilt rack. That would be good enough.

The rain was the final straw. They had decided to go back to Austin. There were no more clues here that would lead them miraculously to the killer's doorstep and if there had been, the rain would have washed them away.

Tonight was their last night and they had all decided to go get raucously drunk, maybe pick up a sweet young thing from the junior college here and get laid. A few of them would undoubtedly be impressed with the title of FBI agent and that usually helped get their panties off.

Tonight was the last night and there were a lot of pretty girls around. It was a shame to be leaving with so many pretty girls in town. A damned shame.

Loren and Logan ate the mushroom-laden spaghetti and noodles Tana had prepared, appreciative of her effort. She was upstairs getting ready for her date, but Logan had thanked her. He had been prepared to inform Loren it was sandwich time. Or a burger. That was what they had eaten for lunch.

"Your daughter is a good cook," Loren commented, rolling the noodles on his fork and dipping a mushroom up on the end. He ate it, enjoying the flavor.

"She opened a can of Ragu, but it is good," Logan commented low enough that Tana wouldn't hear.

"That may be true," Loren said, "But I've tasted Ragu spaghetti at other people's houses and they weren't as good. She added some mushrooms and probably some garlic or powdered onion to get this taste. Plus, she used less than a pound of ground hamburger in it. I know good spaghetti when I taste it."

Laughing softly, Logan acquiesced, "Okay! She's a good cook. Her burritos and cheese enchiladas are top notch."

"It's a wonder you aren't as fat as a pot-bellied pig," Loren stated, drinking his ice tea.

The sound of a vehicle in the driveway caught their attention, Logan looking through the window. It wasn't Randy and Milly. The vehicle was a car, a red Cadillac.

"I think your date is here, sweetheart," Logan called, hearing a muted response that he couldn't quite make out. At a guess, he would say that she was brushing her teeth.

Logan went to the door, opening it before Tim could knock. "Hello Tim, come on in," Logan greeted, ushering him inside to sit at the table. "We're just finishing up supper. This is my friend Loren Chadley. Loren, this is Tim Kresser."

Shaking the youth's hand, Loren nodded his head to wards the stove. "We have some spaghetti left, Tim. You hungry?"

"No thank you," Tim answered politely. "I'm taking Tana to the new steak place over by Mazzios and in front of the old Wal-Mart."

"It only opened last week," Logan informed Loren. "What else do you two have planned for tonight?"

"A movie. They made a movie out of one of my favorite books. We want to see it. We will probably go to Keller's Hideout for a while after the movie is over."

Tana came down the stairs, the forest green shorts on, the blouse tucked in with a thin, black belt around her slim waist. A blue topaz necklace encircled her neck, resting prettily on her chest above the hem of her blouse. Her dark-blonde hair was pulled back, and spread loosely across her shoulders after being held in place by a green holder, a purse that matched the belt on her shoulder. She wore low-top Reeboks and socks that barely covered her ankles. Her strong, tanned legs were set off by the green and she looked radiant.

"You have your cell phone?" Logan asked, knowing it was an extension of her usually.

"My battery is dead and I have it charging. Tim has his with him," she replied, looking at Tim.

"I have mine Mr. Denton. Mrs. Denton made me write the number on the notepad on the door of the refrigerator," Tim said.

"Our informal registry," Logan said to Loren as the other man smiled, thinking all of this awaited him in the near future.

Tana smiled at Tim, giving her dad a kiss. "I'll be home between twelve-thirty and one," she promised, drawing a nod from Logan before she said good bye to Loren. Tim said good-bye too, following the lovely girl out the door. The sound of the car disappeared and Loren looked at Logan with a grin that was annoying.

"What?"

"You let her stay out past midnight?"

Frowning, Logan asked, "Why not?"

"No reason. Just that Tim reminded me of you," Loren commented blandly, his face suddenly showing no emotion.

"You son-of-a-bitch," Logan grunted, shaking his head at Loren's implication. "Tim is a good kid."

"So were you," Loren said, chuckling at Logan's remark. He saw that he had Logan's mind ticking and that made him want to laugh hard, but he didn't. Logan would realize that he was just aggravating him and that would spoil it entirely.

"God was punishing me when he gave me a daughter," Logan finally groaned and Loren laughed, unable to keep it in any longer. Logan laughed too, holding his stomach.

"Why are you laughing so hard?" Loren asked, wiping tears of mirth from his eyes.

"You," Logan said, doing the same to his eyes. "I have one daughter, but you have two."

Loren grew quiet, then chuckled some more, but with less humor. Damned if he wasn't right!

"You look gorgeous tonight," Tim commented after they got in the car. He folded the umbrella up, glad that they had snatched it from the hall closet before leaving, laying it in the back for later.

"I can't believe your dad let you borrow his car," Tana commented, rubbing the plush front seat. "Too bad they're bucket seats. I can't sit right next to you." Tim grinned, moving his hand to her knee and squeezing. He didn't tell her he had practically begged his dad to let him take his car. She smiled and watched the road. Her stomach rumbled. The spaghetti had looked good, but she hadn't eaten any except for a taste or two of the sauce after it had simmered.

"Dad didn't want me driving my old junker on a night like this. He would hate for me to wreck his car, but he would rather have a wrecked car than a dead kid. That's why he let me drive the Cadillac," Tim explained, obviously reciting something that he had heard his father say.

"He loves you, Tim," she said sweetly, leaning over to kiss his cheek as though saying that she did too. Tim grinned warmly, keeping his eyes on the road. He could hardly wait for the movie to be over. He was going to suggest to Tana that they go parking somewhere. Taking a deep breath, he hoped she would agree.

Randy and Milly were unloading the Blazer as Loren and Logan walked out the door. The two women looked harried, though the kids were going full bore, unencumbered by the long trip to the mall.

"Hectic day?" Logan asked, trying to keep his expression friendly.

Randy said, "It was interesting. The kids went everywhere at a run and so Milly and I followed at the same speed. When one tried on some clothes, the others wanted to try on clothes too. It was maddening." Stopping what she was doing, she took a deep breath of remorse. "I forgot to pick something up for your supper."

"No problem. Tana fixed us some spaghetti before she left. Besides, I should have had supper waiting on you," he replied.

"I'm too tired to eat," she said, giving him a kiss. Loren had just given Milly a kiss and then the two men climbed into the Bronco, Logan slipping on his holster before getting inside.

"Still carrying that .45, huh?"

"Yeah. It's been with me too long to be put in the house and retire it. I carry a revolver sometimes. But, I usually carry this pistol." Logan touched the butt of the .45 and then started the vehicle, pulling around the driveway and out to the highway.

"Alright, Adam 12, here we go," Loren joked, leaning back in the seat and watched the wet trees go by. It was sprinkling again and then it started raining. This seemed like a good way to spend the evening anyway.

The fork stopped its rise to his mouth and he could not take his eyes off the girl. She was gorgeous. He took a deep breath before putting the steak in his mouth, chewing out of reflex, not tasting the steak. It was rare and he liked it that way. For some reason, he liked it even better than he ever had before. But, he did not taste it now.

That girl was beautiful. Her legs were exquisite; powerful in an athletic way, the forest green shorts displaying the full, curvaceous buttocks beneath the material and the sexy vee of her pubic area. Her flat stomach was taut and the prominence of her pert breasts voluptuous for her slender frame. There was a stirring within him. It was not a sexual stirring, but the hunger awakening. It was awake and it had focused on her, even as she turned to where he could see her face. He almost dropped his fork when he saw her face. He knew her!

Well, not exactly, but he had seen her before. She was Sheriff Denton's daughter. He smiled wolfishly, taking a deep breath, sniffing of the air and scowling when he received the scent of cooking meat, a hint of garlic from the salad dressings and a dozen different perfumes wafting through the air. That was a disappointment.

Last night, he could smell the fear in the woman when she approached him in the parking lot. It had been a heady rush that had almost drove him into a frenzy. To smell fear! The hunger was giving him such wonderful powers. He was growing more powerful every day and the hunger was responsible for it. He knew that!

The other agents had gone to a bar, drinking and getting drunk, but he did not drink. Not much. Liquor numbed one's thoughts and he did not like that. Never had liked it, so he did not drink except a beer from time to time.

His vacation through here had not allowed him to stop long enough to realize the potential in hunting this small town and county. There were a lot of pretty girls in this rural part of Oklahoma and they would be easier to take. Tonight was the last night and that girl was beautiful. The hunger wanted her and so did he. To let the hunger consume her as he ravaged her would be enough fuel to let the hunger provide him with immortality. He knew that immortality was what the hunger held dangling before him. To think otherwise would be foolish.

He got up, dropping a one-dollar bill on the table for a tip, no longer hungry for food though he had only finished half of his meal, a T-bone steak and potato. Walking out the door after paying for his food, he got in his car, driving across the street to a business that was closed, sitting in the car and watching the restaurant. They would come out later and he would watch them, stalk them like a predator stalks its prey. Then, when the time was right, the hunger would be given full control of his body and he would take her. Maybe once or many times, whatever it took to sate the hunger. And, the hunger was ravenous tonight. It took everything within him to keep it in check.

Only a while longer, he thought while looking at his watch, absently rubbing the bulge in his jeans while thinking about her. Only a while longer.

The theater was dark and the movie was scary. Tana was against him as he let his hand rub her arm, holding her close. She had her hand on his leg and he had leaned over and kissed her on the side of the face several times. He had suggested that they go parking later, after the movie was over and she had nodded her head.

He was excited. She really did look pretty tonight and he had enjoyed himself with her. Letting his hand move under her arm, he stroked her side, letting his fingers roam across the side of her breast, Tana seeming not to notice. He would be glad when this movie was over!

The popcorn had been oily and he had not watched much of the movie. Sitting three rows behind the girl, he watched her bastard boyfriend kiss her, his arm around her while his hand rubbed her arm. He could see the boy's fingers move down and guessed what he was doing.

The girl belonged to the hunger now and the boy had made a mistake. Those fingers must not have been very important to him.

One fender-bender near Heavener and that had been the extent of the night. The two men had talked, catching up on a lot of different things as well as reminiscing about high school experiences.

"You ever think about what might have happened if we hadn't went up in those mountains, Logan?" Loren asked, face stolid as he peered out into the night.

"Yeah. Jerica and Kent would probably be alive. The others would be alive too. And then, maybe not."

"Maybe not is what I think too, Logan. Someone would have had to stop Madden and maybe we were the only people to do it," Loren postulated.

"There are other people a lot tougher than us," Logan stated, inclined to disagree with Loren's theory.

"True, but would they have had the mindset we had. You know we all came close to dying at one time or another out there. Yet, we survived."

"Milly ever mention Martin?" Logan asked quietly.

"No, it's almost like he didn't exist in her life. There have been times when she has had to conduct business to get his name off of her belongings, but she takes care of it herself. He was a bad man, Logan. Don't reckon he had a bit of good in him. He used everyone he ever came in contact with in life. Even his own parents," Loren stated rhetorically. It was obvious he thought about the subject at times.

"Randy doesn't like to talk about it either. That was a rough time for her."

"For all of us," Loren said. "My first wife was a cold, heartless bitch, but it still tore me up to tell her parents how she died. Her folks were okay and it almost killed her mother to lose Cindy."

Loren had lost his first wife during the massacre in Idaho and numerous friends had went up the mountain to never come down on their own.

"How many people have you told?"

Loren looked at him, shock on his face. "No one. No one would believe it anyway. Werewolf stories have given way to world-ravaging mutant strains of bacteria, alien invasions or serial killers. Werewolves were creatures of the Old World, before men knew what was lurking in the night." Chuckling sardonically, he scratched the top of his leg. "If people only knew what the night held, they would lock themselves in at night."

"Most werewolves have never killed anyone, Loren," Logan reminded him.

"I know, Logan. Most haven't. The ones that have may have done it for the right reason. Hell, I've killed people myself. It just gives me a creepy feeling when I think about people out there that are something else within."

"Have I changed?" Logan asked.

Shaking his head feebly, Loren said, "No, not really. You're the same hard-headed bastard I knew in high school."

"Do you feel uncomfortable around me?"

"No," Loren replied. "Nor do I feel like that around Vitoro. Maybe I don't feel exactly the way I explained myself. It's hard to understand or explain."

"Why don't we grab a soda pop instead," Logan suggested, turning at the Quik-Stop in Heavener. "I'll buy."

"Sounds good. I need a new pouch of tobacco anyway," his friend replied.

"We'll go through Holsom Valley, swing by the lake and mess around the mountains, watch the creeks running off the sides," Logan suggested.

"Just don't get us stuck," Loren warned, getting out to go inside with Logan.

"I haven't done that in years!" Logan said indignantly.

"So long as you can say that tomorrow," the dark-complected man teased, spying the tobacco rack as he went through the door. The Coke could wait.

The crowd was tightly packed as they walked up the ramp to the exit of the theater. Tim's right hand was on Tana's hip, the other carrying out their trash. They were going to hit Keller's for a few minutes and then go somewhere to be alone. That way Tana had not lied to her dad.

Neither of them noticed the man shadowing them, walking unobtrusively behind them, keeping a half dozen patrons between them and himself. They talked animatedly, the girl laughing and the boy grinning at her response, pitching the trash in the large open mouth of the trash can at the door.

He could smell her now. She had gone to the bathroom once and he had made his way to the concession stand, purchasing a box of chocolate-covered almonds to munch on. He followed her back inside the darkness, sniffing of her, the scent of her perfume light, the scent of her body even more enticing. It was pure and sweet, a fragrant ambrosia that clutched him, dragging him to her like an iron nail to a magnet.

The hunger had its tendrils out. He could trail her by her scent now and the hunger had marked her to be consumed as surely as those that accepted the mark of the beast were destined for the fires of hell.

The road was dark, the tall pines reaching high above it, making it seem like they were driving down a winding corridor. Tana had her hand on Tim's leg, watching the rain splattering on the windshield and the occasional flash of lightning that illuminated the spooky shadows and movements of the trees beside them.

The road had fresh gravel on it, keeping the mud beneath from splattering on the side of the car. They listened to a country station out of Ft. Smith; the music turned down low and soft from the speakers in the back.

The road ended at a gas well, the pad thick with gravel. There was no resounding thump of the compressor as it sit idle.

Parking the car, he turned off the ignition, bringing it on around to allow the radio to continue playing. The patter of the rain was louder with the motor off and it ran in torrents down the windows.

Looking at the constraints of the bucket seats, Tim asked, "Care to get in the back seat where there is more room?"

Tana chuckled. "Sure," she said, sliding between the two seats to the back, situating herself on the passenger side in the back as Tim struggled to get out from under the steering wheel.

"Thought I was going to tear my butt off," he said with a shake of his head.

He got in the back and looked at his girl friend. She moved close to him and their lips met. They were kissing passionately as the radio played soft, country music and the rain trickled off the roof of the car.

The forestry map did not show the road that the car had taken, but the metal sign beside the entrance gave him all the information he needed. It was a gas well road and a new one from the look of it. It couldn't be more than a mile to the end.

The rain had slowed to a steady drizzle, but small streams of run-off were everywhere. There was a forgotten logging road less than a hundred yards away. It had been opened up and was wide enough for a car. He parked his car in an area that the gas company had used to off-load equipment, enough brush around it to keep the vehicle from being readily visible to a passerby. It was far enough away from the other road to be forgotten. He was sure it was used only because of convenience. It wasn't on the old map either.

Stepping out of the car, he dropped his jacket back inside, the rain slowly drenching his shirt. It felt good to him, not cold at all. Reaching behind the front seat, he got a nightstick, newly acquired from a police car and just the kind of blunt instrument he needed for this kill.

Wiping his forehead, he felt a surge go through him, his head pounding momentarily as he staggered forward, using the night stick as a cane for a few steps before regaining his balance. The hunger was not to be denied and he began walking alongside the road, staying less than fifty yards away. He would find the object of his desire soon.

The rain was picking back up, but neither of the two people in the back of the Cadillac noticed. Tana's shirt was folded in the back window, her bra beside it. Tim's shirt was crumpled, thrust hurriedly beside them. They lay chest-to-chest, mouths locked hungrily as they kissed, hands grasping each other as they explored each other's body. The heat and closeness of their young bodies had a light sheen of sweat glistening on their skin. Her back was dark from the tanning booth and her body was like velvet as he touched her.

Clad solely in her shorts, her Reeboks still on her feet, Tana was eager to kiss Tim, loving the way his lips felt on her mouth. He had a habit of moving from her mouth to kiss her neck, ears and breasts, then back to her lips. He always lingered at her chest, causing small spikes of pleasure to race through her. Tim's shoes were in the floor.

A flash of lightning lit up the car and for a moment Tim could see Tana's magnificent body, his heart pounding heavily in his chest. He lowered his head to her firm breasts, Tana moaning softly. Tim wished the night would last forever.

He ran his hands down her legs, across her shorts and to the belt at her waist. Her eyes held his as he unbuckled it, releasing the buttons on her shorts as he kissed a fiery path across her muscular stomach. She was reticent, but his confidence helped to relax her. Tana wanted to stop, but couldn't bring herself to say the words. Her body was smoldering and she felt like a spark would set her aflame.

Lifting her hips, she let Tim slide her shorts off, folding them and placing them beside her blouse. Clad only in a pair of pink, lacy bikini briefs and her shoes, Tana looked like a golden goddess, a caricature of the goddess Aphrodite in living flesh. His fingers gripped the lacy waistband of her panties, easing them down her body, his breathing heavy as her nubile body was exposed in full naked glory in front of him. Unbuttoning his pants, he took them off, unable to believe what they were doing. The lightning flashed and he saw her nude body again, awaiting him. Struggling to get his jeans off without falling over, he had to slow, calm himself. It wasn't easy with such a beautiful girl lying before him.

A half-mile was the distance he calculated that he had already covered. He could see an opening ahead and assumed it was the gas well. It was still a quarter of a mile away if he was judging distance accurately. They were still up there; the car had not came out and he was positive that he could approach unseen. Gripping the nightstick, he felt a lurch in his stomach. It was time. Past time.

They kissed heatedly, Tim touching Tana, exploring the intimate parts of her as she held him to her, kissing his face and lips. She responded to his fingers as they moved gently, searching her, Tana arching her back and kissing him desperately. Her breathing was very hoarse, chest heaving erratically as the passion drove her wild with a tension that culminated within. Moving on top of her, Tim felt her tense momentarily, hesitate, and then spread her legs to receive him. His mouth covered her lips as he ran his right hand down her side. She looked hazily into his eyes, her body relaxing beneath him as he began entering her.

Tim felt sweat roll down his forehead as the damp warmth of her engulfed him slowly, Tana undulating her hips in a small circle before he was totally surrounded by her moist, heated sex. Tana gasped sharply as he entered her, the filling sensation wonderful to her as her back arched in response. She moaned, her chest pounding inside as her heart raced. She loved him so much.

The tightness was overwhelming, but Tim realized Tana was not a virgin. The rumor about Steve Becker was true. He lay across her, unmoving as his emotions faltered, but only for a moment. He loved her. No matter what, he loved her. His hands gripped her slender waist, Tana's knees pulling back even with her chest, then they were moving together. The young girl's chest was heaving, her hands on the small of his back as they made love; new lovers that could only see one another in the mist of their desire.

Their passion was an undeniable thing they could no longer ignore and they had finally answered the powerful yearnings of their young bodies. They writhed against each other passionately, desperately seeking the release that had drew them to this act like iron to a magnet.

This was so different from her first time. Tim was so gentle, so caring and his whispered words of how he loved her made her want him even more. Her first lover had been intense, but lacked the feeling, the subtle nuances that made this experience so wonderful and Tana realized she was learning the difference between being with someone and being with someone you love. Especially when that someone loves you back.

Her lovely face was a frozen mask of sublime pleasure as a fire built within her. His lips kissed her lips gently, pulling at them as his sighs made her own pleasure greater. She moaned loudly, a swarm of butterflies exploding in her stomach as something seemed to grip her; squeezing mightily and throwing her forcefully into the throes of sheer ecstasy.

Closing his eyes, Tim pushed himself as deep into Tana as he could, his face going slack as his climax shook through him from his head to his toes, gut-wrenching pulses that finally slowed. Burying his face in her neck, he moaned softly, striving to catch his waning breath as she did the same.

Afterwards, they lay beside each other awkwardly, unable to speak to the other as confusion settled in their minds.

Tana felt sick to her stomach. She had been with her second lover and all the advice Randy had given her was swept away in a moment of intense passion. Her face perplexed, Tana said, her soft voice strained, "I don't think I was completely ready."

A wave of disappointment and fear went over him like a thrown bucket of ice water at her tone. "What's wrong, Tana?"

Pushing up on her elbows, she searched for words, having a hard time talking. Taking a deep breath, she said, "Are you ready to be a daddy, Tim?"

Shaking his head, he leaned against the door. Why didn't he bring a condom!?

"I mean it, Tim. I wanted to be with you. I really do and it was wonderful!" she assured him, "But, I want it to be done responsibly. If we are going to act like adults, we need to be responsible like one too. Do you understand what I mean?" Her face was still flushed with passion, but she was serious about what she was saying.

He loved her. He knew that and didn't mind admitting it to himself. Nodding his head in defeat, he said for the first time, "I love you, Tana. Yes, I understand and I think we will be more responsible from now on. We can make the next time very special too." Laughing to himself, waving his arms as he flamboyantly indicated the inside of the red Cadillac, he added, "Our love should call for something better than the back seat of a car. Even the back seat of a Cadillac."

"I knew you would understand," she said.

"You weren't a virgin, were you?" he asked hesitantly.

Tana's face grew somber and she shook her head. "No."

"Those rumors about Steve Becker at the prom were true?"

"Yes," Tana said, "most of them. I made a mistake, but I cannot change it. Does it matter?"

"Not really," he replied with soft smile, kissing her lips. "I love you and that won't change."

Laughing, relieved that Tim had not grown angry, Tana said, "I love you too, Tim. Can we put on some of our clothes in case someone drives up on us?"

"Who would drive up on us?" he asked with a bemused look on his face.

"I . . . well, I told Jennie we were coming out here," she answered, a sorrowful expression on her face.

"That'll do it," he agreed, getting her panties and handing them to her.

Slipping her panties over her shoes and on her waist, she said coyly, reconsidering the odds of them being discovered, "We don't have to get completely dressed - at least for another hour." She checked her watch as she added the last part. Tim lay beside her, still naked as they began to kiss some more, their hands resuming their exploratory role. He loved the way her silky panties stretched across her firm, rounded bottom. The sounds of the storm were far away and the rain-washed all other sound away. Tana loved Tim and Randy had been right. If he loved her, he would share in responsibility.

The Cadillac was near the well house, the windows tinted too dark for him to see inside. He could see someone's shadow raise up from the back seat earlier and had frowned. The girl did not belong to the boy. She had been chosen by the hunger within him!. Didn't the little slut know she was special?! Clutching the nightstick, he circled the location, putting the well house between him and the car. That way he could definitely be on top of the car before anyone saw him.

Where there had been unbridled passion before, now they needed to talk, insure their friendship, the bond that linked them more powerfully than the sex act they experienced with one another. They talked of things they had done together -- last summer at the beach near the Arkansas River and skiing at Cowlington Point. Tana had been trying to talk her dad into buying two PWCs of some type to play on the water with during the summer vacation, but so far he had adamantly refused this request. She smiled when she mentioned that he did seem to be faltering on it more and more as she brought it up.

They paused to kiss and hold one another, their new intimacy actually bringing stronger feelings of love into their young lives, their awareness. They were still naked except Tana was wearing her panties and he was in his briefs. It might be embarrassing if Jennie and Greg came out here, but they could not say they actually caught the two making love.

Tana moved over Tim, kissing him lovingly and he encircled her chest with his arms, returning the deep kiss with all his passion. They did not break for air as they kissed for several long minutes, Tana finally breaking the kiss and smiling at him.

Tim lay gasping as Tana moved off of him. She kissed his sweating forehead and sat up as he moved his legs to sit in the seat, trying to catch his labored breath. Glancing at his watch, he thumbed the light and checked the time. They had another forty minutes before she had to be home for her curfew.

"I'm going to put on my pants and go to the bathroom," he announced boyishly.

"Out there?" Tana questioned.

"When you gotta go, you gotta go," he quipped, looking for his jeans. He appeared to be on the verge of getting out with just his underwear covering his body.

"You better put on your pants," Tana warned, finding his jeans and handing them to him. "What if someone drives up with you out there in your shorts?"

"You're right," he said, putting on his jeans, shifting the lump in his pocket that was his cell phone. "It would be hard to explain." He put on his shoes, leaving the laces loose and then reconsidering that idea. Tying them tight to keep them out of the water, he opened the door, whistling sharply at the cool drops of water pelting his arm and upper chest.

When the door shut, Tana pulled on her panties, picking up her shorts, contemplating putting them on. It felt strange sitting in the back seat alone, wearing only her panties. Leaning back against the door, she decided she would wait a while longer. It seemed provocative to be waiting on Tim like this. She giggled at her boldness, smiling happily. Tim did love her and she had finally told him that she loved him too.

Tim was exhilarated at what had happened between them. He did love Tana and the act was from his heart. Maybe it was early, but she loved him as much as he cared about her. The rain was refreshing and he felt like shouting aloud.

Maybe some of his friends would brag about what happened, but Tim would never consider doing something like that to Tana. His parents had told him he was too young to understand the complexities of love for another person. True love. Not puppy love.

What a crock! He didn't know where they came up with such archaic terms! He did love Tana and they had been discussing college. Tim was going to attend the same college Tana chose. That would keep them together and away from a long distance relationship, which almost always ended in disaster. Tim was actually considering marriage in a few years and though it scared him to have such serious thoughts; it excited him too.

Groaning as he urinated, he had let his bladder swell until it had been very uncomfortable. No pain, no gain was another saying that came to mind as he zipped up. Turning, he caught the movement out of the corner of his eye, throwing up his arm to block the blow.

Laying her shorts aside, she grimaced when she saw that her shirt was wrinkled, having been mussed when Tim put his pants in the window. Straightening it out, she saw something dark loom over the window and then it crashed heavily, spider-webbing the back window as the car shook violently. Tana heard herself screaming as she recognized Tim's back before he rolled off the side of the car. Another shadow detached itself from the well house and moved towards him.

Tim had managed to block the blow, but the pain that shot through his arm made him grunt, paralyzing his arm to his shoulders. He could feel the smashed cell phone in his pocket that took the full force of the club once, the small parts sharp and uncomfortable, though he had no time to attend to them. The man that attacked him raised the club to strike him again, but Tim leaped at him, seeking to shove the man off his feet in the slick footing of the mud. They grappled, the stronger man punching him across the face, Tim falling with a grunt. The sharp gravel scraped hide from his ribs and he felt a burning sting from the small of his back to beneath his right arm. Getting his feet beneath him, he started to stand.

Raising the club, the attacker hit a glancing blow across his shoulder, but Tim was fighting hard, throwing a punch to the man's groin. The man was unaffected, grabbing him by the shoulders and waist band of his pants, lifting him until Tim was above his head, casting him effortlessly into the car in a tangle of legs and arms. The metallic whump was heavy and his back shattered the back glass.

Pushing himself off the car, he could feel the bones in his arm grinding and he screamed. Landing beside the car, he yelled, "Get out of here, Tana! Leave!"

Tana looked at the ignition, leaning over the seat and struggling to make it to the driver's seat. It was empty! They were in Tim's pocket! She remembered them jingling when he put them there! She knew the cell phone was in the same place and her helplessness struck her like a punch to gut as she sucked in her breath in fear.

Opening the door to help him, she grabbed at her clothes in the seat. She stepped out in the rain, horrified by what she saw.

Tim was fighting a losing battle. His left arm was dangling crazily, a dozen bloody wounds marking his shirtless upper body, which was literally covered, in watery blood and one eye was swollen shut. His face was lumpy and the terror in his eyes scared her beyond belief.

"Run!" he yelled, his voice slurred with pain and fear. She hesitated, rain pouring over her naked body, her panties soaked through as she let her eyes go past Tim to the man on the other side.

"Run dammit!" Tim demanded, throwing himself feebly at the attacker to give her more time. Tana turned, racing into the darkness of the woods, whimpering fearfully as she ran. The limbs of the brush and the low hanging briars cut her skin and she grunted, letting the pain pass as though it was nothing. She was frightened beyond belief and ran straight into the woods without looking back.

Stopping after she had ran for a few minutes, she looked back, unable to see the gas well location or hear the awful struggle that she prayed was still going on. Glancing at the shirt in her hand, she put it on, covering her upper torso, the cloth sticking to her wet body.

The shorts weren't with the shirt and she wished she had put them on when she had thought about it. She was wearing panties and her shirt. Luckily, she had kept her shoes on. But, she wasn't thinking of any of that. She was remembering the face of the man she had seen. It had bristled with dark hair, the lupine features contorted grotesquely with insanity and something that chilled her to the bone. The man was a werewolf and he would be coming after her next.

Tim had never seen anyone so strong or this ugly. In the flashes of light he had seen a relatively normal human face, then the next light it looked darkened, hair sprouting around his cheeks, the eye sockets bulging. The cold eyes themselves remained the same, insane with maniacal fury and something indescribable.

The man had become annoyed. Several times he had fallen to his knees, shivering for a few seconds before leaping to his feet, more agile than he had been when he fell. Once, his face had seemed to run like liquid only to revert to his human self. The hunger was giving him strength and then abruptly taking it away. He didn't understand why, but he did not doubt its fury and power.

Tana was in the woods and Tim knew he would not last much longer. Diving for the car, seeking to lock himself inside, he almost made it, the end of the nightstick clipping his ankle, the sound of the bone breaking like a crack of thunder as he screamed. Falling to the gravel, he pushed with his legs to get under the car, the nightstick pounding his body. He grunted, laying still, the mad man beating his body savagely for several seconds before stepping back.

The hunger had enjoyed this, but the real reason he was here was out there, in the dripping rain beneath the canopy of the forest. He sniffed of the air near the place she had stood. Her scent was faint, but it was there. He pulled a knife from his belt, lifting the right hand of the boy on the ground. Putting the blade in the joints of the index and middle fingers, he wrenched the blade violently, casting the severed digits to the mud with a satisfied snarl.

Opening the door of the car, he went to his knees on the seat, almost overcome with the scent of sexual arousal in the vehicle. She had been very aroused, her secretions providing a plethora of information to his nostrils and her scent filled the entire car, masking the scent of the boy almost completely. He shivered momentarily. Only the smell of sweat and semen were strong enough to be noticed over that smell.

Turning to the woods, he grinned lewdly, loping awkwardly into the forest like a strange two-legged animal. He had never run like this before, but it felt natural. And, he was moving very fast.

The cut on her leg was bleeding and she looked at it fearfully. A wild animal easily smelled blood and the animal chasing her would home in on it like a shark in open water. She picked up a handful of mud, clogging the wound with it and running again. She knew that she was in serious trouble. The woods were the werewolf's home and the creature would catch her if she could not outsmart it.

"Tim will be pissed!" Greg giggled, unconcerned with the fact that Tim would be giving him a cussing when they pulled in on Tana and him. They had decided to find Tim and Tana and give them a hard time.

"He will be if we cut him off like we did last time," Jennie laughed, pointing out the turn to the gas well location as it came up.

"Were they . . .?"

"Not yet, but they were thinking about it seriously. I'll bet Tana gave in tonight," she speculated after giving him her own opinion as to Tana and Tim's relationship. "They have went together long enough!"

Greg gave her a strange look under the cover of darkness. He had only been going with Jennie for a month and had heard some wild rumors about her since. He had dismissed them, but he was beginning to wonder if he had been dismissing the truth.

The headlights cut through the night like a knife through warm butter and they could see the Cadillac parked beside the well house. One door was open and the back window was crushed, a wide dent across the rear compartment.

"God! The car's destroyed!" Jennie gushed, tears filling her eyes. Greg stopped the truck, his heart pounding in his throat.

"Don't get out!" Jennie cried, clutching his upper arm, terrified by the destruction of the car.

"I've got to," Greg said, gently removing her hand from his arm, opening the door and pulling something from behind the seat of his truck. Speaking to Jennie, he ordered, "If something happens and it looks like I may be down, leave me." She nodded her head, sliding behind the wheel of the truck. He hoped she wouldn't take off and leave him before he looked at the car.

The single barrel shotgun was shiny in front of his lights, the dark barrel wet with rain and he walked to the car on pin-and-needles. The legs protruding from under the car caught his attention and he pulled at them, gasping in shock, vomiting beside the car.

Tim's face was mangled and swollen. His chest was lacerated with a hundred cuts and contusions.

Greg was scared. He looked in the car and saw a pair of shorts and a bra lying in the seat. He shook his head and then backed away, eyes searching the darkness for whatever or whoever had committed this assault.

He was white-faced when he got in the truck. Jennie had moved from behind the steering wheel. "Are they dead?" Her face was frightened and Greg still felt his stomach tumbling ominously.

"Tim is," he replied as she gasped, tears flowing down her cheeks. "Tana is missing. We got to go get help." He shut the door and threw the truck in gear, showering rocks from under his back wheels when he took off down the gas well road. He was driving too fast for safety, but he didn't care. His friend's mutilated face was stuck in his mind and all the trees whipping by beside the road couldn't erase it.

"I can smell you," the man said to no one in particular, his voice almost a growl. She smelled like fear now, but he could smell the other scent too. That scent had stirred him to an erection.

"So sweet," he muttered gutturally. "So sweet and delicious."

He lost her for a second, pausing to test the wind. Lifting his nose in the air, he caught the scent, lips curling back to reveal his teeth as he smiled, changing directions to trail her. He couldn't be too far behind her now.

Tana ran through the creek, hoping to mask her scent, praying that her plan would work. Soaked, she didn't feel the coolness of the air. Her blood ran hot with fear, though she had got control of herself. She wasn't whimpering anymore and she was thinking, seeking to outwit the werewolf. She climbed the bank, gasping for air. She was in excellent shape, but the exertion was tremendous.

That it followed her was a certainty. She cringed at every snap of a twig, every sound that was not natural. It was back there and it wanted her.

Running along the bank, she cried out when a saw briar tore a gash in her shin, hopping a few steps as blood dripped down her leg into her sock.

"Damn!" she said, her face a dual mask of fear and the determination to live.

Smearing mud across this wound too, she ran, falling twice and picking herself up to keep running. There was no one to save her and she would be forced to do it herself. The odds were definitely against her.

The truck shot out on the highway, careening wildly as it fishtailed towards the ditch, barely righting itself as it headed down the highway.

"Got one!" Loren said excitedly as Logan flipped on the flashers, pulling in behind the truck. The truck stopped, skidding to a stop so fast the rear of the truck spun to the right

"Might be trouble!" Loren suggested suspiciously.

Logan was silent as he stepped out of his truck, recognizing the vehicle as belonging to a boy in Tana's class. The young man half fell out of the truck, his face pale as he cried out.

"Sheriff Denton! He's dead! Dear God, he's dead!" the boy cried, hands clutching Denton's shirt, eyes wild with fear. The girl was Jennie Tolbert, Tana's best friend, and she was scared to death too. Loren had grabbed her and she shook violently in his arms as though from a chill.

"What is it, son?!" Logan asked when he saw that the kids were terrified.

"Tim! Your daughter! Dead, oh God!!" Greg mumbled, breaking down as the Sheriff grew more alarmed at the mention of his daughter.

Shaking the boy harder than he intended, Logan demanded, "Where?! What happened?!"

Catching his breath, Greg said between breaths, "The new gas well. Car . . . Cadillac with door open. Tim dead! Tana gone!" He was shaking and crying again.

"Get in your truck and go to the court house, son. I'll be there to talk to you later," Logan said more calmly than he felt.

The boy agreed, taking Jennie's hand and racing back to the truck.

"And slow down!" Loren yelled as he crawled back in the truck. Logan was already driving, the four-wheel drive flying down the muddy road.

Logan called in back-up, getting an answer from the closest unit over twenty minutes away.

"Give me the key to this rifle lock," Loren demanded.

"Said you'd stay out of it," Logan mumbled, his mind on the horrors that his imagination concocted.

"That was before Tana was involved, gawddammit! Give me the fucking keys!" Loren yelled, the Marine in him shining through.

"Glove compartment," Logan said, the truck jerking violently as he barely missed the ditch when he made the second turn. It was a mile from here to the new gas well road. He prayed he wasn't too late.

The air left her lungs and she grunted when her feet shot out from under her, Tana sliding pell-mell down the hill side as the low brush added a dozen more scratches and cuts to her body. She felt a jerk followed by a short breath-taking fall before her suddenly bare buttocks splashed in a pool of cool water below. Her underwear was gone, ripped to shreds and hanging on the limb of a short scrub oak ten feet up the steep, muddy bank.

Standing, she looked around her, pulling her shirt down instinctively to hide her nakedness. It was dark. Very dark, but her eyes were somewhat accustomed to the night and the woods were not too thick with brush to blank out all of the light. Wiping the sore areas of her legs for a moment, she picked her route more carefully. She crossed the creek, running down the low side, hoping she didn't run into the creature she sought to escape.

He was amazed at how well he could see in the dark. He had never had great night vision, but the darkness had not been a hindrance to him. In fact, he could see almost as well as he normally did during the evenings at dusk.

Something caught his eyes as he looked at the small troughs of mud, the furrows made by the girl's elbows or knees. Something hung on a low limb of brush and he growled hungrily, catching the feminine scent and recognizing what it had been.

Hurrying to it, he smiled happily, his chest rising and falling as he saw he was correct. The girl had fallen and lost her panties here. She was nude except for her shirt.

The hunger twisted his guts as he pulled the torn panties to his nose, inhaling deeply. He laughed hoarsely, putting them in his pocket. He was behind her and the hunger would be sated yet. It would not be long now.

The Cadillac was like Greg left it and Loren hit the ground running as the truck came to a stop. Logan was a moment behind him, the Springfield Armory .45 in his hand. The Mini-Thirty was in Loren's right hand when he peered into the car, then laid in the seat while checking on the boy. Logan looked inside the car.

"He's alive, Logan," Loren announced, pulling the boy from under the vehicle. "Not by much, but he's breathing shallowly."

"Let's get him out of the rain," Logan said, water dripping from his face.

They moved him to the truck, laying him in the seat. Logan went back to the car, picking up his daughter's bra and shorts. Loren was behind him, getting the semi-auto rifle from the seat.

Logan dropped them in the seat, his face a mask of worry.

"I think she took them off willingly, Logan. I think this boy took them off of her, not the man that beat him like this."

Logan shook his head in agreement, holding the blue topaz necklace in his hand. The chain was intact.

He searched the ground around the car, seeing the nightstick on the gravel. A dim, rain-washed print could be seen on the ground in a muddy area, the track was leading towards the woods. The nightstick was close, obviously discarded by the man that had beaten Tim. Picking it up, he staggered in shock, "Oh my God!"

"What?"

"His scent," Logan said weakly, as though he was out of breath. "The man is a werewolf!"

"Shit!" Loren cursed vehemently. "What are you going to do?"

Stripping the gun belt from his waist, Logan said, "I'm going to save my daughter if I can!"

Loren watched, unable to take his eyes off his friend as his body changed in front of him, taking the form of a powerful animal as the boots he wore were destroyed. The man- beast ripped the clothes from its form with two quick swipes of the clawed hands. Then, Logan was running for the forest, changing into a wolf as he ran. It was the first time he had witnessed a change and it sent chills up Loren's spine.

The boy groaned and the radio crackled, a disappointed voice saying, "Logan, this is Andy. The water is over the bridge between me and you. It'll be another fifteen before I can get there."

Picking up the mike, Loren said, "This is Loren Chadley. I am riding with Sheriff Denton tonight. We need an ambulance with a life flight unit ready at the hospital! I repeat: I need an ambulance with plasma and a life flight unit ready at the hospital. We have one victim down with cuts and contusions across most of his body. He probably has head injuries."

"I'll relay the message," a voice said over the radio. "I'm Bill Jackson. Caught Logan's message on the scanner at home and I'll be at your position in less than ten minutes. Is there anything else I need to know?"

"Yeah. I'll be the man carrying the rifle," Loren replied, dropping the mike on the floor. He watched the woods, prepared for any eventuality. He prayed Logan would be in time.

CHAPTER FOUR

Lying on the rock shelf, Tana fought to keep her breathing from being loud enough her stalker could hear it. The wet rock was cold against her bare flesh and she shivered as much from fear as the cool rain. It was unseasonably cool for mid-summer and she felt small chill bumps across her legs and buttocks. Her shirt was soaked clear through, the front torn badly to expose her stomach to the elements.

She had seen him a few seconds ago, further down the hill, following her trail like a bloodhound tracking an escaped convict. He swayed back and forth when he walked, horrifying her when he raised his head, seeming to look right at her as he sought her scent in the air. Finding it, he turned right, still following her trail.

Disappearing towards the creek, she waited a few seconds before getting up, running quietly along the rim of the hill for over a hundred yards before stopping to rest. She was getting tired and the creature was as tenacious as a bulldog. She no longer thought of him as a man or human. He killed more wantonly than an animal. He was determined to find her and she doubted her ability to shake him off her trail. There was nothing of the loser in Tana Denton. She refused to lay down and die. Taking one deep breath, she sprinted another hundred yards, going partially up the hill and back down in the running water of a run-off creek that made a small waterfall in its course to the valley. Whether her ploy actually worked or not, she didn't know, but she was still alive. That was her way of judging the success of her ideas.

Rocks tumbled down the hill behind her, the sounds faint, but definite and she felt her heart skip a beat. He was on the ledge! She ran, panicking now as the threat of death came closer with every passing second.

The large beast was covering the ground like a gazelle running from a cheetah, leaping large boulders and fallen logs with the grace of an Olympic athlete. The rippling muscles beneath the dark, coarse coat of fur belied the true power that lay within the beast. With a single bound, it crossed a swollen creek, leaping twenty-five feet to land like a cat on the far side, and its gait never slowed.

Stopping its advance, it ran up a fallen tree, standing six feet off the ground as it raised its shaggy head and howled.

The hauntingly lonely howl pierced the night, wavering forever in the valley between the mountains. It split the relative silence of the rain-dampened forest with its feral tone and savage beauty and Tana Denton stopped when she heard it, knowing that it was meant for her. Only one creature could make that heart-stopping noise and that was an adult wolf. The man behind her was still in the form of a man and the howl had been too far away to be him anyway.

Looking over her shoulder, she dropped down the hill, hide scraping on the rocks as she slid to the bottom. Running down the hill, she could hear the grunt of surprise when the man saw her and she yelled, hoping desperately that the night beast would hear her. "Daaadddddyyyyy!!!"

The man stopped, forgetting about the gnawing hunger driving him. The girl had yelled something and now the chilling howl of the creature that screamed in the night cut through the air again and it was closer, the fierce note insinuating danger, and the promise of death.

It had answered her!

The thought was foolish, but he knew it was true! It had been answering her. Indecision caused him to hesitate.

That howl had been for him too. There had been a threatening note of finality in that howl. The hunger was within him, but he sensed that the predator had just become the prey. He could see the girl, the tawny flesh of her naked buttocks enticing him as she ran away from him. The sharp tangy scent of her blood was hanging in the air, the sweet musky scent of her sex lying subtly beneath the scent of her blood and he almost leaped from the cliff in pursuit.

But, the creature that howled was out there and he knew in his mind that it was coming to her.

Grunting disgustedly, he turned, running back along the ridge and heading for his car. That thing was coming to the girl. Then it would be coming for him.

The limbs slashed across the fur coat, but the beast did not pay attention to the tiny pinpricks of pain, shoving its body through briar tangles to explode through to the other side. The small cuts were healed before he made two leaps. He had heard her voice and knew approximately how far she had been when she screamed for him.

Crossing another creek, his back feet slipping, he grunted and then was moving forward. She was close and he would find her soon.

The scent of the man was in the air too and he knew that he had been close when Tana yelled. It had been taking a chance that she would recognize the howl of the wolf as belonging to him.

He rounded a thick cedar, skidding to a halt when he lay eyes on the figure of his daughter. She was standing with her back against a tree, facing him with her eyes wide in terror. Her hands held a thick stick and he could see she intended to fight. Logan changed as he moved forward, taking his daughter in his arms as she began to cry with huge sobs that shook her entire body, tossing the stick to the mud.

She almost collapsed and Logan picked her up, one arm under her legs, the other beneath her shoulders as he carried her across the creek, helping her to sit on the bank as he washed the mud from her face with water he cupped in his hands. His eyes searched her for wounds, ignoring her nakedness as he confirmed she was unharmed.

Tana sat for only a few seconds before she said with a catch in her voice, "Tim's dead, Daddy."

"He wasn't when I left, sweetheart, but he's badly hurt," Logan informed her. Pointing towards a dark cloud hovering in the distance, he instructed her, "Walk towards that cloud and keep the breeze at the back of your left ear. You'll come out at the gas well and Loren is waiting there. Can you go by yourself?"

Her face was woebegone, but she hadn't given up. She had struggled to survive. "I can do it, Dad. Are you going after him?"

He nodded his head, splashing through the water as he ran towards the last place he had scented the man, changing into the wolf as he ran. Tana watched him disappear, feeling strangely safe in the dark forest now. Her father was in the woods and he was the most dangerous beast in the forest.

Plunging head-long through the wet brush, the man instinctively knew where his car was hidden. The distance was over a mile, but he had several minutes head start on the creature. If the beast that howled went to girl before it came for him.

Why would a wolf call to her? Why had she screamed for her daddy? Why was he so positive that the beast that howled would be hunting him? He wasn't for sure, but the hair standing on the back of his neck was for real.

The hunger wasn't bothering him now, strangely aware that there was a threat to its existence as well as the man it shared a symbiotic existence with in his body. It urged him to run faster.

The leaves were wet, no noise coming from them as his full weight came down on two feet, his back legs swinging in front of the front legs as he kept the scent ahead of him. Twice, he had to stop, catch the scent before taking the change in route the man had taken.

Logan recognized the scent. The man wasn't a werewolf yet. If he had been a wolf with the full powers of the change, his daughter would be dead now.

This was the same man that killed the woman from Tulsa. The scent from the body had been too faint, too intangible for him to get a good feel of it, but his instinct told him that this was the man. Vitoro had told him that his instinct would become more powerful and it had.

He was going to kill this man. This man would not go to prison. He was a danger and would continue to be one until he was killed and Logan had taken an oath that was much older than the one he had taken as a law officer. The highest level of that law demanded that he kill this man, to destroy him before he could draw attention to a species that had remained hidden for over two hundred years with success.

The scent grew stronger and he was nearing the county road. There was no sound of a car, but he was sure that the man was close to the point where he had parked his vehicle. Logan began running faster.

He was going to die. Loren's face was flushed with helplessness. It wasn't the first time he had seen someone die. In fact, he had seen too many people die, beginning with his own sister before he was five years old.

The boy had woke up earlier and Loren had told him to rest, to conserve his strength to fight. Tim had mouthed one word and it was the name of his girl friend. Loren told him she was going to be fine. He didn't think Tim believed him, but he had closed his eyes to rest.

Walking a few steps from the boy, he checked his watch, curling his lips in anger when he saw it had been over ten minutes since he had spoken to the deputy. Something caught the corner of his eye and he spun to face it.

Loren slowly swung the rifle towards the movement in the woods, walking away from the boy when he thought he might have to fire. Closing his eyes thankfully when he recognized Tana, he lowered the rifle and mouthed a quick prayer of thanks before grabbing the rain slicker in the truck and taking it to her to cover herself with.

She ran to him and he averted his eyes from her nakedness as he put the slicker around her, appalled at the cuts and bruises across her arms and legs. A long rash-like abrasion across her hip was seeping blood even now. She clutched Loren tightly and he felt an almost paternal surge of love for his best friend's daughter as she buried her face in his chest while she sobbed. He rubbed her head, unsure of the words he felt he should say as he remained quiet. She pulled her head back, starting towards the truck. Loren had Logan's pistol in his hand, turning to check the woods before they walked back to the truck.

Tana was quiet, unable to speak as she cried softly. Headlights were coming down the road and Loren said, "That's Bill Jackson. Your Dad told me about him." Looking at his watch, he added, "He said he could be here in ten minutes. That was fifteen minutes ago."

Walking towards the truck, Loren gripped her shoulder, stopping her. "He's hurt bad, sweetheart, and he don't look like he did when he picked you up. I bound up his hand. That bastard cut two of his fingers off."

She sobbed, looking at Loren. "I want to see him, Loren. I love him."

He shook his head, letting her pass. Holding her shoulders, he hugged her as she cried, decimated by the sight of his brutally assaulted body. His face was caved in and blood covered him like a second gruesome skin. She almost cried out when she saw that one eye was open and he blinked.

"Alive," he mumbled, closing his eye.

Putting her hand on his arm, she said, "Your alive, Tim. Fight! Fight for it, Tim!"

Loren hugged her, stepping away to meet the truck that was parking between him and the Cadillac, a stern-faced man wearing a revolver stepping out. Loren didn't tell Tana that she had misunderstood him. He wasn't declaring himself alive; he had been happy to see that she was alive.

The man stuck out his hand, Loren shaking it politely as Bill surveyed the scene. "I'm Bill Jackson, Loren. Logan's told me a lot about you."

"He's mentioned you a few times too, Bill. How long before that ambulance arrives?" Loren was all business and Bill thought that he could get to like the taciturn man.

The swirling red lights rotated across the trees and the ambulance came into sight before Bill could answer. Glancing to Tana, Bill asked, "You all right, Tana?"

She nodded quietly, standing beside Tim. Bill looked the boy over, grimacing sadly at the battered features of the young man. Angrily, he shook his head, stepping away from the truck as the ambulance pulled in behind the truck. When the ambulance stopped, Tana waved for the medical technicians to come to her, eager for them to take Tim.

Stepping back to where Logan's friend stood, Bill asked, "Is Logan in the woods after the man that did this?"

"He's out there and I think that he'll find the man that did this. Don't send back-up out there, Bill. Logan ain't bringing him back alive and he sure as hell don't need any witnesses," Loren warned, his voice low as the emergency medical technicians squeezed in beside Tana, checking out the boy in the seat of the truck.

Bill spat on the ground, eyes locking on Loren's, face grim, but he didn't speak. If that man had done something like this to his daughter, he would want him dead. If Tim were his son, he would kill the man himself. "All right Loren. I'll have the other deputies to put up roadblocks coming out of this area. There is only about five roads that the man could take if he's parked anywhere near." Pausing for a while, Bill glanced at Loren cautiously, noting that the man was holding Logan's handgun. "What is Logan carrying?"

Looking at the handgun in his palm, Loren grunted, peering straight into Bill's eyes. "A whole lot of anger."

His lungs ached as he pushed himself, cursing in his mind as he heard the engine turn over and start. He urged his legs to cover more ground and abruptly, he saw the red taillights through the openings in the brush. The car had been backing up and now it was moving forward as the engine revved up. Logan changed as he ran, losing a few precious seconds as he took the strong, lupine form of the wolf-man, his tall, lean body combined with the savage ferocity of the wolf. Long claws extended from his fingers, fangs protruded from his lips and he was many times as strong as any man.

The white car was moving on the mud road and he slammed into the side, claws grasping at the metal as they shredded the thin skin of the car to grip the metal frame of the door. For a moment, he saw wild eyes that were trapped in the body of a man that was no longer just human.

Jerking hard against the car, his legs dragged in the muddy road, a rooster-tail of mud behind his feet. Reaching up with his other hand, he pulled himself forward, determined to sink his claws in the vulnerable throat of the man behind the wheel.

The driver was terrified by the creature clinging to his car. He was whipping the car from one edge of the road to the other, pushing the accelerator desperately as the vehicle picked up speed, dancing in the potholes and slinging Logan wildly, threatening to dislodge him from his perch. Logan wanted to be on top of the car, but he could not do get there. Then, the car slid sideways, turning a full three-hundred sixty degrees and he felt the metal give and the door opened, the hinges snapping as he briefly floated in the air, door and werewolf slamming solidly in the bank of the ditch, his back and hip breaking from the impact, the scream of rending metal screeching in his ears, the door bouncing across a boulder that had been pushed off the road when it was built.

Laying in the muddy water of the ditch, Logan gasped at the pain, feeling it gradually grow less as his body healed itself until he could no longer feel a tingle after thirty seconds. Standing exhaustedly, he looked down the winding, country road, shifting shapes to his human form. The car was gone. Yet, he knew the man he had seen behind the steering wheel. He knew him and the car. The killer was a government agent. And, he was instrumental in the FBI's investigation of this serial killer.

He turned and walked into the woods, hoping that Loren would come back for him and he would not be forced to cross two or three mountains to get home. There was a man to kill and he had a face. One that he knew and one that he had never suspected.

He had to hurry. His bags were packed, but his car would be easy to track. Looking around the parking lot, he spied a late model Chevrolet truck and smiled. That one he could hot-wire if he had to do something drastic.

Gripping his bags, he hurried across the parking lot, glancing over his shoulders to see if any of his companions were showing up from club hopping. Undoubtedly several of them went to Ft Smith tonight. Putting his bags in the back, he cursed beneath his breath when the door in front of it opened. Drastic was in high gear now.

A blonde woman was giggling as she stepped outside, her pants gone, the long T-shirt hanging over her panties. She was talking to someone behind her, looking over her shoulder. "I'll do that after I get the beer out of the pick-up," she insisted with a drunken giggle.

"The beer" was never gotten. The man stepped towards her as she gasped at his surprise appearance, abruptly aware of the danger in his presence, the silenced automatic belching quietly. She gulped, slumping forward with a round, bloody circle above her right eye, a spray of blood splashing the doorjamb.

"Sandy! What's wrong?" a man's deep voice said from inside, alarmed by the sharp slap of the spent round in the wood of the doorjamb. He was wearing his underwear, socks and a cowboy hat. He had a beer in his left hand. "What the hell . . . ?"

He never finished. The man shot him three times through the chest, the man jerking spasmodically as his cowboy hat rolled off his head. Falling, his body crushed the hat under his weight. He tried pulling himself to the phone as the agent calmly carried the dead woman inside, laying her on the bed and putting a fourth round through the back of the wounded man's head. He had only managed to drag himself a few feet, leaving a wide bloody path beneath him and the final round slammed his face in the floor where he died with a harsh, gurgling sigh.

Searching the man's wadded blue jeans, the agent found the truck keys and his wallet. There were a few dollars in the wallet and he took them, tossing the wallet on the man's bloody back contemptuously.

Pulling the DO NOT DISTURB sign from the doorknob, he hung it on the outside. "No need for an early checkout," he said cheerfully, pushing the semi-automatic in his waistband before shutting the door.

Going to the truck, he opened the door and climbed inside, frowning as he shoved over the sack with the leftover six-pack carton. A half-eaten hamburger fell in the floor with a plop. Some people were such pigs!

The motor sounded good and he drove the vehicle out of the parking lot. He had parked the car down the block in the back lot of a church. They wouldn't find it until in the morning and by then, he would be long gone.

Miranda blinked back the tears of her fear, silent as terror clutched her heart. Bill had told her to come to the hospital and bring some clothes for Tana. She was all right, but she needed some clean clothes, something loose.

Logan Jr. was quiet, wide-eyed as he watched his mother drive at speeds that he had never witnessed in the past. Milly and her two girls were in their Blazer behind them.

Going up the hill, she could see the hospital at the top. She grunted as the truck went over the train tracks, jostling them both. There was a parking spot in the front and she pulled in, grabbing the bag beside her as she hustled inside. Logan had to run to keep up with his mother.

Bill met her as she came through the emergency room door. "Slow down, Miranda! She's okay! She's okay," he repeated, catching her in his arms. He was amazed at her strength and she would have been hard to hold if she hadn't slowed, breathing deeply to fight away the tears.

"What happened, Bill?" she asked, vaguely aware that Milly and her girls had entered behind her.

"It was that serial killer. . ."

"Oh God!" Miranda sobbed, hand going to her mouth as her legs went weak. She moved to a chair and sat down.

"Tana is alright," Bill insisted, kneeling beside her and holding her hand. "She's having antiseptic put on her cuts and bruises. They wanted to observe her to make sure she didn't go into shock. From the sound of her voice when they put the antiseptic on her wounds, she ain't in shock," he added wryly, a faint grin on his weather-beaten face.

"Tim?" Miranda asked, feeling her heart thumping solidly in her chest as Bill's face went blank.

"Don't know, Miranda. He was too bad for the doctors to take a chance on a life flight to Tulsa. The boy is hurt bad and his folks were in Ft. Smith visiting his sister. They haven't got here yet. He took on the guy while Tana escaped in the woods," Bill explained.

"The woods? What were they doing in the woods?" Miranda asked in disbelief. They were supposed to be dancing.

"They were doing what all kids do sometime, Miranda. They were parking, both of them in the back seat and they were . . . doin' what kids do," he said, finding it hard to explain to her.

"I don't care, Bill. Just so long as she's not hurt," Miranda stated, having caught a second wind. She stood, following Bill as Milly and the kids walked behind her silently.

Logan had stepped out on the road and Loren picked him up, shaking his head as his friend got inside, covering himself with a jacket.

"First time I ever picked up a naked man off the side of the road," Loren commented gruffly.

"Yeah, you usually go to a club to do that," accused Logan, unable to add the smile of humor that was behind the comment.

Grunting, Loren asked, "Is it over?"

"No," Logan replied, looking down the muddy road as the windshield wiper beat a steady cadence. "I'm afraid it has only begun."

"He got away?" Loren asked in bewilderment.

"Not entirely. I ripped the fucking door off his car," Logan growled, shivering from the cold water and the sudden heat of the defroster.

"So we're looking for the one-armed car?"

Logan gave him a look of disgust at the poor joke and Loren chuckled to himself as he drove to Logan's house. He knew Logan needed some clothes before he did anything else.

"What happened? Tana wouldn't talk after she saw her boy friend in that condition."

"He still alive?" Logan asked, ashamed that he had let Tim's condition slip his mind.

"Was when I saw him last. He's a tough kid, Logan. He may make it," Loren said hopefully.

"Sure hope so. How is Tana taking it?"

"She rode in the ambulance with him. Couldn't talk her out of it and Bill said it was fine if the technicians didn't care."

"Bill call Miranda?" Logan asked.

"Yes, and he should beat her to the hospital. We won't be far behind."

Logan thought about the man he had seen. Would he run? Not that it mattered for now. He was going to check on his daughter and the young man that fought off the monster that sought to kill her.

That sickened Logan. He knew the man was after Tana. He could smell the musk of the man's excitement as well as the faint scent of his daughter's previous activities. Only barely though. The killer had been reeking with pent-up passion and . . . madness? The man had wanted Tana badly, and he would have ravaged her if he could have caught her, leaving her in a bundle of severed limbs in an attempt to hide his own hellish desires. Tim had simply been an obstacle. The kid was brave. Logan gave a short prayer for him and sat up as the driveway to his house came up on the left.

He dressed quickly, belting on his revolver before coming out the door, picking up a magazine for his .45 that had been hidden behind a glass candy dish on a bookshelf. A speed dump with six rounds for his .357 went in his pocket too and then he was out the door, climbing back in the truck with Loren.

Handing the magazine to Loren, he said, "They're silver. Seventy-three percent silver with some other metals as hardeners mixed in. There's enough silver in it to wipe out a half dozen werewolves if you were to shoot through them."

Loren put the clip in his pocket beside the gun. Pulling from the driveway, he took a deep sigh. Werewolves again! He just wished that Logan had given him more than a single clip of ammo. The last werewolves he had dealt with came in packs!

Randy hugged Logan as he gripped her, rubbing the back of her hair as she sobbed. Logan kissed the side of her face. "How's Tim?" he inquired, knowing the boy's condition was far more desperate than his daughter's.

Shaking her head, she said, "Not good. His parents are on their way. Tim's father and him were friends when they were teenagers. Bill called them and I think it's the hardest thing he's ever done, Logan. He . . ." She was unable to say anything else as she started crying again. "Tana could have been killed," she sobbed.

"Is Tana with Tim?" he asked.

"No. She's having her wounds cleaned. Bill says she's doing fine."

"I know who it is," Logan said softly, feeling her go rigid in his arms.

"Who?" she asked, her face buried in his chest.

"I'll make the accusation in the morning. After, I've killed him," he stated.

She looked in his face. "Logan, you can't kill him for this!"

"He's a werewolf, Randy. I scented him and he's a wolf that hasn't completed the change yet. He might not even know he's a wolf."

That changed things in Miranda's mind. "Do you want me to call, Vivian?"

Vivian Denton was his brother's wife and a close friend. She was a werewolf too and had been elected to the role of Protector of the Law. The Law of the Wolf was a code that all werewolves followed to keep their existence secret. The law had come into existence after one crazed wolf cost the lives of thousands of werewolves and even more innocent humans.

The Law of the Wolf stated: *No werewolf may take the life of a human or werewolf except in the defense of life or family, and any who break this law will be hunted and slaughtered by a council-appointed Protector of the Law.*

"No," Logan said hesitantly. "She doesn't need to be involved. Not yet."

Miranda didn't say anything else about the killer. Her thoughts were filled with Tana and Tim. "The doctor says that Tim will lose most of the sight in that eye. He sounded certain. He didn't sound certain that Tim would last out the night."

Logan nodded weakly. He felt sick to his stomach. Maybe it was partially his fault. Any parent that thought they could prevent their teenaged children from having sex were fools. Why hadn't he talked to Tana?

If she was going to . . . If they decided to make that very adult decision, he would prefer they rented a motel room than park on a deserted road and do it in the back seat of a car. Maybe that wasn't a proper thought for a father, but he would rather she was safe and taking responsibility for her actions than putting herself in danger and taking a risk at getting pregnant.

It was too damned late to curse fate. He couldn't change things, couldn't take that boy out of harm's way though he wanted to very badly.

The nurse had given Tana her clothes and Logan saw her as the swinging doors banged open. She was covered with small bandages and he saw her face lock on him as she ran to him. He grabbed her, hugging her tightly, smelling the antiseptic and soap they used on her. She had taken a shower and her hair was still wet, smelling of the shampoo. It had the mild scent of a baby shampoo.

"Daddy. I'm so sorry, Daddy! Tim . . ." Her sobs were racking her entire body and he kissed the top of her head.

"It's okay, Tana. It's not your fault. It's not your fault or Tim's, baby." Tears fell from his eyes and Loren's face was solemn as he met Logan's gaze. Randy held Logan Jr. against her legs as he watched his dad hold Tana while his eons older sister sobbed grievously.

Logan looked up as two people entered the hallway and he recognized Tim's parents. They look half-awake, that aura of disbelief parents had when their children were in a horrible wreck. Logan released his daughter and started walking towards them. He felt someone at his side and was proud to see his daughter striding with him.

"Mr. Kresser, I . . ."

Jacob Kresser was ten inches over five feet, his shoulders wide, but not as wide as his belly. His eyes were red and his hands were nervously plucking at his pants pockets. He was finding it very hard to speak calmly.

"Our son is alive?" interrupted Beth Kresser. She was a thin woman with dark hair and a pinched face. She reminded Logan of Loren's first wife that was killed in Idaho. The thought was not flattering for either woman so he kept it to himself.

"He is alive, but he is in bad shape," Tana said, her voice stronger than Logan expected. "He will make it," she added confidently, her chin lifted as though her small defiance would be all that was needed to save Tim's life.

"What were you doing parked out in the middle of the country?!" she snapped, eyes blazing with hot anger. Logan could sense her aggravation, but her sudden eruption into anger had caught him unaware. His daughter was facing it calmly.

"We were wanting to be alone. We should not have gone there, but we did. That part is impossible to change now," Tana said, her voice beginning to show the strain of facing Tim's grief-stricken mother.

"I should have known you were a little whore! You and that . . ."

"That is enough of that, Mrs. Kresser," Logan said, his normally calm face tinged with anger at her words.

She turned towards him, unleashing her wrath on him as easily as his daughter. "What are you doing here instead of trying to find the man that did this to my son?! Why . . ."

"That is enough, Beth!!" Jacob had finally found his voice and his words made her clamp her mouth together. She turned on her heel, walking to the nurses' station, leaving Jacob alone with Logan and Tana.

"I apologize, Tana. She almost went off the deep end when we got the call. She will be sorry for what she said to you later." Facing Logan, Jacob said, "Is this the same man that killed that woman?"

"I believe so," Logan said with a nod of his head. "I am going to do everything in my power to put a stop to him, Mr. Kresser."

"Yes. Well, I'm going to join my wife and see if we can get inside the room to see our son." Jacob Kresser turned and walked away as Logan watched helplessly. He saw that his daughter had tears flowing from both eyes and he placed a hand on her shoulder.

"You did good," he said, releasing his grip and walking back to his wife and friends. Tana followed silently, feeling sick from her encounter with Tim's mom.

"We're going to stay here for a while," Randy said, placing her arms around Tana's shoulders. The girl gave her an appreciative nod and Logan didn't disagree.

"What now?" Loren asked, his eyes on Logan's somber face.

"Now I'm going to get some answers from a certain FBI agent," Logan replied.

"I'm going with you," he stated firmly. "I would really like to hear what that son-of-a-bitch has to say."

"That makes two of us," Bill added, walking up from behind them.

"Okay," Logan agreed. "Let's go talk to the sons-of-bitches."

CHAPTER FIVE

The parking lot was black and wet, but there were cars parked in the lot. The FBI was here waiting and he scowled wryly when he saw he would not have to call them. He went up the steps two at a time as Loren and Bill followed him. The lights in the Sheriff and Deputy offices were on and beckoned at the end of the hall.

There were six agents inside, standing quietly as they waited on the sheriff to step inside and start cussing them. They had been cussed before and it meant little to them any longer. They were the government and the government had to keep secrets sometimes.

Logan strode inside, spotting Scott Hale standing in front of a desk, peering at him almost guiltily. Never missing a stride, Logan walked to within arm's length of him and punched him. The blow was unexpected and powerful as it caught Scott flush on the jaw and propelled him over the hard wood desk in a crash of pens and papers. Logan moved around the desk, even as the other agents moved for their pistols.

"I wouldn't," Loren warned, the cocked .45 auto in his right hand and pressed behind the ear of an agent. Bill was holding his revolver on two more men.

"No need for a blood bath, gentlemen," Bill said. "He wants to beat the hell out of him, not kill him."

"He will play hell," grunted a blond agent, a sneer on his face.

Impassively, Logan grabbed Scott, the younger man lashing out with both feet, driving his heels in the pit of Logan's stomach. Logan doubled over as the man tried to kick him in the face. His shoe glanced off Logan's head, but Logan slammed a big fist into the man's face.

Grabbing him by the jacket, Logan lifted him to his feet, pitching him across the desk as Scott's men watched in disbelief. Scott was known for his hand-to-hand skills, but this man had never allowed him time to get into action.

"Start talking to me, you son-of-a-bitch," Logan said calmly, kicking the man across the chest and into a ball as he rolled across the floor. "Give me the fucking answers you've been keeping to yourself."

Scott pulled his pistol, Logan kicking it from his hand. He stepped back, allowing Scott to struggle to his feet. The agent was bleeding from his mouth profusely and he looked to be missing a tooth. "I wasn't allowed the liberty of telling you . . ."

Scott blocked the right, throwing a hard right of his own. Logan weaved to the side, bringing a knee up into Scott's groin, the man's face turning pale as he retched. Logan side-kicked him to the chest, Scott slamming into the wall with a crash.

"He almost killed my daughter," Logan said, his rage diminishing as he saw the FBI agent was gasping for breath. "She would have been just another victim to you."

Scott coughed, feeling his ribs. Several were broken and he was having difficulty seeing from his right eye. "I didn't know until tonight," he muttered with a lisp.

"But, you suspected," Logan correctly suspected.

Scott nodded his head and Bill cursed vehemently. "She could have been killed!"

"Her or anyone else," Scott said, pushing himself to sit in a chair. "We thought we had him, then the DNA sample was screwed up."

"You shouldn't have let him take the samples!" Bill said angrily.

"We didn't," said one of the other agents. "He took samples, but so did we. Our samples were bad. We assumed he would taint the samples he took and we believe he did, but somehow he screwed up both samples. He was not the only suspect"

"Exactly," Scott said, groaning. "I'm going to need to go to the hospital."

"You're under arrest, Sheriff Denton," said the agent that had been doing the explaining. Logan thought his name was Ken Bailly or Ballard or a name similar.

"No," Logan said. "Not tonight."

"You attacked a federal officer!"

Loren prodded the man at the back of his ear with the .45 auto. "I'm holding a gun on one. Don't make me use it."

Scott wiped blood from his face. "You fight like a wild man, Denton. I'll drop the attack charges against you if you stay away from my man. We'll take care of him."

Logan shook his head, peeling the badge off his shirt. Picking up the phone, he dialed some numbers and waited.

"Ralph, this is Logan. You have a decision to make right now. I have an emergency on my hands. You can retire today, now, take a position as a deputy or I can fire you. It's up to you."

There was a quiet spell and Logan glanced at Bill before speaking. "I accept your retirement over the phone. Turn the necessary paperwork in within forty-eight hours. I'll defer it for three months so you can get your time, but you will be working from a squad car. Your position as assistant sheriff is now vacated." He hung up the phone, his mind steering away from the bewildered man on the other end. Looking at Bill, he said, "You're assistant sheriff, Bill."

Bill knew what he was intending and he said, "Logan, don't do it, man?!"

Logan pitched the badge to Bill. You're the sheriff at eight this morning. I'll sign papers."

Loren cursed beneath his breath. The FBI agents watched in shock as Logan filled out his resignation and pitched it on the desk too. "I'm going to hunt a man."

"You can't!"

"He is walking out that door or the shit goes down now," Loren said ominously, backing out as Logan passed him. They both trotted to Logan's truck and jumped inside.

Bill lowered his gun and sighed. Moving to the desk, he retrieved Logan's badge and resignation. Putting them inside his jacket, he glanced at Scott. "You want an APB put out on him?"

"No. Just get me to the hospital and let them check out my ribs. I'm not pressing charges. I've seen his daughter and she is a nice girl. Maybe I'm lucky he didn't kill me."

"Bullshit! He assaulted a federal officer!" Ken cried in indignation.

"No, he attacked a man that endangered his daughter," Scott said with a groan while he stood. "Can't say I wouldn't have done the same." Ken and Bill moved to him quickly, helping him hobble out the office door and to a car one of the other agents pulled to the bottom of the stairs outside.

"Hell! Why not?!" Loren was asking angrily as they drove towards Logan's house.

"You're a family man now. You don't owe me or this county your life tracking this bastard down."

"That's weak!" Loren exclaimed.

"You're not a werewolf," Logan finally stated.

"No, but I've killed a few," Loren assured him.

"I'd rather have you with me than anyone, including Vivian, but your place is here with Milly and your girls."

"That your last word on it?" Loren asked, his anger dissipating slowly.

"Yes," Logan replied succinctly.

"Fuck you then," Loren said wearily, pulling the .45 auto and placing it in the seat between them.

Logan began chuckling, Loren looking at him strangely for a second before joining in. They were both laughing loudly by the time they got to the turn to Logan's driveway.

The truck was not in great shape and he dumped it at a truck stop in Sherman, Texas. He needed another car. He looked across the street at the two motels, thinking about the people sleeping early this morning. There was a nice sub-division of homes to the east and he considered making a selection from one of the homes.

His stomach growled angrily as he remembered the scent of Tana Denton while he chased her. It had been a searing combination of so many things and he found he could categorize each one. God, what power he was being given!! He could tell exactly what he was scenting! Fear. Passion. Sex. Her pussy had been leaving a faint trail of feminine essence that made him swoon weakly as he chased her through the forest. That scent had been weak compared to the scent of fear and the lingering smell of recent sexual escapades with the poor young bastard he smashed to a pulp.

He laughed to himself, entering the truck stop and ordering a Western omelet and a cup of coffee. The waitress was an old woman and he could smell age on her, mingling with the second hand smoke of the smoking section that lay dormant on her clothes. Sweat and the nauseating scent of cheap bubble bath made him grunt disgustedly looking out the window.

A police car pulled in the parking lot and he tensed checking the position of his weapons. They may have put an APB out on the truck and him too by now. He watched the two men get out of the car talking to each other and ignoring the other vehicles in the parking lot. Relaxing, he avoided their eyes as they entered the restaurant.

The waitress brought his food and he sniffed it, his stomach rumbling again. It was good food, far better fare than he was accustomed to in the truck stops he had frequented in his career. Scratching the backs of his hands, he cursed to himself. His hands had been itching badly for the past three days and the rest of his skin had been about the same though to a lesser extent. Those hicks must put some chemical in their water that made him itch.

He looked up at a redhead peering at him from across the room. She was wearing lots of make-up and he guessed she was a prostitute though a town as small as Sherman wouldn't have any streetwalkers. Undoubtedly she was one of the few that frequented the truck stops to work the continually arriving masses of truckers. Her body wasn't bad, but she could have been anywhere between the ages of thirty and fifty. He smiled at her, sipping the coffee. Her car keys were lying on the table in front of her.

He took a refill on his coffee, glancing at the woman who seemed interested in him. She stared at him, smiling surreptitiously at him once. He glanced at the police officers, then back to her as she nodded knowingly. When the officers left, she joined him.

Amanda Walters was thirty-seven years old and she had been a prostitute for twenty-one years. She had worked johns from San Antonio to Amarillo and back to Dallas. Sherman was not a large city, but it had been quiet and the police here had not bothered her yet.

More attractive than most prostitutes her age, she managed to stay busy at the truck stops and she had been working this one for three months now. A small hotel to the north was where she lived with a cheap rent she could afford. The owner had an understanding with her and it worked out well for both of them. She got a cheap weekly rate and he got a couple free ones from time to time.

This john seemed different. He was handsome and clean cut. His eyes were piercing and she felt them on her when he glanced in her direction. This man wasn't a trucker, but he was definitely interested.

She liked men who were interested. Prostitution was a hard job and the years were telling on her. She was not in demand like she had been when she was a fresh-faced twenty or even twenty-five, but her sexy butt still pulled them in.

Normally, she wouldn't mess with someone who did not drive a truck, but this man had been appealing. Besides, a blowjob and one straight-up screw had netted her only one hundred ten dollars tonight. She had experienced worse nights --much worse -- but not recently.

The man was nice, talking to her in this rich, mellow voice that she liked. She told him her rates -- straight up and hourly -- and he nodded in agreement. He talked easily and suggested they leave. When she told him they would need to park his truck in a darker place, he shook his head, saying he preferred going to her place.

Amanda balked until he placed two one hundred-dollar bills in her hand. "For one hour," he said with a smile. She nodded, slipping the bills in her purse and standing. The man paid for his meal and her coffee. She started towards his truck and he digressed, saying the water pump was going out. She didn't like taking her car, but she couldn't turn loose of two hundred dollars either. That was double her hourly rate!

The car was five years old and well kept. The man rode quietly beside her as they went to the motel. She could hear his soft, rhythmic breathing as he glanced at her with a charming smile.

She opened the door and he stepped inside. "There is a small light beside the bed. I want you to wear a condom," she stated, knowing some johns would not complain and others left in a huff.

"Okay," he answered pleasantly, watching her slip her blouse off, staring vacantly at her pendulous breasts.

She leaned over to take off her shoes and he took a deep breath. Amanda said, "You like my ass?"

"Love it," he replied with a warm smile.

Amanda smiled seductively, her eyes going to the large bulge in the front of his jeans. A veteran prostitute, Amanda had no problem dealing for more money, even when she had a generous john that paid her cash before he got anything. "I usually charge seventy-five dollars more to do anal, but you already paid me double my hourly charge. We are using my place and I drove us here. That ain't free, but I'll let you do my ass for another twenty-five."

"Let me think about it," he answered, his voice guttural, his breathing becoming heavier.

"You got an hour," she said with a laugh, stepping out of her skirt and panties. She moved beside him on her knees, kissing across his stomach after raising his shirt. His hands were on her buttocks as she worked at his jeans.

He stood, unbuttoning his jeans and removing his shoes. Dropping his jeans in the floor, he added his shirt before lying across her, still clad in his underwear. Amanda opened her legs as he lay across her, kissing him as he eagerly pulled at her lips. Some johns wanted to kiss her, some didn't. This one seemed ravenous and she let herself enjoy it as he kissed her passionately, pressing his bulging manhood against her.

"That's it, baby!" she exclaimed as he covered her bosom, shoulders and neck with his kisses. She felt a fluttering of desire and realized that this encounter might be better than a simple moneymaking proposition. He licked her shoulders and she hugged him tightly.

His chest was so hairy and she used her professional expertise to elicit a deep moan from him that became a strange growling. He was really horny! She chuckled softly, seductively while rubbing her palms across his back. His face remained buried in her neck as she pulled at his underwear before he ripped them savagely off himself. Her hands went to his back and it felt hairy too and she didn't remember . . .

He raised up from her neck and she opened her eyes to tell him how wonderful he was making her feel when she felt her breath catch in her throat. His face was covered with short dark hair, two fangs thrusting from his mouth and his eyes were feral, inhuman. She tried to scream as he lunged forward, burying his teeth in her throat and ripping out her larynx and jugular with one huge bite. She pelted him with her fists as she wheezed for breath, no longer concerned with the sex as she fought for a life that was already fading. He took another bite from her neck as she weakened, splashed with blood as the deadly creature finished its hellish orgy of feasting.

Her arms dropped beside her and the man fed from her, liking the taste of her flesh better than the Western omelet, better than a T-bone steak.

After taking a shower in her bathroom, he looked at the hideous remains without emotion. Her eyes stared at the ceiling, the flesh from her neck, shoulders and chest missing. He looked at his hands. They seemed normal, but they itched.

How had he managed to bite through her neck like that? She had seemed terrified by the sight of him. Had his intentions shown in his face? He opened her purse, adding her money to his own before searching the room, finding another stash. Her car keys went into his pocket and he dressed hurriedly.

Hanging the DO NOT DISTURB sign on the door, he chuckled as he thought they might change his name to the DO NOT DISTURB killer. He got in her car, pleased to see it was almost full of gas. It started easily and he pulled out of the lot, careful not to spin the tires in the gravel. He drove north on Highway 75 until he hit Highway 82 east to New Boston outside Texarkana. They would find the truck in the parking lot and start flagging down truckers. He giggled like a child. The owner of the seedy little motel would wait at least a day before he bothered the whore. It would be plenty of time for him to get out of the immediate circle of the search.

They might splash his picture on the television and every newspaper in the country. He would buy some hair dye. Rubbing his chin, he felt some stubble. Letting his beard grow out would be too cliche', but it might not hurt to grow a Van Dyke and mustache. They would help hide his features while lending a different character to his face a full beard might enhance.

He knew how the FBI worked and that was how he managed to stay one step ahead of them. That bastard sheriff was too smart for his own good and deserved to pay for his intrusion on the yearnings of the hunger. His sweet daughter would have been so fucking good to take like he took the whore. Only he would have taken her many times before eating her flesh. He shivered deliciously behind the steering wheel. The hunger wanted it and he wanted it. That desire had not faded, nor did he believe that it would over time. The hunger did not forget.

"His name is Phill Sturgis," Logan said, walking around Randy as he shoved another pair of underwear in his leather bag. He was wearing his .45 auto and he had explained to her briefly what happened at the courthouse. Tana and Milly were still at the hospital, but Loren was downstairs.

"I never saw him," Randy said, trying to remember the agents she had seen.

"He knew Tana. He had seen my pictures on my desk if nothing else. The bastard knew who he was after, I feel it," Logan said, his voice hiding the anger he was still feeling.

"Are you calling, Vivian?" she asked, wanting to tell him that she would call her if he did not.

"I will once I get an idea of which direction he is heading. No sense in both of us running pell-mell all over the country."

He was packed and he stood in the middle of the room, going over his mental checklist as his wife approached him. Putting her arms around him, she said, "Be careful, Logan."

Leaning over, he kissed her warmly, passionately as she growled at him. "I'll take that as a yes," she said as he smiled, patting her rear lovingly before grabbing his bag.

Going down the stairs, he knew Randy was following him. Loren looked sullen, but Logan wasn't changing his mind.

"How do you know which way to go?" Loren asked.

"Instinct tells me to go south first. Vitoro said my instincts would grow and that I must learn to trust them. I think I'll go with that. It's the best I got for now," Logan replied.

Loren nodded. "I called my foreman and he is going to cover for me for another week or two. Milly and I are staying here with Randy and the kids while you run around playing the furry avenger."

Always his friend. That was an apt description of Loren and Logan shook his hand. "I appreciate it, Loren. Watch them for me."

The thoughts remained unspoken between the men, but both knew the killer might return after a brief chase. The man was insane, but he was a werewolf. The man would want revenge on the man who discovered him. The werewolf would displace the fear that might prevent his return with the courage of a wild animal. Loren was wearing his pistol and it was loaded with silver solids that he had made almost ten years ago. He never went anywhere without a box of them in the truck. A man never knew when he might need them.

Logan hugged Randy again before disappearing out the door. He drove away and Loren placed a strong arm around Randy's shoulders. "He will be fine."

"I know. I don't have that sick feeling I felt before Kent and Logan went to look for Martin and Jake at the oldest cabin. It was almost a psychic awareness, but I knew I would never see the same Logan Denton again."

"He seems unchanged," Loren commented.

"There is a wildness about him sometimes. The wolf in him calls to his soul. I am a werewolf too, though I have not changed more than ten times in six years. It doesn't call to me like it does to him. It was like the wolf completed an incomplete puzzle with a mysterious missing piece that fits, but changes the entire concept of the puzzle."

"Have things changed between you?" Loren asked, genuinely concerned for his friends.

She smiled, shaking her head. "No. We love each other, Loren and we have never talked about the things I just told you. It is simply something I can sense. Logan might not even be aware of it."

Loren removed his arm and sat down. Little Logan and his daughters were in bed and asleep. He offered to stay with them while Miranda went back to the hospital with Milly and Tana. She accepted and he watched her pull out of the driveway. He took a deep breath. Checking the strap on his pistol, he went upstairs to check on the kids. They were sleeping quietly and he smiled as his youngest daughter turned, snuggling into the shoulder of the oldest.

"People change, Randy, and they don't realize it until it has already happened," he mumbled, feeling the joy in his heart at being the father of such lovely girls.

CHAPTER SIX

She sat in the waiting room, stunned beyond words. He was dead. The life flight helicopter from Tulsa was in route and he died while they were prepping him. Tana had already thrown up once, her hands quivering as Milly held her with one arm around her shoulders.

He had died and she had not been with him. She was not there to hold his hand, to say goodbye. Tana had tried to come inside and Mrs. Kresser had forbid her to enter. She was not immediate family so the nurse made her leave as gently as possible. Tana saw the nurse had not wanted to make her leave, but she had no choice.

Mr. and Mrs. Kresser had not left his room yet. Mrs. Kresser blamed her for what happened to Tim. She had meant it earlier and she meant it now. If Tana had been able, she would trade places with Tim. Tana would give her life for Tim's.

Randy walked into the waiting room as the Kressers walked past. Mrs. Kresser looked at her accusingly, sobbing hysterically and Randy closed her eyes as the realization hit her. She stepped closer to Tana. Milly met her eyes and stroked Tana's hair.

"His body was too damaged inside," Milly said. She had been talking to the doctors. Assertiveness had never been a problem for Milly and she questioned the doctors and nurses involved with Tim's care. "She tried to see him and Mrs. Kresser forbid her even stepping into the room."

"I am so sorry, Tana," Miranda said sadly, kneeling in front of her daughter.

"I want to be a werewolf," Tana mumbled, peering into Randy's eyes.

"Not while you are so emotional," Randy said quietly, knowing that the younger girl was not thinking straight in her grief.

"If I had been like Daddy or you, I could have stopped him from hurting Tim." Her voice was pleading and Randy hugged her, crying with her and Milly. They stood after a few minutes and Randy led Tana out the door, Milly following closely behind.

"Mrs. Denton?"

Miranda turned, walking away from Tana as she and Milly went to the trucks. Mr. Kresser was red-eyed. He blinked his eyes several times before he spoke.

"My wife does not want Tana at the funeral," he said.

Randy shook her head in frustration. Why couldn't these people see Tana was devastated too?

"I know she wants to come and I know this isn't her fault. I want you and her to know that. Still, in deference to my wife's wishes, I would appreciate it if she would not come. I will call her with a time she can come by the funeral home . . ." He was choking up and Randy waited patiently for him to gather his wits.

"Mr. Kresser. Your wife is hurting, but so is my daughter. My daughter was genuinely in love with your son. Your son was in love with my daughter and Tana is well aware of the sacrifice he made for her. She watched Tim fight a madman so that she might live. Her guilt was already enough before you and Mrs. Kresser forced more on her. I can forgive the cruelty your wife is showing towards my daughter for only so long. She may not come to the funeral, but she will go to the funeral home when she damn well pleases!"

Kresser was startled by the woman's animosity and he stepped back, flinching, his eyes going wide. He calmed, nodding his head. "Of course, Mrs. Denton. Forgive me."

"Forgive me, Mr. Kresser. I was praying with all my heart for Tim's recovery."

He nodded, walking away and Miranda felt sad for him. She walked away, going through the door and down the stairs. Milly and Tana had left in Milly's Blazer. Miranda looked at the sky as the dawn approached. She had been up all night and she was exhausted.

"Damn," Loren muttered sadly, popping the knuckles of his hands. Tana had gone to her room and Milly was informing Loren of Tim's death.

"His parents were very mean to her, Loren."

"People are mean at times," he commented, seeing the headlights of another vehicle turning in the driveway. Miranda was parking beside their blazer and he saw her briefly as the dome light flashed while she opened her door.

Loren remembered the battered kid, his concern focused solely on his girlfriend. He hoped Logan found that son-of-a-bitch soon.

Instinct. Logan knew much about his instinct as a wolf. He had spent years in the form of a werewolf, able to shift between wolf and wolfman, but not man. It was a sacrifice he made willingly to save the life of his wife, though they were simply lovers at that point. Lovers and friends.

Lovers and friends. He could say the same about Vivian. She married his younger brother in a double ceremony with Randy and Logan. She professed love for Logan's brother and they were happy together, but he would have went utterly insane without Vivian's company while he was stuck in the wolf form. They were more than friends. They were soul mates in the wolf form. Randy was his soul mate in human form. His human form had control, but at one time his wolf self reigned his soul.

He understood how rogues could go crazy, killing and destroying all who were unlike them. The battle between man and wolf was a constant thing in their bodies.

The wolf had been supreme in his body and it was constantly fighting for its former position. It demanded its time and that was why Logan ran the woods at night as a wolf. It was why the wolf was at the edge of trans-mutation when he was angered. Whenever the wildness came to surface, the wolf wanted to be in control. Sometimes he allowed it, but most of the time he did not. There was too much danger in it keeping control.

Vivian understood this as Randy never would. Logan found himself drawn to Vivian when they were together. He wanted her -- not as a man wants a woman -- but as a wolf wants its mate. There was a difference and God knew his soul could tell it apart. He and Vivian had never been together long while alone, but he sensed she felt the same way. He felt the longing to change into the wolf with her at his side, running free on four legs. It was why he would not call her until he was near the killer or believed he could not take him alone.

He shook the thoughts from his head as he entered the small town city limits of Van Alstyne. It was less than fifty miles to Dallas now. He had felt like he was going in the right direction this morning, but now he wasn't sure as the morning sun came up on his left.

When he got to Allen or Plano he would stop and give Randy a call to check on Tim. He was not confident in the boy's chances at recovery. Logan wasn't a pessimist, but he was a realist about the youth's chances: they weren't good.

The radio droned on, Logan ignoring the songs as he thought about the man he was chasing. He was not a fool and he had passed the psychological exams of the FBI without flagging anything. Strange, but not impossible. He was a psychopath. He knew how the FBI would try to trace him as well as the police too. He would know how to avoid them.

The odds were in the man's favor except he was becoming something more than human. He was nearing the time of the first change where his body would slip in and out of the human and wolfman form anytime he got highly emotional. The full change would occur within a week and when it did, the man might go on an orgiastic rampage. It would be devastating to the werewolf community if he was destroyed or video taped killing numerous people. The deaths alone would be horrifying and the addition of exposing a race long forgotten could teeter the civilized world on its axis.

His stomach rumbled and he decided he would stop in Plano or Richardson at the first place he thought he could get some breakfast. He could make a call from there. Tana would be all right whatever happened. She was a strong girl and he believed in her strength. Her strength had saved her tonight. Her strength, and the courage of a young man fighting something out of his worst nightmares.

The hooker's car was in good shape and Phill Sturgis looked in his back mirror. He had listened to a Dallas radio station until he lost the signal. Nothing came over the radio about a grisly murder and he thought the murder in the motel would be bad enough it might make the state news.

He was a master. A master artist and a man to be reckoned with in any situation. He considered what he done with that woman's body. He had eaten her or parts of her. It would have sickened him once, but now it made him feel more powerful. He did not kill her. He consumed her. Her flesh. Her blood. Her very soul!

Embarrassed, he found he was getting an erection. A damn woody from thinking about how he ate that woman.

"She should be happy," he said aloud, laughing at his own voice. It was not every day one had the opportunity to be nourishment for a new god. A new creature that was far more superior than man. She was lucky. An aging whore given the opportunity to be useful to one so powerful as he was becoming.

New Boston was behind him now and he was on the outskirts of Texarkana, heading for Hope, Arkansas. Hope was a nice, clean town in Arkansas that claimed fame as the home of a former president. Phill could care less about that fact. He knew he could find a place that he could hole up.

A friend owned a deer lease near here and the cabin sat empty all summer. He would stay there for a couple days after dumping the car. There was plenty of money in his suitcase. This trip had been long in planning. He knew someday they would catch him. The sheer numbers of women he killed made it almost impossible to believe he might not be caught. Psycho maybe. Phill was not a fool.

He might drive around and see if he could find someone with a car for sale. First, he would dye his hair before searching. No need to make someone famous by reporting him to America's Most Wanted. A car he had not stolen would increase the likelihood of him making it to the East Coast if he decided to go.

Phill wasn't sure if he was going to continue east or not. There was a beautiful teenage woman he scented back there and the hunger selected her. She was so beautiful, so hot, he could not get her off his mind. He closed his eyes momentarily, remembering the overpowering scent of sex and the aroused essence of her. He squirmed uncomfortably in his seat.

She had been selected by the hunger.

It would be foolish to try to take her. Her father would be ready and he still didn't understand what in the hell that thing was that jumped on the side of his car. It looked like a man, but like no man he had ever seen before.

There was something out there and she knew what creature had howled in the night. She was the reason he had to flee. She and that bastard she was fucking ruined his entire set-up with the FB-fucking-I!

The little hussy needed to be taught a lesson. The hunger wanted her to understand how important she was to it. He wanted her to know no one had ever escaped the hunger once they were selected.

He wanted to fuck her. He wanted to strip her clothes from her and fuck her until she begged him for mercy! Phill smiling thought about how he would acquiesce as she sobbed after he finished. She would be whimpering and he would tell her one more time and it would be over. One more time humping her hot, young body and he would let her go! He would do her a second time and as he climaxed, he would rip out her throat!

He swerved, muttering to himself as he barely missed the bridge embuttment. His thoughts had incited his lust too much and he must concentrate on driving. The new power that fed the hunger was hard to deny. It pushed him to do the things he considered and he liked this new aspect of the hunger. It destroyed his conscience. He had never had much conscience anyway, but now it was non-existent.

Hope was at least a half-hour from Texarkana and he would be there soon. Maybe he could find his friend's cabin before long. He wanted to get off the road as soon as possible.

The news made him sick to his stomach. He hoped the boy had a good chance once they took him to the hospital. The injuries were severe, but . . .

Hell, he was just being hopeful. Tim was a good kid, a young man who had a whole lifetime ahead of him. Only a maniac cut his lifetime short. Tim had stepped into a nightmare where werewolves exist and men were more dangerous than the mythical monsters of television. The nightmare consumed him and with him, a portion of his daughter's heart.

Now, the nightmare existed, but the child, the victim did not. The nightmare lurked in the darkness, in the daylight, waiting to creep into another unsuspecting life. Logan Denton was part of that nightmare and he prayed his instinct was correct, that he was close behind the man who was becoming a wolf.

He did not want anyone else to die at the hands or claws of a werewolf. The soul of the wolf lived within him, a part of him he could feel with every beat of his heart. Yet, he feared that power within him. He feared it as much as men fear power-mad dictators or insanity.

Did Jack the Ripper enjoy killing those women? Of course most serial killers did enjoy the killing. It was the act that made them a god in their minds. Deciding who lived and who died was the ultimate achievement of a god.

Logan had gone east out of Dallas. The interstate to Texarkana was not crowded with traffic. He was not sleepy, though he had not slept through the night. There was a rest area about an hour from Texarkana and he would pull over there to catch a nap.

His .45 ACP lay under a newspaper on the seat beside him. He had three magazines lying on the seat. They were filled with silver bullets. There were two more with high velocity hollow points. He ejected the magazine with the silver bullets, working the slide to remove the round from the barrel. He put a magazine with the normal rounds in the gun and fed one to the chamber. Easing the hammer to half cock, he put it beneath the paper again. He was more likely to encounter a nasty human than a slobbering werewolf at the rest area.

Tana lay on her bed, sleeping restlessly. She had cried herself to sleep and Randy had felt helpless. The girl did not want anyone to comfort her. Randy hoped she would sleep and that would take her away from the sadness she was feeling. The way she tossed and turned, Randy doubted even that now. She looked to be having nightmares and Randy felt a shudder at the thought. Nightmares had came to her when she and Logan went through that horrible experience in Idaho that changed them all.

Milly and Loren were asleep. Milly slept in her room, but Loren fell asleep in the living room, perched comfortably in the big recliner near the picture window. His pistol lay within easy reaching distance, though Randy doubted the danger was still in the area. Always the soldier and ever vigilant.

The children slept too and she walked to Logan Junior's room, peering inside at the youngster who was sleeping so soundly. He did not understand what was happening in this adult world . . . or maybe he did. Maybe he understood all too well and preferred remaining on the level his childish innocence could tolerate.

She did not like Logan being by himself. Yet, she knew he did not feel comfortable with her along when he sought to confront a werewolf. She knew that as well as she knew he was in constant battle with the wolf living within him. She knew.

Vivian should be with him, but she could sense his indecision when he and Vivian were together. Miranda did not doubt his love for her, but too much had passed between Logan and Vivian for them to act as though nothing happened. She believed Corrie noticed it too, but he had never said anything to Logan. Maybe Vivian explained something to her husband that Logan had been unable to impart with Randy. Maybe she was just being stupid and letting her mind run wild. She knew she wasn't

.

If Logan wouldn't call Vivian, then Randy would. Vitoro never intended for a protector of the law to face a rogue alone. Two wolves against one would ensure the death of the rogue. She scowled. That wasn't true, but the odds were so much better. Glancing in her room at the phone, she bit at her lower lip. Maybe she should call Vivian and just let her know what was happening.

Vivian Denton listened to the phone ring, her face frowning as she reached for the receiver. Corrie ran his hand along her hip and around her stomach as she gripped the phone.

"Hello?" she muttered, irritated that someone would wake them so early this morning. The voice on the other end was instantly familiar and she perked up at the sound. She considered Randy a friend as well as her sister-in-law.

"This is the guy who has been killing these women?" Vivian asked, causing Corrie to raise his head, looking at her speculatively.

"Oh my God! How is she?!"

"Tana?" Corrie mouthed, his face growing gray with worry.

Holding the phone from her mouth, Vivian mouthed, "She is okay. Her boy friend was killed last night by that killer that killed that woman in Logan's county a few weeks ago."

"Damn," Corrie whispered, his eyes wide open, the sleep erased from his face. He wished he could hear his sister-in-law in person now.

"How long has he been gone?" Vivian asked.

"Logan went after him," Corrie stated, not needing a reply to know he was right.

"If he told you he would call me when he got close, I imagine he will do exactly that. I don't know why . . ."

Vivian covered the mouthpiece. "She wants me to join Logan."

"Why?" Corrie asked.

"Werewolf," she said softly, listening as Randy explained everything about the man and Logan's obsession with finding him.

"Damn," Corrie swore again.

"If the man is a werewolf, Logan is doing it because it is his duty to the pack," Vivian replied to something Randy had said. She was silent for a few moments. Her voice was friendly, but firm as she said, "I will join him when he calls me, Randy. I can't make him call me, nor is it likely that I will find him if I just try to search for him."

Corrie lay back on his pillow, running his fingers through Vivian's long, bright blond hair. He knew she was Logan's partner as a Protector of the Law. It scared him to think she would be facing another werewolf, one who killed savagely, but he was comforted by the fact there were few werewolves who turned rogue. Now his worse nightmare was confronting him.

"Keep us informed. When Logan calls, I'll be there fast," Vivian assured the woman at the other end. Vivian had been a werewolf since birth and she had killed with tooth and claw. She was not helpless and she knew how to fight as a werewolf. Vivian was a veteran and Vitoro had known this when he paired her with Logan. That and the two wolves had a special relationship, a bond unlike anyone else in the pack that was not married.

Hanging up the phone, Vivian lay back beside her husband. Corrie placed his hand under the tee shirt she slept in, allowing his hand to roam across her flat tummy, loving the warmth and the taut muscles of her abdomen.

"How is Tana?"

"She is okay. Some cuts and bruises, but nothing permanent physically. Randy thinks she is dealing with it okay mentally right now, but she is afraid that too will change."

"Did she call Mom and Dad?" Corrie asked.

Shaking her head, Vivian said, "I do not think so. I think she will prefer to tell them in the morning rather than wake them this late."

"Are you going?" he asked.

"If Logan calls me," she replied, smiling as his hand moved to her breast, cupping it gently in his palm while he nuzzled her neck.

"It scares me that she was almost killed. Did Randy tell you how it all happened?"

Vivian told him what Randy had told her. It had been little enough for an explanation and left questions in the minds of both. She expressed her confidence in Logan and she noticed that Corrie nodded when she said it. There were other things concerning Corrie too.

"Do you think he will call?"

"If he needs me . . . to help with taking out this killer," she added, hoping she did not add her words too quickly. Corrie knew she and Logan had been lovers. It did not bother him because Vivian really loved him; he knew that and she did as well. Still, there was something between them that made one or the other uncomfortable. Not all the time, but he saw a glance pass between them sometimes when they were together. A wordless, unspoken communication that no one else could ever be privy to without being telepathic. It was though they could read each other's thoughts.

They couldn't. No more than Corrie could read Randy's thoughts or his own wife's mind. A werewolf was strong, had the instincts of the wolf, but they weren't telepathic. The bond between Vivian and Logan was uncanny in both the human world and the wolf world. It frightened Corrie.

Randy noticed it too, but she remained quiet. He knew Vivian had been Logan's constant mate while he was stuck in the form of the werewolf. Of Logan's entire family, Corrie was the only one who knew the real story. It was a harsh, chilling story of survival and later, determination. He respected his brother, he loved his brother and he feared his brother when it came to his wife.

Corrie had not taken the decision to become a werewolf lightly. He considered it and decided that to truly understand it, he would have to make the leap of faith required to become one. The wolf dwelling inside Vivian's heart was foreign to him though he understood her from many aspects of both his humanity and his lupine nature. She rarely changed anymore, but sometimes he awoke and found her gone. He would get out of bed, look out his window at the rolling scrub of Western Oklahoma and knew a blond werewolf stalked the night.

She took a few animals, but mostly she simply became part of the night.

The wolf must be free.

Vivian told him that once, trying to explain to him in the most eloquent of speeches, yet he did not understand until he became a wolf himself. All her words came down to those five words she spoke last: The wolf must be free.

She would return to bed silently before the dawn, freshly showered and sleep exhaustedly. The wolf had experienced its freedom and she would be content for a long time. He did not encourage it and maybe that was where he erred.

Logan understood her. She understood Logan. Corrie was unsure if he could ever understand them. Randy was a werewolf and her understanding was no better than his as to why her husband had strange longings, stirrings in the night that had nothing to do with human instinct or drives.

Yet, his brother had been human once.

Vivian rolled over, interrupting his thoughts. Her face was aglow. "As long as we're up, we might as well make good use of the time."

Corrie smiled softly as she nibbled at his chest and shoulders. He locked his arms around her, stroking her powerful buttocks beneath the filmy silkiness of her panties. She snarled teasingly and he kissed her warm lips tenderly, feeling the power in her arms as she pulled herself closer.

He loved her. Vivian loved him and he prayed Logan did not call.

CHAPTER SEVEN

The ceiling had a few cobwebs running from rafter to rafter and the heat was stifling, but the shadows of evening would cool the interior quickly enough. Sweat poured from his pores, trickling across his forehead and Phill Sturgis stared silently at the pine ceiling.

When had he become a killer?

His father was a normal man who worked hard to support a wife and three kids. They were raised in Colorado where the aspens turned yellow during the fall. He could remember hearing the bugling of the elk across the mountains before his parents moved to Arkansas. His father worked for the railroad. Phill was not sure which company, but they had lived near Durango. When his father lost his job, they moved to DeQueen, Arkansas and his father became a truck driver. His dad had not been home much, but he was a good father.

His mother. Susan Sturgis. She was pretty, her figure good for a woman with three children and he remembered his dad telling her he was lucky for having such a fine-looking woman. She would laugh and blush, but she did not seem to take him seriously. There was something about her . . . Well, his mother had been a quiet woman, her character entirely reclusive and she had never made friends well. Phill got the same characteristics from her, even at a young age. She was content to be a humble housewife while his dad drove that big truck across the country, getting some satisfaction that he was taking part in a shift of transportation that would eventually derail the railroad industry.

She treated him well though he was the middle child. His older sister had always been more responsible and very close to their mom. That was normal too. The oldest child was supposed to be more responsible. His younger brother was an idiot. He lived in Little Rock, working in a mall as the manager of a clothing store. Phill had not seen him or his loud, pudgy wife in four years. He preferred to keep it that way.

His older sister was married to a preacher in Durango, Colorado. The lure of home had taken her back where she remembered home being the best. They had two boys of their own. His older sister was beautiful and he could remember her long hair draping across her shoulders in the morning, the faint smell of cinnamon in the air as his mother prepared cinnamon toast in the kitchen. White lacy dresses on Sunday for church and modest dresses their mother made herself for school were his sister's only wardrobe, yet she was gorgeous. Karen had been his best friend and he believed he had a faint crush on his own sister.

He had seen Karen and Brandon last Fall. Brandon set out to save Phill's soul and Phill was amused by his brother-in-law's intentions. It had been a good visit and he took the opportunity to take a drive to Las Vegas. The young brunette whore he picked up there had never been missed. She was a runaway. She told him so before he killed her. Phill buried her somewhere in the desert. No doubt she was simply a skeleton now, the heat aiding the soil in decomposing her body. Another lost soul no one had ever found.

Phill swallowed, wiping the sweat from his sticky forehead. He had been on suspension then because he crossed the line with a racial slur to a higher-ranking agent. The son-of-a-bitch took him before a review board. It resulted in a suspension while he was investigated for racial prejudice in his work. They found none, but that was because Phill could control himself when it came to dealing with people he did not like. He scowled hatefully. He hated blacks. They investigated him, but they never found out how hate-filled his heart was towards the black population of the United States.

Smiling candidly, he remembered the lie detector test they gave him at Langley during his initial training. He passed with flying colors and that was when he found he had a power few men were granted. He could control his emotions, his mind, to where his heart rate did not change when he lied. Nothing changed, his emotions remaining steadily normal. He could take a lie detector test on every bitch he killed over the last ten years and pass every question. It was not a trick, simply a gift.

Where had he first felt the twinges of the hunger?

He had thought about this question many times. It was like a victim with a virus trying to decide where he had become exposed.

Had it been after Dad died? His father was killed during a grain house explosion one summer. It leveled the grain and feed elevator as if a huge bomb detonated above them. Everyone except one man was killed. They never found all the pieces of his father.

Phill had been in junior high school, his sister a junior or senior best he could remember. He remembered his mama crying and a man telling her it was all she had coming. She got a check from the trucking company, but she weeped, tossing it aside. Phill had picked it up, shaking his head in disbelief. It was his father's pay for the hours worked and a two thousand dollar accidental death payment. It was not much money and he knew his mother feared losing everything they owned.

She had picked him up from school one day, driving toward the section of town Phill knew was owned primarily by blacks. What was she doing?! Did he hate Negroes then? He thought so, but he couldn't remember for sure.

They parked in front of a nice home, his mother getting out of the car and going to the front door. A tall black man opened the door inviting her inside. Phill watched from the car and his mother was gone for less than ten minutes. When she returned, her face was pinched and pale, but she wasn't crying.

"What did you do, Mom?" he asked, unable to comprehend why she had came to see this man.

"He owns the house we live in, Phill. We ain't got much money and I need a job to support us. Never worked and no one is goin' to hire a woman my age without no skills for a high payin' job. I got a job cleaning rooms at the Traveler's Motel, but it won't do much more than put food on the table and pay our 'lectric and gas. Our rent is too high, but me and Mr. Carter worked out an agreement," she said, her voice strong though she still had that pinched look on her face.

He did not ask her to explain about the agreement, but he could see she did not entirely like it.

It was three months later he came home from school early and the back screen door was open. He had been sick and a friend had drove him to his driveway. Phill went to the back where he knew Mom left a key for them. The open door surprised him and walked inside.

He could hear strange sounds emanating from the back rooms and he listened, wondering what could be making the noises. Walking silently on the hard wood floor, he eased stealthily into the hallway, padding to the back room. His mother's bedroom door was open and he could hear the grunts of two different people.

Peering hesitantly inside, he watched that tall black man on top of his mother. The joining of their bodies was explicitly displayed. He was wringing with sweat and his mother was moaning softly as the man lunged into her, his cries guttural and tense. Phill felt ill, his stomach quivering when he saw his mother's face as she arched her back, clutching Mr. Carter's shoulders.

Phill turned, walking quietly away, going out the back door, his pace increasing with every step as he ran for the big creek running behind the house. He stopped when he got to the steep bank, dropping to his knees, tears rolling down his cheeks. He was still a kid, but he knew what he had seen. It was his mother's agreement that allowed them to live in this house. He cried for half an hour, then Phill Sturgis never cried again.

Standing, he walked to the house, hesitantly peeking through the window. He could see his mother on her knees in front of Mr. Carter, doing something . . . disgusting. He cringed, the sight driving all emotion from him as Mr. Carter lewdly swayed back and forth. Phill walked away from the window, retching near the storage building before sitting in the dark shadows beneath the shed.

He sat there for an hour, waiting outside until Mr. Carter left through the back door. Phill watched him and he contemplated murder for the first time, a tingling in his belly. Maybe that had been the birth of the hunger. Maybe not, but he hated niggers and he intended to kill Mr. Carter.

The realization that corruption came in all colors of humanity did not surface in his teenage mind. In his eyes he saw only the man who desecrated his mother's image and made her enter into lasciviousness because of their plight. That man was black and for that he blamed an entire innocent race.

He never did kill Mr. Carter. Mr. Carter died in a poker game in the back of a country bar, a gunshot to the chest a few years later. Mr. Carter's son had allowed his mother to buy the place with what his mother called, "very fair terms." By then, Susan Sturgis was working as manager of the restaurant in the motel and she made more money. She could afford to pay a house payment. Phill did not believe she was required to pay Mr. Carter's son the same way she paid Mr. Carter.

It didn't matter. He still hated niggers.

After graduation, Phill went to the army for three years. He was a military policeman and liked doing police work. It also allowed him to make more money than he had ever saw at any time in his life. He saved for school and entered the police academy immediately upon receiving his discharge from the armed forces.

His mother remarried after he had been in the army for a year. She married the man who owned the motel. His wife had died of cancer two years prior and Susan had found a man who needed someone. They were good together and Phill liked him all right. He often wondered how the man would feel if he knew his wife used to fuck a nigger to keep a place to live. Phill was quiet about it and his mother never knew he had caught her and that bastard Carter as she paid their rent.

They gave the house back to Mr. Carter's son when she moved in with her new husband. All the payments were for nothing. She had paid little of the principal on the house and she explained to Phill they thought it would be easier to let the house go back rather than try to sell it. Mr. Carter's son was pleased with the arrangement.

After all she had given for the house, she let it go back to the bastard's son. The memory made him shiver with anger.

He went to work on the East Coast, working along the piers in New York City. That was when he knew the hunger was inside him. Maybe the hunger had always been there and it was the piers, the stagnant scent of the docks that awoke it once more.

There were several hookers populating the waterfront, plying their trade with the merchant seamen. He knew many of them and did not bother them as long as they were not selling drugs. They knew him by name and he used some of them from time to time himself. He carried rubbers in his pocket all the time. He didn't want to catch any diseases.

The waterfront was where he killed the first girl.

She had been white, pale, but attractive. He had never . . . ever wanted to do what Mr. Carter had done to his mother when he stared through the back window. The girl had been beautiful and she talked him into trying it one evening. They had been together a few times and she was always eager to see him. He remembered her kneeling in front of him, leaning forward. The sensation was incredible and he groaned loudly. He felt himself swaying, looking down to watch the pale woman as she performed the act professionally.

Closing his eyes, he winced as he remembered watching Mr. Carter. The old bastard swaying hypnotically, his black member disappearing in his mother's mouth. The caress of the hooker's mouth on him as the thoughts ran rampant through his head left him confused. It felt so good, but he felt the anger boiling up inside him as he remembered the intense expression on his mother's face. The rage grew like an Atlantic storm. It was a horrible black rage accompanied by the awful tingling in his stomach, his vision blurring as his breathing became more hoarse and erratic. The rage seemed to envelop him, trying to suffocate him.

When it dissipated, he was standing over a dead girl. Her head was caved in, his hand gripping his nightstick. He did not know how it happened and he started to run. Glancing around the wharf, he took the girl's arms, dragging her to the end of a pier and dropping her into the water. Quickly, and without anyone seeing him, he walked away.

They found her body the next evening and he was the investigating officer. He found it absurdly easy to cover it up as a random killing, an act of violence on a person that society had already forgotten. No one searched hard for the killer of a whore. It was incredible to believe a person could be killed so brutally and the killer walk without fear of retribution. Maybe that was when the hunger started to spread. It was already there, but it seemed to swell into something tangible within him.

And, he began remembering parts of what happened when he blacked out. He had raped her. He had pushed her away from him and raped her, though she had performed the act with the thought that he was going to be paying for more services. When he climaxed, he stood, pulling his nightstick and calmly beat her damn head in with it. He was relieved to know he had not completed the disgusting act they had started.

Phill thought about the murder a lot, but he did not kill a second time for a long time.

It was a year and a half before he killed again. It was a pretty black hitchhiker he picked up while driving through Pennsylvania near Pittsburgh. The winding mountain roads had been making him sick to his stomach anyway and maybe that was what triggered the hunger that time. Maybe it was because she was black and alone. They found her body in the Allegheny River. It was too decomposed to determine whether she had been raped or not.

The third time was in Texas. He came to Dallas to apply for a position with the Border Patrol. The test was applicable to the Border Patrol or the FBI. He interviewed with both branches of the government before leaving that evening, picking up a fourteen-year-old girl as she walked home from school.

It had been necessary to render her unconscious before loading her in the car. He used gray tape to seal her mouth, loading her easily in the trunk. She was very pretty and innocent. He raped her many times in a deserted barn between Dallas and Commerce before slitting her throat and stacking rotted hay over her body. The hunger was an entity he recognized now and it had begun to talk to him. It had selected the teenager as she walked by in the designer jeans, her bubbly buttocks enticing any man to touch her. Phill had touched her well.

He did not categorize people into objects. Phill never called his subjects an It. They were people and he selected them as sacrifices to the hunger. The hunger desired people, not objects. This made him different from many serial killers he would later start tracking.

Phill was a very good agent in the Department of Behavioral Science. He attended school while in the army, during his stint as a police officer in New York and he had a degree in psychology. His knack for figuring out the methods of a serial killer was well known among his colleagues though he was not an out-going person. He had associates, but few agents called him a friend.

He killed. He killed on vacation. He killed twice while investigating another killer, but found that was too dangerous. One killing was bad, but two made the FBI hunt that much harder. Phill was too smart to get caught by a mistake.

It was easy to take a vacation to kill. He bought a ticket to fly somewhere overseas or across the country. Guaranteed late reservations for the first night. Often he would call the next morning and cancel, telling them he was moving across town or some story to dilute the trail if someone ever did search his back trail. He paid for a ticket and one night in a motel while he roamed the back roads of America, preying upon its women and youth like a lion upon the antelopes of Africa.

Only this past year had he become suspect. Scott Hale was a friend, but Scott had begun suspecting. He tried to keep it secret, but Phill knew the look Scott gave him when he thought Phill wouldn't notice. Phill had been more careful in the way he doctored evidence.

Now they all knew, but it didn't matter. He had killed over thirty women in ten years. It was a respectable number, but the hunger craved more. It was giving him these wonderful powers and it craved, needed so much more! Why didn't it give him these powers before? My God! If he could have smelled the fear at first he would . . .

He would have gotten caught.

Phill began to understand. The hunger had evolved as his skills evolved. It did not give more power until he was ready. He sat up on the edge of the bed, looking at the dusty window. More power. He wanted it and he wanted to evolve faster.

That hooker had been filled with fear and her flesh was like a succulent steak to his palate. Never had he dreamed eating flesh would be so . . . orgasmic?

He was hungry and maybe killing his victims for food was the next step. It was growing dark outside and he squinted his eyes at the sun setting in the west. He was hungry and he would find food. If the hunger required human flesh, he would feed it. He would have to leave tomorrow, but he would consciously take the next step to evolving. The thought made his stomach stir and he lay back on the bed.

There had been a house a few miles down the road. It was white, two story and there had been a vivacious brunette mowing the lawn while two kids played in a pool. Her legs had been tan, full breasts, perky butt and he was depressed that he had not gotten to scent her. The smell of cut grass was overpowering and the speed of the car too great anyway.

It would be easy to return when the sun went down. She and her kids might be there alone. Her husband could be home. It didn't matter. A man would simply be an obstacle he could eliminate. He had eliminated them before.

Logan looked out the window of the motel. He was in Texarkana. There had been some really strange people at the rest stop and he drove on. No need to invite trouble. He wasn't far from the mall in Texarkana and traffic outside attested to it. Randy had been asleep when he called and Loren talked to him. He was glad his friend was there, but he could detect the bitterness in Loren's voice at not being allowed to accompany him.

There was nothing new except Tana surprisingly ate a few bites of a sandwich Milly made for her. Milly had cleaned the house today while Randy sat with Tana. Randy was afraid to leave her alone, but Loren finally convinced her that Tana needed some time alone.

When he hang up, he lay on the bed, closing his eyes. He had ordered a small pizza and waited for it to be delivered. It arrived about the time his eyelids grew droopy. Paying for it, he opened the box, tasting the sausage-Canadian bacon-onion-Japaleno pizza with a growl indicating his pleasure in the taste. He had bought a six pack of beer and it rested in his sink with two ice buckets of ice to keep it cold. Logan took one, popping the top and drinking it while he ate the pizza. It was good and he ate ravenously. This was his first meal since breakfast. He drank two more beers as he ate.

There was a killer out there and he could almost feel him. What was it about his instincts that led him along, but would not allow him to home in like a laser-guided bomb?

They were alike in some ways. The man was becoming even more of a predator than before. Yet, Logan could do nothing more than predict his movements. He would kill and Logan would recognize the method if it made the news. Soon, he would kill as a werewolf kills and it would be bloody enough to make the regional news.

He hoped.

If it happened halfway across the country in the opposite direction, he would . . .

He guessed he would catch a plane. Hell, he wasn't a fool was he?!

No. Logan knew he was on the man's trail though maybe not directly behind him. He was close, but he did not know how close. It made him sick to know the man would kill again and Logan would be able to get a little closer. Swallowing, he decided that was a poor way to have to track a monster.

Showering after he finished eating, he collapsed on the bed, closing his eyes. Logan slept without dreams. He had expected to have nightmares, but that didn't happen either.

There would be plenty of time for nightmares when he caught this guy. He had no doubts about that.

CHAPTER EIGHT

Vitoro lifted his head and howled deep in the night, the cool of the mountain air refreshing, invigorating as always. He had been trailing the elk for an hour, head to the ground, his shaggy pelt grayish in the pale moon. He wound around the mountain trail, going to the upper ridge to where he could look down in the cavernous darkness of the valley. Angling through a stand of aspens, he approached the bedding area of the elk, the wind hitting him straight in the face.

A poacher had wounded one elk and he was going to take it, feed on it like a wolf. He was a wolf. Vitoro was over two hundred eighty years old.

The elk was an old cow, her milk sac long dry as she became barren, unable to reproduce, but the scars of battle shown on her flanks where she had fought a mountain lion in her youth. She was old and the winter coming would likely be her last. One knee was swollen on her front leg where she had fallen on a slide a few months ago as the spring snows melted. It was this knee that allowed the poacher enough time to shoot her. Vitoro's nose did not tell him these things though, his wolf instincts helping him as he stalked into the wind. He knew she was wounded and suffering. The elk would be nervous with the wind blowing from this direction.

The night belonged to the predator. The night remained the same through the eons. The predator hunted while the prey grouped together in protective societies or groups to combat enmasse the threat of danger. He could hear the sounds of elk ahead and he lowered himself, utilizing the sparse cover to bridge the distance without alerting the animal to his presence.

He could see the slight movement as the elk stirred, some browsing before lying down to sleep. His eyes searched the herd until he found the one that he believed would be the wounded animal. She lay by herself, lowering her head to her flank, her rough tongue caressing the wound.

With a burst of speed, Vitoro crossed the distance, launching himself as the elk became aware of his presence. A mad scramble ensued, Vitoro's fangs hamstringing the wounded elk as she bleated in terror, trying to fight the creature killing her. He crushed her neck as the herd ran into the night and he stood over her as her heart beat its last beneath the clear Idaho skies.

Vitoro ate, tasting the fresh meat, enjoying it like it was a delicacy. He ate until he was stuffed, moving to a warm place on the ground where an elk had lain earlier. He dozed for a few hours, arose and ate a second time. The carcass still had meat on it, but the voracious appetite of the werewolf had allowed him to eat much of it.

The scent of three different bears was on this hill and they would find the carcass. He left it uncovered, eagerly sharing his kill with nature's denizens of the forest. Padding back the way he had came, he wondered how his friends fared in the south. Logan had become like an adopted son to him and he found himself closer to him than he had been with his own son.

Perhaps he would call Logan in the morning, he decided, picking his way down the slope of the mountain. His gait was slow because of the meat in his stomach. It would take him many hours to get home, but that was fine. He would lie down to rest at least once before he arrived at his home.

It was a beautiful night, a clear night and he did not look upon his deed tonight as savage. Who could commit savagery on a night like this one?

Sandra Collins brushed her pretty auburn hair back from her forehead. The hot bath had done a world of good for her exhaustion. Her muscles were sore, tired, but she felt good about the way her yard looked. Jim had been happy when he got home from work. It would give them tomorrow together without worrying about yard work. Jim had even commented on the neatness of the edging around the house. He had thought the gas-powered weed-eater would be too heavy for her.

He was cooking supper downstairs, the kids in bed after she fed them soup and sandwiches tonight. Jess had felt betrayed after helping her this evening. He felt like his age (12 years old) should allow him to have more privileges (It did), but she still made him go to bed at nine this evening. This evening was to be her night with Jim alone. Jim was preparing his culinary specialty with two large slabs of Red Snapper he had bought in Texarkana this evening. She could smell the blackening seasonings and the aroma made her stomach growl.

The wind was blowing lightly outside and she thought she saw a movement at the window in her bedroom. The air conditioner was on downstairs, but she chose to run a ceiling fan in her room at night except when it was very cool. The French doors to the balcony were open, a thin screen across the door to prevent bugs from getting inside the house. The shadow had been a play of imagination. Scowling, she vowed again - one of many vows over the same subject - to clip the morning glory vines from the lattice and burn it all. It was beautiful, but hard to keep attractive. It was too thick for her to feel comfortable on her balcony. She had seen snakes get in the vines before while hunting for the small nesting sparrows that took refuge in the greenery.

Sandra hated snakes.

She retrieved the lacy white body suit, smiling as she put it over her nakedness. Jim would be speechless when he found this beneath her sexy short set she intended to wear to supper. If she really dressed for supper, he would get suspicious. Sandra wanted to spring a surprise on him. The teddy would be sure to get his attention.

A shadow crossed the window and she glanced quickly, the window empty as before. She frowned heavily, moving to the French doors to shut them. The night was cool for the summer and she languished in the breeze, looking at her freshly cut yard, the bluish glow of the light casting an eerie glow on it that made her nervous when they first moved into this house two years ago.

Stepping out on the balcony, she could not conceal a smile when she thought how it would look to a passerby if they saw her standing on the balcony in this sheer white body suit. She stretched cat-like; turning to walk inside when something scratched her leg. Jumping, she turned, cursing the small, barely discernable nail protruding from the banister. She had scratched herself on it before and believed she should be able to remember it was there. There was some blood from the scratch and she wiped it from her leg. Stepping back inside the room, she shut the French doors and went back to her bathroom to clean the scratch. It wasn't very bad.

The scent of fresh blood wafted on the air like gourmet food from a kitchen and the creature lurking beside the well house felt his stomach grumble ravenously. The stack of firewood concealed his mass easily and he watched the woman stand on the balcony, stretching deliciously in the sheer bodysuit that left nothing to imagination. He looked at his arms, growling in a tone that was not normal. His hands were covered with hair and he was naked, a soft mat of coarse fur covering his body.

The hunger had given him more power. He was so strong, his legs like corded steel and he sprang easily to the top of the well house, swaying from side to side as he sniffed the lingering scent of the blood. It disappeared finally, almost driving him wild to find it again, but he forced himself to be patient, to wait until the time was right to move forward.

He was a creature of the darkest night, a child of the moon. Every instinct told him that he belonged under the night, that he was no longer a daylight dweller and he could see easily in the night as a predator, a night hunter should to see his quarry. His lupine eyes searched the windows, marking the movements of a small high window where he had seen a man earlier tonight.

Dropping soundlessly to the ground, he covered the expanse of the yard in three bounds, standing in the shadows beneath the kitchen window. He could smell fish, pepper and other spices that no longer brought saliva to his lips. He no longer ached for things human . . . except for the flesh to rend in his teeth, to fill his gullet. The smell of human flesh was tantalizing, the desire to taste it like a huge rope dragging him to an abyss of pleasure that held no escape. It was a pleasant thing, something he desired and he did not fight the rope, choosing to allow it to guide him.

Moving stealthily to the back porch, he froze when he heard the door-knob rattling. He slunk against the wall, crouching, watching the thin patch of light grow as the door opened widely. The man stepped one foot outside, turning in surprise at the swift movement beside him. His body fell forward as his head arced in the air, his lips screaming silently, the head landing in the freshly cut grass, the red blood staining the green to where it looked dark black. The scraps in the plate fell to the grass too, landing beside the body of the man and the creature that was Phill Sturgis dragged the body towards him, slinging the man's body carelessly against the foundation of the house.

The door creaked as his clawed hand opened it. Stepping inside, he could smell the cooking fish before he entered the kitchen. His feet were long, covered with hair and thick, razor-sharp claws. They clicked ominously on the tile floor as he crossed it. The woman was upstairs and he felt the hunger boiling in his stomach.

He saw his reflection in a mirror and he barely stifled the growl. He was a werewolf. The hunger had turned him into a werewolf! Phill wanted to laugh aloud in joy at his discovery! He was a werewolf!

The woman spoke, calling to her husband and he licked his lips wetly, thinking about the woman's hot flesh, the food she was becoming in his mind. He went up the stairs four at a time, moving faster than an Olympic class athlete. She was moving in her room, nearing the door as he crossed the hallway, liking the distinct click of his claws on the hardwood floor. He met her at the door.

She stepped back, opening her mouth to scream as he lunged forward, emitting a roar that shook the rafters of the house. Slamming her on her back, his mouth sank long fangs into her throat, tearing her jugular out, swallowing hot flesh and blood greedily as she feebly fought against his greater strength. He watched her eyes as he ripped off her right arm with his powerful claws, biting another mouthful of human meat from her neck and shoulder as her eyes glazed. They glazed over, life surrendering to a greater power as he howled loudly into the night.

Voices in another room. Terror! Young voices filled with terror screaming for their mother. The werewolf stood, swiping at its lips with the back of a paw, grunting in a bestial manner, sniffing the air. Weaving back and forth, the thought of tender, young flesh in his gullet was tantalizing. Walking out of the dead woman's room, he loped apeishly to the door where the children had screamed. He could smell them as they hid under the bed.

Phill tried to laugh, but it was weird, whining growl that brought more humor to his blood-flecked lips. He sniffed like a hunting dog, whuffing lightly as he heard a gasp under the bed. Leaping across the room, he landed on the bed, hearing the scrambling kids beneath it, their whimpers bringing him untold pleasure. Ripping the mattress violently with his lower claws, he snarled at the two kids hiding under the frail cover of the bedsprings. Dropping to the floor, he pitched the bed to one side with his right hand, the entire frame crashing into the closet and a wooden dresser.

A sharp spang and a burning sting in his chest made him recoil, a tremendous roar erupting from his throat that would have drowned out the king of beasts. The oldest boy worked the pump on the .22 rifle and shot him in the middle of the stomach. Phill screamed in rage and pain, running into the wall, knocking pictures from the wall and cracking the sheet rock as he tried to get away from the sharp pain of the weapon. The rifle spat a third time and he felt the little bullet punch through his neck, gouging an aching hole that dampered his desire to attack the little bastards. The rifle fired again, the bullet missing and he did not want to feel another bullet rip through him.

Whirling, he careened wildly into the wall in the hallway, running on all fours for the bedroom where he killed the woman. Entering the room, he no longer felt the pain of the first two wounds, but the boy had shot him! Grabbing the woman's carcass under his left arm, he crashed through the French doors of the balcony in a spray of glass and wooden splinters. Leaping from the balcony, he landed effortlessly on the grass below, his hideous package under his arm. With a harsh growl, he disappeared into the night, frustrated at being foiled by a child, elated at retaining his supper beneath his left arm. He regretted ripping her arm from her body now. It was a waste of good meat.

The woods were dark, but not for him and he stopped only when he was several miles away. Gorging on Sandra's body, it was only when he finished that he realized the hunger did not rear itself to push him to rape her. Had the hunger shifted its aim or did he evolve with the hunger to a higher level? Thinking about Tana Denton, her nakedness winking temptingly as she ran away, he knew the hunger still held similar demands. Now it demanded different things from different subjects. It evolved as it allowed him to evolve.

Something told him he could not fully evolve until he had the girl the hunger had selected. It was frustrating, but hardly worth worrying over on a full stomach. His car was still two miles away, but he could cover the distance in minutes. The police would bring hounds to find him, but it would be later, maybe hours later.

Looking at the woman's remains, they were hideous, but not so bad as some of the dismembered victims the police had found before. Phill Sturgis left the body where it lay, moving through the forest like a deadly wraith, sated, yet willing to deal death if it encountered anyone. No one else was unfortunate enough to encounter him.

"You want to go don't you?" he asked softly, his hand resting lightly on her elbow as she looked out the window of their bedroom.

"It is my duty," she whispered, brushing her blonde hair from her face. Her bosom rose and fell evenly, the gentle ache of their lovemaking evident in her muscles, in the very scent of the room.

"The night always calls to you," he stated, moving to stand behind her, slipping his strong arms around her flat, muscular stomach.

"I would not be a wolf if it did not," she said, unable to present a better explanation.

He pressed his lips to the back of her head, kissing her, smelling her hair. "Sometimes I wish I could smell you like you smell me. Sometimes I wish I understood what the night does to you."

"Perhaps if you were a wolf?" Vivian suggested.

"Randy is a wolf and she does not understand Logan," Corrie offered as an argument.

"Randy is a human. The wolf in her is secondary. Her psyche fights the wolf and she finds the wolf forms repulsive where I revel in the form of the wolf. So does Logan. If Randy would allow herself to change more often, allow herself to become the creature that dwells within her, she might come to understand. The heart and soul is the realm of the wolf. She does not allow the wolf its place within her heart and her soul might not ever accept it. If what I say is true, she may never understand. I could tell her what I tell you, but it would change nothing. Either she will find it herself or she never will."

"Do you wish I was a wolf?" Corrie asked.

"Yes, at times when I run through the woods at night. I wish you were beside me. You would understand, Corrie. You are like your brother in many ways."

"Is that why you love me?" he asked teasingly, shocked as she whirled around to look at him in surprise.

Her eyes narrowing, she said, "Never have I loved you because of Logan." Caressing his face with her fingers, she looked into his eyes. "My love is for you, Corrie. I fell in love with a human and that human is you. If you never accept the wolf into your body, I shall love you forever. It is you whom I love."

"I'm sorry," he apologized.

She smiled, touching his shoulder, letting her hands roam down his slim waist to his powerful buttocks, squeezing them playfully. He leaned forward, kissing her lips tenderly as she let him lead her back to bed. She lay on her back and he lay across her, their mouths pressed desperately together.

Corrie woke, feeling the bed, knowing she was gone. He stood, looking out the window. Her car and his truck were still in the driveway. He breathed a sigh of relief, worried that she had left to join Logan.

The night had been calling to her and she had given in to that call. At least she had not given in to her sense of duty to Logan. She would eventually, but Corrie hoped his older brother would find the killer before that happened. He went back to bed, closing his eyes, drifting off to sleep with the vision of a blonde wolf padding silently through the brush covered ravines behind the house.

CHAPTER NINE

Walking around the police line, Logan felt sick at the scent of carnage assailing his nose from afar. The two children were gone, lucky victims of a monster that did not know his own powers yet. He heard the oldest boy shot the crazy man several times with a pump action .22 rifle. The police had not confirmed that as true, but Logan heard enough to know that the boy had hit something.

Something was a good term. None of the cops were telling the boys' story without pausing at the description of the killer. They were hiding something that they were having a hard time accepting.

The police were bewildered; both by the boys' unlikely description and the disappearance of Sandra Collins' body. The imprint of the man's feet indicated he had been carrying the woman's body, but the feet were huge and unlike the feet of a man. He heard one of the officers say something about Sasquatch or Big Foot. The other man had cursed him mildly.

They were bringing dogs in and Logan knew it would be too late for them to find the beast that killed these people. They would find the ghastly remains of Sandra's body out there somewhere. Undoubtedly he had fed from her and the body would be grotesque. Logan had seen the bodies of people who had been dined upon by lycanthropes. It was not a pleasant memory. Those people had been his friends.

Phill had completed the change last night. He was a full-fledged werewolf and a rogue prior to changing. Logan had hoped to kill him before the first change occurred. It would be easier to keep the werewolf's existence secret. With a sad sigh, he knew there were two little boys who would never lie down to bed at night without worrying about the return of the hairy creature that destroyed their lives.

"You want to come inside with me," said a voice behind him and Logan turned, meeting Scott Hale's eyes. The man's face was puffy, bruised and he walked somewhat stiffly, but he did not have an unfriendly expression on his face.

Logan's first response was to tell him to go to hell, but he did want to go inside. "Yes," he replied succinctly.

The FBI agent motioned for Logan to follow him, going through the police line with a show of his badge. Logan walked behind him, his eyes squinting as he got closer to the origin of the death scent.

"Got another one this morning in Sherman, Texas," Scott said. "You hear about it?"

"Hooker ravaged in a cheap motel room. Yeah, I heard about it. Was it him?"

"You know about the dead people in Poteau?"

"My wife told me on the phone yesterday. Man and woman shot several times, their truck stolen. Figured it was your boy who did it. His car was in bad shape."

Scott nodded his head, frowning as he opened the back door for Logan to enter. "Car looked like a lion or bear attacked it. The door was tore all to hell. You know about that?"

Logan said, "I almost had him. Car sideswiped a bunch of brush beside the road. Tore it up pretty bad. Threw me off before it happened."

"Yeah," Scott said, his voice indicating that he didn't believe everything Logan implied. He thought Logan was hiding something from him and maybe even his own people, but he could not put his finger on what motive the man would have for doing something like that.

The dead man's body was gone, but Logan had seen the blood on the grass. The kitchen floor was spotless, the black skillet still on the burner. Someone had turned the burner off when they first arrived. A thin man with a gray cowboy hat was standing in the living room. He noticed them immediately and Scott walked towards him.

"Sheriff Fowler," Scott acknowledged, shaking the man's hand. "I'm Agent Hale. This is Logan Denton."

Sheriff Fowler's face was grim as he shook the men's hands. "Man who did this is sick, Agent Hale. He tried to kill those kids. Boys were hiding under the oldest boy's bed. Crazy bastard ripped the mattress to hell, then flipped the whole damn bed off of 'em. Oldest kid popped him with a pump .22 rifle. Thought he lied about the hit, but we found the bullet embedded in the sheet rock. Little sucker did hit him, maybe more than once, but it didn't slow him down."

"Seen it before from a .22 long rifle," Scott said, unaffected by the sheriff's story.

"Not much knock down power, but there ought to be some blood," Sheriff Fowler asserted.

"Did you find any?" Logan asked, his eyes meeting Fowler's momentarily.

"Specks, a few drops that don't belong to any of the victims. The man was wounded, but it must have been a grazing wound." The sheriff's frustration was evident and Logan didn't press for more details. The absence of a small blood trail or even drops of blood somewhere outside the room appeared to disturb Sheriff Fowler a lot.

"The man was killed outside. Where did the woman meet her death?" Scott inquired, moving on with the questions lurking in his mind.

"Upstairs in her bed room. Go up the stairs to your right. Can't miss it with the county coroner's people in there. The state boys will be here shortly and your people too, I imagine." Fowler removed his hat, pushing his hair back from his forehead. His eyes held on Scott's face as he asked, "This guy the man that killed that woman in Sherman?"

"And the people in Oklahoma," Logan stated, drawing a look of irritation from Scott.

Fowler glanced at Logan, noting the FBI agent's hesitation at telling him the facts. He looked directly at Logan. "You think he will stay in the area?"

Shrugging his shoulders, Logan said, "Maybe. I doubt it though. We know what he looks like and will be on top of him if he is identified."

"You get the APB on him?" asked Scott.

"Yeah. Didn't think he would come through here," Fowler stated wearily. He wished he had retired this past term like his wife suggested.

Logan and Scott went upstairs, finding the bedroom using the sheriff's simple directions. The woman's arm lay where it fell, Logan noting the savage claw marks. The coroner would note it too, though he might find it too strange to list as having been done by claws or a vicious animal. He had a reputation to worry about in the community and the community did not believe in werewolves.

Logan walked out on the balcony. It was a romantic type of balcony made for peering at starry nights and the full moon. Last night it had been a stage for terror. He could not help feeling pity for the people who died here as he peered curiously at the ground below. He could see where the killer had landed after leaping from the balcony. It was an easy jump for a werewolf, even with a woman's body under his arm.

Stepping inside, he noticed a picture on the wall. It was a family picture and Sandra Collins was a beautiful woman. Her auburn hair was long in the picture, curly around a pretty face that was rounded in a gentle way that indicated friendly smiles and a person that found it easy to laugh. Her husband was handsome, his eyes clear, proud of his family like a man should be on such an occasion. His hair was brown with blond streaks trying to take over. His moustache was light over a mouth with white, even teeth. The boys were copies of both people and they were a few years younger than they were now.

Happy times. Good times. Times in the past that could never be repeated.

The man was dead, his head separated from his body and somewhere lay the devoured corpse of Sandra Collins. They would find it today when the dogs arrived. He could smell the scent of the werewolf and the dogs would be able to trail him too.

Logan did not think the man raped her. There was a lot of blood and the scent was overpowering, but he trained himself to detect the underlying scents, the subtle ones that lingered. The scent of sex was a strong scent, but it was not in this room. Bath oil, a perfume and the tangy scent of a body powder Sandra used before she was killed. No sign of sex, forced or otherwise.

The werewolf had killed to eat.

"Dogs are here," a deputy announced, sticking his head in the room. Scott followed him out of the room. Logan could hear the rumbling of a diesel engine and walked out the door. Looking down the hallway, he went to the room where the werewolf attacked the boys. A few seconds was all it took for him to confirm the boys' claims. They had shot the bastard. By the scent in the room, Phill had been hit at least twice. The scent of splattered blood was too strong for one wound.

The wounds were healed before he left the main bedroom, but he did not know enough about the type of creature he had became to turn and attack the weapon wielding boys. He still feared the weapon, but Logan knew that fear would not last much longer. Thank God for his ignorance last night.

He trotted down the stairs, slowing at the bottom before going outside where the sheriff was assisting the men with the dogs. He heard the bang of the tailgate drop and the scrambling of canine feet as the dogs fought to escape the dark prison of their box.

Scott was near the sheriff, but Logan stayed back, careful to position himself downwind from the dogs. He didn't need them going crazy over his scent. He smelled mostly human, but the scent of the wolf was there too. The dogs could smell it if he let them get in position for the wind to carry it to them.

"You going?" Scott asked, taking a vest and a shoulder holster from an agent Logan recognized from Oklahoma.

"I'll stay here. Seen enough dead bodies in my time."

"I want to see you before you leave. Hang around until we get back," Scott requested, glancing at a deputy that nodded his head.

Nodding, Logan watched them leave, trotting behind the three dogs who had already struck the scent. It amused him that Scott thought that deputy would keep him here if he wanted to leave. He did not want to leave; he simply did not want to see Sandra's body. One dog was holding back, but the other two were pulling their handlers. They would find her within a mile or so. Logan was positive he had not taken her far before he fed.

There were a few deputies and agents mulling around, but none of them paid Logan any attention -- even the man that Scott spoke to about keeping an eye on him had went inside the house. Logan walked around the yard, finding where the werewolf had entered and hidden as he watched the house. The woodpile was in perfect position to allow someone to see the balcony and the small kitchen window. The werewolf had stood behind the pile before leaping to the top, then to the roof of the well house. He dropped off the other side and Logan lowered his head, smelling that scent too. It was on the grass, though the dew made it harder to detect this morning.

He had hunted the people like they were prey for a large predator, taking them unaware where they believed themselves safe. Man was unaccustomed to being looked upon as prey. Except perhaps in Grizzly bear country, that fear had been long gone in the United States.

He whistled with the music over the radio. Phill felt better today than he felt in years. He was the most powerful creature on earth. Those wounds from the bullets had healed to where there wasn't even a scar where they penetrated his skin. His stomach was full and he hadn't even had to pick his teeth with a toothpick.

They might figure out where he was going. Scott was smart and Phill genuinely liked the man, though he held him in contempt for working so closely beside a serial killer and never suspecting it until now. He burped, blowing it out the window and singing along with the words of a song he knew. DeQueen was ahead, but he would circle around it. They might suspect he was going home and that would be entirely too simple. First, he would go to Little Rock in a roundabout way, or maybe Jonesboro. Eventually he was going back to Oklahoma and the girl the hunger selected.

The hunger should not be denied. Phill was convinced the hunger had given him these wonderful powers strictly on his convictions. It trusted him to do its will without veering from the path along the way.

He would not fail the hunger. Tana Denton would be sacrificed in time and he would move on to the next selection. His mind wondered how much stronger the hunger would make him. What other wonderful powers would he inherit from this powerful entity living within his belly?

He could only wonder . . . and hope.

Jacob Sessoms screamed as he saw the remains of his youngest daughter. Jacob had worked for the county since he quit school before the war with the commies in Korea and no tax-paid officials were telling him he couldn't search for his daughter! A large pistol on his hip was strapped in place and two deputies were standing on either side to grab him if they did happen to corner the perpetrator.

He had forced his way through the group to see the mutilated body of his daughter. It had almost driven him to his knees. Two deputies had to restrain him from destroying the scene by rushing to the carcass of the young woman.

All the meat from her thighs and legs were gone, the muscles of her chest and stomach laid bare, an empty hole where her heart should have been. Scott felt the bile rise in his throat and he turned his head. Some of the deputies were puking, stepping away from the scene, and closing their eyes in an attempt to force the image out of their minds.

The burly man with the dogs opened a can of snuff, gathering a dip between his thumb and forefinger, packing it in his lower lips with a strange smile. He was looking at Scott and he said, "Tole' you my dogs would find it!"

Scott looked at the woman's mutilated carcass. The redneck was right. She was no longer human and "it" was as apt a description as anything else was for now.

The shadows flickered behind her like an ever-changing kaleidoscope as she cried out, running through the trees, limbs tearing at her flesh like small sickles harvesting winter wheat. She panted, running, her breath flowing from her mouth in visible vapors like the fog of London. Her blood pounded in her ears, heart hammering in her chest like the rat-a-tat-tat of a machine gun.

It was behind her, flitting from shadow to dark shadow, a fearsome specter of violent death with slavering fangs and horrendous claws. It wished to kill her.

She slipped, falling across her belly as the wind was driven from her lungs. She cried out, surprised by the hollowness of her voice, the terror ringing like a church bell in her ears.

"Run!"

The voice was powerful and it was Tim's voice. Tana leapt to her feet, sprinting to a clearing beckoning in the distance. A sliver of moonlight sliced the darkness to illuminate the open field. It was as if the pale light represented everything safe, everything untouchable by the hands of evil.

A coarse howl erupted behind her, wavering like a somber melody in an operetta. Every hair on her neck stood out and she felt clutching fingers of something unnamable circling her spine, seeking to freeze her before she reached that light.

"Argghh!" she grunted, feeling her legs growing stiff, the sound of heavy feet behind her. The feet were coming closer, but Tana refused to quit, pushing herself desperately. "Nooo!" she cried, feeling her feet become lead, her legs marble as she slowed, a figure appearing in the light. He held out his hands, his face easily recognized as she neared him. It was her father, both hands extended from the light, but his body would not break the rim of the light. The light was a fence that held him in place, his face in agony as he tried to help her, straining to reach her before the monster overtook her.

Tana was within a few yards of the clearing, the sounds of the monster behind her so close she could hear the labored breathing, the crack of individual twigs snapping beneath its weight. She lunged forward in a desperate bid for safety, reaching for Logan's outstretched fingers, but she missed, falling a few feet short of the safety net within the light.

The creature dug its claws into her legs and she cried out, screaming shrilly and she was still screaming when Randy gripped her shoulders, pulling Tana to her chest as she awoke from the nightmare. Randy held the weeping girl, tears in her eyes as Tana sobbed helplessly. This wasn't the first nightmare that drove Tana into a screaming terror as she awoke. Randy closed her eyes, feeling more helpless than she ever remembered feeling in the mountains of Idaho. How do you comfort someone else when all your thoughts are thoughts of confusion?

The werewolf had killed to eat.

That thought stuck in Logan's mind as he sat on the woodpile, looking over the grain field separating the house and the forest. He selected a woman to eat when he had already killed a man. That was easily explainable under the circumstances. The man was accustomed to killing women, eliminating men only when they got in his way. His feeding took on the same characteristics as his serial killer MO.

Would he have eaten the children or simply killed them so they could not report his identity? Logan thought about it, deciding he would kill them simply because he could do so without fear of retaliation. That gutsy kid shooting him in the stomach made Logan smile. Too bad the kid had not been armed when the killer came up the stairs. Sandra Collins might be alive now.

The men were coming back across the field and Logan felt something turn in his stomach. He could see the sunlight glint off the bright black body bag in the far rear. There was no desire to examine the body and no need either as he scented the werewolf in the house. It was Phill and he was far more deadly than ever.

Logan dropped to the ground, knocking a chunk of wood out of place. He put it back on the woodpile and waited for Scott Hale to return. He was curious what the man had to say to him. It was unlikely he wanted Logan to join him in the investigation. Logan thought he might want to ask him politely to stay out of the Bureau's way.

His finely tuned hearing could hear some of the men talking. They were mentioning coyotes or a wild dog pack must have mutilated the carcass after he raped and killed her. The man he heard was her father and he had to be helped as he sobbed openly. Logan saw Scott looking directly at him, his lips tight with suppressed anger and the stress of forcing the horror of the woman's condition out of his mind.

Two deputies helped the woman's father to a vehicle and Scott walked directly to him.

"Why didn't you let the body lay for a medical examiner?" Logan asked when Scott was close by.

Shaking his head, Scott said, "A wild dog pack or coyotes had ravaged the body. Any evidence was destroyed."

Grunting, Logan turned to walk to his truck. He heard Scott walking behind him and he stopped, facing him. "If you believe that you are crazy as hell. Where were the tracks? Did you see any animal tracks around her body?"

Eyebrows narrowing, Scott admitted, "No, but the ground was torn up some." He wiped a hand across his face and stared back across the field. "I'm not a zoologist or even a country boy really. The Sheriff believed that was . . . ate her like that." Putting his hands on his hips, Scott Hale was beginning to suspect Logan Denton knew more than he was telling.

"What is your explanation, Denton? You are acting awfully all knowing about this guy. What is it you are hiding from me?"

Disgustedly, Logan said, "I ain't hiding nothing from you, Agent Hale. The goddamn evidence is in front of your nose and you ignore it."

Scott wanted to turn and punch the man, but he knew that would not solve anything. Besides, he was not sure Logan would not mop the floor with him again. He had fought some tough men, but this man enraged was the strongest man he had ever fought.

"Denton, I didn't run you in for assaulting me, but I can have your ass for interfering out of your jurisdiction! Quit beating around the bush and tell me?"

Stepping close, Logan said, his voice forced, "He is a monster, Hale. A werewolf that is killing these people like they were cattle. You know what those boys said they seen!" Pointing towards the house, his voice remained low, but harsh. "Can't you see his MO has changed?! He is no longer fucking and killing them!! He is eating them too!!"

"It happens with psychos," Hale said, unable to believe this man was trying to make him believe those kids had seen an honest-to-god werewolf. "Listen, I thought you were a good officer, but if this carnage convinces you to believe in fairy tales . . ."

Grabbing, Hale by the shirt front, Logan jerked him close to his face. "Look into my eyes, goddamn you!! What do you see?"

Scott was looking into the gray eyes of the larger man and he felt his soul turn cold as they became savage, animalistic, a frightening sight that made him shiver. The man gripped his wrists and Scott was unable to shake them off. He tried to tear his eyes away as Logan looked into his face. Whatever that was behind his eyes did not speak of madness, insanity, but those were the only concepts Scott could relate to what he saw.

"You're crazy!" Scott muttered.

"Come with me," Logan said, pulling the man along like a child. He saw the sheriff and his deputies looking at them and he released his hold on the agent. They stepped in the small storage building near the well house and Scott shut the door behind him.

"What?" he asked as Logan turned. His eyes grew wide and he backed up a step. "Jesus!!" He swallowed hard as he looked at the apish face and long fangs. The man looked normal except his face and it suddenly appeared to melt and became as normal as the rest of his body.

"Now what do you say?" Logan asked, his eyes cold and steady.

"I think I need a drink," Scott muttered sickly.

Logan gripped the man's arm. "I'll buy if you want to go somewhere and talk."

"I appreciate it," Scott said, opening the door and finding the air refreshing. It seemed stifling inside the storage room with Logan Denton.

The cafe no longer did a booming business since the Interstate bypassed it, but there was enough local patronage that it remained profitable. It was not empty, but there was plenty of space inside to keep eavesdroppers from hearing what they had to say.

Sitting in a secluded corner of the small cafe, Scott drank the coffee Logan bought him, looking across the table at the man or creature that had finally convinced him Sturgis was a real monster. He pulled out a pack of cigarettes and put one in his mouth, fumbling with a match. "Quit smoking a year ago," he said with a weak laugh. His hands shook nervously as he tapped the knuckles of his left hand against the table. "What the hell are you, Denton?"

Logan looked at the young agent without emotion, his eyes studying the man's nervousness. "I am a lycanthrope."

"That a werewolf?"

Wryly, Logan said, "Yes, or loupe-garou if you are French, lobo-hombre if you are Spanish. There are many names for us."

Scott was calmer as he inhaled on the cigarette. "You been one all your life?"

"That don't matter," Logan said with a shrug. "Just understand that this monster is going to keep killing until we stop him. You go against him with the attitude that he is another psycho and a bunch of cops or agents are going to die when they try to take him."

"Why? What is so special about being a werewolf?"

"It takes silver to kill one," Logan said, sipping the tea he had bought when they sat down at the table.

Scott laughed sardonically. "This sounds like some kind of movie!"

"It isn't a movie," Logan said seriously. "It is a nightmare and people are dying. I know you people are reactive instead of proactive, but I know this nut has just changed for the first time and you saw the results!" The words spoken by the deputies as they crossed the field came to mind. "A coyote did not eat that woman! He did!" He leaned closer, his face stern. "He is getting stronger! He will get stronger every day and he will keeping killing!"

Curiously, Scott asked, "You aren't in this just because he came after your daughter. Is it because you are afraid he will expose your people?"

He was silent for a moment before answering. "Can you imagine what it would do to our explosive society?" Logan asked. "It would rock the entire world. That is why it must be kept a secret. He must die, Agent Hale and his body must be destroyed."

"This sounds too wild." Taking a deep breath, he said, "Look. Suppose I go along with this story you are telling me and he flips out anyway and exposes your people. What will you do then?"

"He must be stopped." Logan would not waver from his convictions. He knew that the potential danger from this man was huge. "I am sworn to stop him. If he exposes us, I must make sure the human population knows we are trying to police our own. He could kill again; tonight or even today."

"I thought you guys were like tied to the full moon and . . ."

"We are not creations of the cinema, Scott. We are true living creatures and we have existed since the dawn of man. We do not go crazy at the time of the full moon though it does pull to the wolf within." He chuckled, shrugging his shoulders. "I am a man. I have a wife, kids and a job. In that respect I am not different from you. My brothers are human. My mother and father are human. My children are human." A thought came to mind. "Do you know an agent named Dane Lewis?"

"Agent? Hell, he is a regional director! Yes, everyone knows Dane Lewis!"

"He is a wolf, Agent Hale, the same as me and the same as Phil Sturgis."

A sudden realization covered Hale's face. "He handled the massacre in Idaho. You disappeared for a long time after that." He studied Logan's face, but the man was not hiding anything. "That is when you became a werewolf wasn't it?"

"Yes. We were attacked by a rogue pack. Dane helped keep it tidy." Logan leaned back, spreading his arms out on the booth top and relaxing. "There are others who have been werewolves, Scott. Names in history that would make you go crazy with disbelief."

"Like who?"

"I am not going to name names, but one of our country's founding fathers and later, a president, was a lycanthrope." He smiled wolfishly. "The werewolves migrated from the old countries too."

Disbelievingly, Scott looked at the table, his hands together around the coffee cup. This was almost too much to digest. "What do we do?"

"We kill him." Sliding a clip of ammo across the table, Logan said, "These are silver alloy bullets. They are accurate and made to mushroom well within soft tissue."

"Who designed them?" Scott asked.

Grinning mischievously, Logan said, "A werewolf."

CHAPTER TEN

Scott had not been surprised by the look of disbelief his field agents gave him when he climbed in the pick-up truck with Logan Denton. They were ordered to continue with the investigation while he went with Denton. He gave no explanation and the men were so surprised they did not think to ask for one until he was already gone.

The truck was high off the ground and Scott liked the legroom. He watched as Logan drove with both hands on the wheel. They were going to DeQueen where Sturgis grew up as a child. The man was making this drive for some reason. They went through two roadblocks that were searching for the man on the highway. The APB on the wire was alerting the police community in Arkansas as to what he looked like and his possible destination. Roadblocks rarely worked, but the Arkansas State police were not going to take the chance.

"You know it did not take them that long to catch Bundy once they had an idea of his location," Scott said, musing over one of the most infamous serial killers in history.

"Bundy was intelligent, but he was an egomaniac. This guy is both, but he is more. He knows how you work as well as you do. Now he has the instincts of a wolf too," Logan commented, his eyes never leaving the highway.

Scott grunted. "You believe in this wolf stuff a lot don't you? Being a wolf does not make you superhuman. The way you talk almost sounds like the werewolf community is a little ego oriented itself."

"You misunderstand what I mean when I refer to the wolf. I mean we have to readjust our thinking. We are no longer following a man. We are following a creature that has two forces raging inside him, both trying to dominate his psyche, maybe even his soul." Logan's voice was calm as he explained what he believed would be going on in Phill Sturgis. "The wolf is a predator, but it is a stealthy hunter. They know the ways of their prey and with the change came a new awareness in his mind and body. He has became more dangerous than he ever was prior to the change."

Puzzled, Scott asked, "Was he always a werewolf?"

Shaking his head, Logan explained, "No. He experienced his first change only recently."

"How would you know that?"

How much should he tell him? "The first change gives your body a different physical makeup. One werewolf can scent another one because it is a scent we recognize. When I met him in the forest the day we were exhuming the remains of Melinda Anderson I could not smell the scent of the wolf on him." He noticed the raised eyebrow on Scott's face. "Yes, I checked you too when I first met you."

"I am glad it does not require you to sniff my butt," Scott grumbled, scooting down in the seat and closing his eyes.

Logan grunted, but did not say anything else to the man sitting beside him. He had decided he did not care much for Scott Hale when the man chose to use his county as bait by keeping his people there. That the monster killed his daughter's boyfriend made him want to kill the FBI agent, but he controlled that desire. He needed the agent's cooperation and he did seem to have it. He hoped they could find Sturgis quickly and eliminate the problem.

Corrie walked into the bedroom after sitting his lunch box on the kitchen table. The suitcases on the bed were open, but she was finished packing. He met her eyes as she came out of the bathroom.

"Did he call?" he asked.

Shaking her head, Vivian said, "No. I am going to stay with Randy." She shut her first suitcase and latched it.

Confused, he asked, "Why? Loren is there." He walked into the room and sat in the chair in the corner near the closet.

Vivian was perplexed as her lips tightened. "He does not think like me," she finally said, unable to think of a better explanation.

Eyes narrowing, Corrie said, "I guess not." He put his hands together. "Want me to take off work and go with you?"

Her eyes met his eyes and she smiled. "If you want to come I would love it." She knew he worried about her. "I can take care of myself, sweetheart."

He smiled. "I know that." He stood, his expression almost sad. There was no need to call in to work for Vivian. She was a florist and had her own business. There were two girls who worked for her that would handle things while she was gone. He did feel better that she was going to Logan and Miranda's house rather than the woods or a large city after some crazed killer.

She paused what she was doing to hug him. Touching his face, she said, "If it would make you worry less, I wish I was fully human."

Corrie smiled, kissing her deeply as his hands roamed to her waist and across her buttocks. He squeezed her playfully and hugged her. "Since you have to help with this guy, I am glad you are a wolf."

She kissed him and he hugged her tightly, her every inner sense feeling his angst at her leaving. They parted and she left, the door clicking quietly behind her. Corrie sighed and sat on his bed. There was an innate wildness there that he might never understand. That did nothing to keep him from loving her.

The distant stars were like a quilt with a patchwork of lights embroidered upon its uneven surface. The late summer night was stifling, humid, but Randy did not feel like being inside. She needed to be here tonight. She needed the message that lingered in the night, that spoke to the wild beast, the nocturnal creature that dwelled inside her. Loren and Milly slept together in the guestroom and she could hear them breathing when she got up to come out here. Tomorrow Milly and the girls were going back home. She had work to do and Randy knew she was worried about leaving her house for so long.

Randy did not do this often. That she had started stepping outside during the twilight hours to feel the night only seemed to fuel the confusion inside her body. There was a yearning inside her heart she did not understand and it often frightened her. In the past, she had felt it swell, making her breath come hoarsely from her throat, her heart to pound in her chest. Usually she would flee back inside to the safety of her own bed.

Tonight, she did not want to run to the lonely bed that waited. Tonight, she did not feel the fear that came with the longing. There was a small part of her that was hesitant, but a more powerful voice coaxed her gently, urging her to do what her soul was demanding.

Unbuttoning her nightshirt, she let it fall to the deck as she stepped out of her panties. The sliver of moon spoke desperately to something within her and she felt strangely comforted by the feeling. This felt so natural. Without a word, she changed, grunting as her bones popped and disjointed to remake themselves into the shape of the wolf. She stood on four feet for a few seconds, allowing the sensation to feel more natural before loping into the woods.

The mountains were different. They were so beautiful at night and she was amazed that she had never noticed it before. There were a plethora of scents she did not recognize and many that she knew instinctively.

Along the mountains she heard the yip of coyotes and wondered if they were some distant cousin to her species. Her tongue lolled out and she felt like laughing at the thought, but there were so many questions that went unanswered about the lycanthropes. She knew Logan did not have all the answers either, but he did know more about it than her.

Vitoro had told her things, but they were hard to understand too. There was an understanding about herself she needed to have first and she had never allowed the wolf to pervade her soul that freely. She almost believed she never would.

Yet tonight there were answers, but the questions did not come to mind. There was freedom and she loped in the forest, aware of the creatures giving her room to pass. She had no desire to hunt -- not tonight, but she knew there was an instinct to do so. She scented a mountain lion and later, a bobcat that circled warily around her.

The animals of the night were aware of her, but they avoided her. The deer that scented her ran from her and she saw an owl look down at her from a perch high in a craggy oak. He wanted no part of her nor did any other creature in the forest.

Logan had wanted her to run with him in the night like this, but she had not done it. She had changed very few times and she almost felt ashamed in her lupine form.

She enjoyed it. That was what she never admitted to Logan or fully to herself. Randy enjoyed the power, the strength of the wolf's heart beating symbiotically with her own. It frightened her -- the human half of her, yet it gave her an inner peace as the wolf was allowed to be free.

The wolf would be free tonight. She felt her powerful muscles rippling beneath her pelt as she climbed the side of the mountain. There were animals moving and she could hear them. Suddenly she had an urge to do something she had never done in this form. Lifting her head, she howled, a lilting melancholy sound that wavered through the night, cutting the sounds of the night woods with its singularity and power. The animals listened to this mighty predator and she sensed their silent acknowledgement of her presence. Lifting her head, she howled again . . .

After a few hours she came home through the back pasture and into the back yard under the fence. She changed in the yard, walking to where her clothes lay and grimaced at the dew wetting them. Going to the shop, she showered, sliding on one of Logan's tee shirts and a pair of shorts that were too big.

She did not feel any danger in the dark as she walked to the deck. Opening the door, she stepped inside. Her eyes saw the man with dark hair in the shadows and she smiled as she stood in the doorway.

"I am going to be embarrassed if you saw me nude," she confided openly as Loren smiled and chuckled boyishly.

"It was not intentional. I saw you cross the yard after you retrieved your clothes."

Her eyebrows raised speculatively and he pointed towards the stairs. "I came downstairs about an hour ago. I had checked on you and you were gone. Found your clothes here and figured you had went . . . jogging in the woods."

"You have been up since then?" she asked, shutting the door behind her.

"Sitting in the den and reading. I was coming in here for a refill of orange juice when I saw you go to the shop."

"Bare ass and all?" she asked candidly, seeing a blush on his cheeks.

He nodded, his slightly glowing cheeks betraying him as he really did not feel very embarrassed. "Bare ass and all," he replied.

"Hmmm," she said in embarrassment, walking to the cupboard and getting a glass. She opened the refrigerator door and took out the orange juice pitcher. Pouring it into her glass, she looked at Loren. "I should be more discreet."

Loren shrugged. "It is a part of you now, Randy. I was not offended and it is your home, your nature now to . . ."

"Is it?" she asked suddenly, her eyes showing her quandary. Loren hesitated as she put the glass down on the bar. "Is it my nature to be a wolf?"

"I would think so," he answered, unsure of his ground.

She sipped the juice and nodded her head. "Maybe Loren. It is not as easy for me to come to grips with as it was for Logan."

The butt of a revolver stuck out of his pants and he wore only his jeans and a T-shirt. His feet were bare and his hair slightly mussed. Randy had always believed him to be handsome and it was especially true here in the dim light of the kitchen. There was a sudden urge to move into his arms, feel his chest against her and allow him to remove the T-shirt and shorts to take her here on the bar. Loren was looking into her face, unaware of the conflict of emotion stirring inside her chest.

He placed his glass in the sink and turned squarely towards her. "Logan had several years with the wolf in control. They fought and his human half won. Even so, the effects of the wolf are still there and he must deal with it. He is different because of it." He saw her start to protest and he shook his head. "Not to me or you, but how he approaches what he is, what he has become. You have only your human experiences to draw from and the human is afraid of the wolf."

"How do you know all that?" she asked in amazement, the urge gone as suddenly as it appeared.

Loren smiled softly, knowingly. "Because Randy, I am human and I know that wolves scare the hell out of me."

She giggled and he joined her. Finishing her orange juice, she placed her glass beside Loren's. They had been friends as long she had been a friend with Logan. Maybe that is why she felt like she did for a few moments. The familiarity with someone who had been so close to her for so long had offered her a door to a brief moment before everything in the world had changed. A time before the change that occurred inside her. She felt the wolf inside her and remembered the powerful features of her husband, briefly feeling ashamed of her previous feelings.

"I am going to bed, Loren." She hugged him, kissing his cheek. He patted her on the back before they parted. "Thanks."

Jokingly, he said, "Well, I guess I can go back to reading. It takes second place to observing gorgeous women traipse nude in the moonlight, but it will have to do."

She blushed a deep scarlet. "You are so horrible!"

"I know," he said, watching her go up the stairs. He went back to the recliner that was against the wall. He could see the front door and the back door near the kitchen. The pistol lay in his lap when he picked up his book. Maybe he was relaxing, but he was the most alert relaxed man in the county.

His human half had not defeated his wolf half. To destroy half of something so integral to his being would have meant death or insanity. They lived in a perpetual partnership. That was where Logan had made his mistake when trying to force the change back into his human form. The change *had came closer* to fruition as he tried to force it, worked at it relentlessly, but it only occurred when he made his peace with his animal side. When the two parts of him worked together, the change became smooth, fluid and without effort.

How do you explain what it is like to be a werewolf to someone with nothing to base a comparison? The words were stuck inside him. For some of the feelings he had there were no words of explanation or wisdom. People who were werewolves were confused. When he was trying to change back to a man so many years ago, he often wondered why there were not more rogues.

After he found the inner peace of communion, he no longer wondered. He was sure of himself and the wolf inside him as much a part of him as the man. That was what he tried to relate to Randy and could not. Her fear that the wolf would dominate the human held back her understanding. Unless she released the wolf spirit to find its natural place within her soul she would always be confused. And, there was nothing he or any other werewolf could do to help her. The answer was inside her. She would simply have to find it on her own.

The search for peace was not in the same league as the quest for the Holy Grail, but it was worth making. Logan knew that he rested far better than Randy did at times and it was purely the wolf suppressed within her that made her restless. The pent-up emotions buried inside her soul would have to be released, expressed and some could only be expressed as a wolf.

"You got quiet on me?" Scott teased, stretching the muscles he could in the cab of the truck. He felt an urge to relieve his bladder and knew it was the result of an entire liter of Dr. Pepper an hour or so back down the road. He rolled along the small of his back, rocking a little side to side a few times before sitting up straight. He had been dozing for at least a half-hour. "I got to take a whiz, Logan."

Glancing at his watch, Logan said, "I could too. We are almost into Mena. I think we will drive to Ft. Smith tonight."

The darkness hid Scott's face as he looked out the passenger window, his irritation covering his face like a grim latex mask. "We do not even know if we are following him or not."

Logan did not say anything. A large semi-trailer went by with a load of cattle and the smell of manure was fresh for a moment. "What are you saying?"

Taking a deep breath and exhaling slowly, Scott said, "We should spend the night in Mena and get some rest. We can get up early in the morning and be in Ft. Smith shortly after day light if that is what you want to do."

Of course he made sense and Logan had no real argument to the suggestion -- especially a relevant argument. "If you think that is best, we can get a couple rooms."

"It would do us both some good," he assured him.

The night was clear and he could hear the sounds of cars ever so often though they were over a mile away. The forest was not a silent domain and he moved stealthily among its denizens, unaware that the wild animals sensed him, moving out of his way before he reached them. He was near the state line on a road that would lead to a small junction called Big Cedar.

He had went through it before and he smiled to himself as he thought about how he had led the fools around in a circle.

God had not created all creatures equally and Phill Sturgis felt the power of his creation boiling in his veins, seething within him to explode, boil over in an orgiastic rampage of murder, savagery and domination. He was the dominant creature. The thought penetrated the blood lust fogged tendrils of his mind -- he was the alpha wolf.

There was a house ahead -- he had seen the lights in the distance and he was padding on two feet towards that beacon. No longer did he have the desire to rape his victim before he slaughtered them. The act of devouring them was by far more sensual, more powerful than the simple act of rape.

He looked more like a slender ape except for the wolfish head, the lower jaw thrust forward, the fangs extending from his mouth in a perpetual snarl.

Resting his elongated hand on a tree trunk, he cocked his head, hearing the sound of a truck moving slowly along a washboard, dirt road. He watched as a single beam of light pierced the darkness a few moments before the twin lights of the truck came into view over the tallest of a small series of rolling hills. Humans!! His stomach growled in hunger.

He snarled, sniffing of the air as he shifted his weight from one foot to the other until he slightly swayed, his eyes locked on the vehicle. With two bounds, he covered over thirty feet to stand at the edge of a small ridge. Below he could sense two deer feed on the browse along the dozer piles, unaware of his presence and only vaguely aware of the truck upon the hill.

It rumbled and shook with the rough road, something rattling in the back. There was something heavy and metallic back there and he growled in his throat thinking about the warm, tender flesh in the cab of the vehicle. He no longer cared if it was male or female - life was life and he was a taker and a giver.

Within him stirred the soul of a god. He has wondered if this is the way all gods were born, but instinctively he knew others were forged in a different cauldron, taking shape according to the metal smith that created them. He was the god of death, the new god of death and war!

Two long bounds and he was into the clear-cut behind a pile of brush. A huge leap and he was on top. Watching the spotlight move across the field, searching for the eyes of the deer. They sought the life of the deer, unaware that they were no longer the hunter, but the prey. His spring-like muscles coiled, releasing and he landed thirty feet from where he stood, loping ape-like to another brush pile as he heard the truck crunch the gravel in a stop.

They had seen the deer and were moving carefully out of the truck to shoot without frightening the animals. One wore a straw cowboy hat, the brim shaped by his own hands. The other wore a red cap with a big S on the front of it, but the rifles they carried were handled with familiarity. These young men had been raised in this backwoods community, their affinity for weapons and poaching a part of their upbringing.

He could see two boys and a girl that sat in the middle of the long bench seat, her long hair barely visible in the reduced light. She was holding a bright spotlight and trying to get it trained on the deer without climbing out of the truck. The deer had moved nervously for the woods, but he could see the driver was walking around the front of the truck to join his companion. The girl tried to hold the light steady as they prepared to shoot.

The echoing shot rebounded off the woods and down the winding ravine. The deer did not move any faster and he could hear one of the boys cussing as he worked the lever on his gun. Phill charged, moving quickly among the scattered hardwood lying scattered from the logging done here in the past.

They had their eyes on the deer as the other boy shot. The lead deer stumbled, falling in a thrashing of legs. The boy let out a whoop of triumph, his face breaking into a huge grin as he turned towards the noise to his left. His victory cry turned into a wavering scream of terror as the nightmarish creature hurtled from the darkness of the deepest pit in Hell onto his chest in a flurry of claws and fangs. His high pitched scream was joined by the girl as she threw the light out the door, pushing herself back inside, fighting to get behind the wheel.

The night breeze blew calmly as the boy with the cowboy hat fired his rifle through the werewolf's body. Phill howled in pain as the impact of the 30-30 rifle knocked him off the boy he was savaging. He spun, his wounds healing as the boy shot again, centering the bullet in the beast's chest as the girl got the truck started.

Grabbing his friend, he jerked as his hand slid off the arm, the wounded boy's arm slick with blood and gore. The wounded boy tried to stand and Phil was gaining his feet, the massive wound already covered with hair as it healed almost instantly. The boy with the cowboy hat grunted, his breath catching in his throat as the werewolf collided with him, ripping the rifle from his hands and gashing his arms. The werewolf's momentum carried him over the boy and he scrambled to his feet, his hat crumpled from the weight of the wolf as it landed on it. The boy dove over the side of the truck into the back with a thump.

"Go!!" he screamed, pounding on the back glass as the werewolf crouched, growling as it looked at him and the wounded boy prone on the ground. Its feral eyes glistened red and they fixated on the girl in the front of the truck. A deep almost jungle sound emanated from the back of the lupine throat before it leaped, aiming for the half open door of the truck like a missile.

The girl screeched, her indecision concerning her friend disappearing in a burst of instinct for her own survival. The werewolf crumpled the door, slinging a long clawed paw inside that sliced through the vinyl seat in long narrow strips. She floored the truck, spewing rocks behind her in a rooster tail as the werewolf tried to pull himself inside the cab with her.

The truck weaved back and forth as the girl screamed, trying to dislodge the hideous thing that sought to snuff out her life. She begged for it to leave her alone while screaming almost hysterically as it growled and snapped, swinging with the door, single-mindedly seeking to rip out her slender throat and taste the rich, red blood. Phil was delighted as he got both hands inside the truck, his powerful muscles lifting him to slide through the window and into the cab with the girl.

The blow on his shoulder was stunning and the werewolf yelped, snapping at the tire tool as it struck him in the shoulder blade, snapping a bone audibly.

"Let go you, motherfucker!!" he screamed, his young face frightened as the werewolf swiped at him, releasing the seat to swing to the side of the truck. His back claws dug into the fender well and he was in the back as agilely as an acrobat.

The slavering jaws clicked open and shut as the boy two-handed the tire tool like a baseball bat. The truck hit a big rut, knocking both boy and creature off their feet. Phil felt himself tumbling over the side and only by a wild grab did he clutch the side of the truck. The wheel burnt his skin and the hair flew from his body as he reached forward with his other hand to pull himself back onto the truck.

The girl saw the creature in the mirror and she saw the heavy Red Cedar leaning out from the ditch. Wildly, she swiped it, the metal protesting as the tree scraped along the side. It tore the wide-angle mirror off the door and she could not see if she was successful or not.

"Yes!!!" came the cry from the back. "Take that you bastard!!!" She glanced to the side as her friend climbed into the seat after pushing the ruined door out of the way. His face was flushed and there was a gash on his arm. "Stop at Mr. Biddles," he said, pointing to the house they were nearing. "They can call the police and we can go get Ray."

"Is he dead, Jimmy?" she asked, her voice low. She sounded like his little sister.

"Not sure about Ray," Jimmy said, his voice wavering. "That creature ain't."

"I ain't sure I want to stop here," she said, glancing at the back mirror nervously.

Reaching under the seat, Jimmy pulled out a short barreled revolver. "I . . . we got to help Ray, Denise." It was all he could say. She nodded and they pulled into the driveway, slinging gravel into the yard. The back porch light came on and an old man stepped out on the porch, his left hand holding the bib of his denim overalls. The two kids ran out of the truck and he recognized them. The story they told was rushed and unbelievable. The two kids were shaken and so was he as he peered into the shadows of the night. It was a crazy story, but something had tore hell out of that pick-up. Ushering them inside, he had his wife to call the sheriff while he loaded his two shotguns with slugs and buckshot. If that other kid was alive, he would have to wait a bit longer. He wasn't going to leave his wife and these kids here alone on a faint hope that the boy was alive after the mauling that monster did to the truck. He moved everyone to the storm cellar entrance in the kitchen to where he could watch only one way in. They all went down the stairs and he stood at the door, watching the door to the outside.

"Do you think he followed?" Denise asked in a whisper. Mrs. Biddle patted her on the arm. She was scared too, but she tried comforting the teenage girl.

"The police will be here soon," Jerry said from the top of the stairs. "We are armed well enough to hold off anything until then."

Clutching the revolver, Jimmy said, "I bet he went back into the woods." He sounded more hopeful than certain.

The slow whining scratch began low and got louder. It was like sharp fingernails on a chalkboard during a test in a high school class. Mr. Biddle squinted, listening to the sound, trying to figure out what made it.

"Oh God! Oh God!" Denise started whimpering, digging her face into Mrs. Biddles' arm as the tears began to flow.

"He's out there," Jimmy muttered, his voice strangely muted as his breathing became harder to control. He gripped the pistol tight in his hand, his voice more urgent. "He is out there, Mr. Biddle."

"Quiet, Jimmy! I got to listen!" The man was suddenly nervous, but he was confident in the destructive power of the shotgun.

Jerry Biddle had served in Korea and he had been on both ends of a gun. His hip had two wound scars in it from a Chicom machine gun and he had walked with a slight list for several years after he came home. He won a Bronze Star for bravery getting those wounds. Many of his buddies told him he should have gotten the Medal of Honor. Unfortunately, most of those buddies came home in body bags, dead from starvation and cold, two realities that killed more men in his unit than any Chinese bullets.

This was different. Something was out there and it hunted them, just like he hunted the turkey behind his house during the Spring. The sound was louder and he thought he saw a shadow cross the window over the sink. Lifting the shotgun, he slipped the safety to off on the Remington 870.

The noise circled around the house, growing quieter, almost disappearing, then becoming louder from another direction.

"What the hell is that?" Jerry asked no one in particular under his breath.

"It's his claws on the windows," Denise said, whimpering, her pretty face red and flushed with tears. "He is walking around the house scratching the windows."

The noise quit after another minute, the silence more frightening than the scratching on the glass. Jerry tilted his head, listening, watching. The back door exploded from its hinges, careening into the kitchen table and splintering both against the wall as though launched from a catapult.

The large, dark blur of fur was moving incredibly fast and Jerry fired, missing as the tightly patterned lead buckshot went over the werewolf's shoulder and into the cupboard. Frantically, he worked the pump as the werewolf growled in triumph, crashing into Jerry with a bone-jarring velocity, teeth digging deep into his shoulder as blood splashed around them. They sailed down the stairs, a tangle of wolf and man, Jerry Biddle screaming horribly as the werewolf savaged his aged body with tooth and claws. His fists pummeled the wolf's upper torso, hitting him with the strength of a prizefighter, but the creature shrugged them off as though they did not exist.

Jimmy fired the revolver, missing the werewolf, but the gunshot got the monster's attention as it slung a gore-covered face toward him.

"Lord Almighty!" Jimmy whispered as the creature dispassionately tossed the dying farmer against the wall and charged him. He fired the revolver again, elated as a red splash of blood appeared on the werewolf's chest and it lurched. The bullet barely slowed him as he broke Jimmy's neck a second before ripping out his throat in a mouthful of human flesh that he gobbled down hungrily. The ripping of flesh was not loud, the sound like wet cardboard, but a red mist filled the room and there was nothing untouched by the blood and violence.

Mrs. Biddle was screaming and Denise grabbed her by the hand, pulling her toward the stairs. She took a few steps, stopping when she reached the mutilated body of her husband. "No," she said, the nightmare throwing her into shock.

Denise screamed as the wolf decapitated Jimmy, tossing the boy's head carelessly across the room as it rolled on the concrete to her feet. The werewolf was splattered with blood, its fur matted into tangles and its jaws flecked with torn flesh as it thrust its mighty jaws into the youth's shoulder muscles. The creature was sating a hunger and had forgotten about them for a moment.

"Come on!" Denise pleaded, holding her hand out to Mrs. Biddle desperately. The older lady just looked from her husband to Denise, then back to her husband. She closed her eyes and stepped across her husband for over forty years.

Phil's mind was aware of the other two people in the cellar. He was in no hurry as he enjoyed the moment, eating from the youth that had angered him so hotly earlier. When the old woman moved toward the stairs, he decided it was time to kill them too. Dropping the body with a wet, slick plop, he leaped onto the old woman's back, his teeth slicing into the tendons of her neck like a butcher's meat cleaver.

Her eyes wide, Denise turned, her young legs propelling her up the stairs as the wolf howled behind her. She heard a scream, realizing it was her own as she reached the top of the stairs. The rasp behind her was the claws of the werewolf digging into the concrete and she knew he was within a few feet of her. Gripping the heavy oak door, she slammed it shut as she raced into the kitchen. The door shuddered with the wolf's impact into it and it pushed partially open, but the wolf had slipped, falling down the stairs.

Denise grabbed the thick board the Biddles used for a latch to keep their grand kids out of the cellar and slammed it into place. The door shuddered again and she heard the hinges and door creak and pop. Turning, she ran through the back door, crossing the yard like an Olympic sprinter, diving through the missing door of the truck. The keys were still in place as she scooted behind the wheel.

The sound of the door being destroyed was loud enough for her to hear as she turned the key. The old truck coughed, then started as a furry blur flew out the door. Denise floored the accelerator, running toward the wolf.

Her actions surprised the creature and it pulled up short, its feet sliding in the dew covered grass. The truck rocked and jumped over him as she hit him center of the grill and he rolled under the entire length of the truck.

"Die you son-of-a-bitch!" she screamed as the truck hit the werewolf, going over it. She turned sharply, tearing up the yard before lining out on the road and giving it all the engine had to pick up speed. In the mirror, she saw the werewolf roll to its knees, covered in gore and watching her with hatred in its eyes. It tried to move, but collapsed and she laughed almost maniacally to herself. She glanced at the speedometer, slowing down from the seventy-two miles an hour it registered.

She saw something ahead of her and she almost screamed as it stumbled toward the road. She saw Ray wave at her and she hit the brakes, sliding the truck to a stop beside him. He looked horrible as he braced himself on the hood and staggered to the door, pushing himself inside with the last of his strength. He was crying unintelligibly and she placed a hand on his head in comfort while starting the truck to moving again. They had not gone over a mile before she saw two sets of flashing lights coming toward her. She turned on her hazards and hi-beams, pulling to a stop as they stopped, one behind her and one ahead of her.

Denise opened the door of the truck, falling to her knees and scuffing them as one of the deputies grabbed her. She heard herself telling them what happened as one of them called an ambulance for Ray. She saw it and she would never forget it. They saw the destroyed truck, the ravaged boy and the blood covering her and they did not believe that the creature she described existed. Even when she finished and they called in back-up, they did not believe.

Calmly, Denise realized that when they saw the destruction at the Biddles' farmhouse they still might not believe there was a werewolf. If that creature was still seeking blood near that house, they would find out for themselves. All Denise knew was that they could make that discovery for themselves. She was going to the hospital with Ray.

Scott had turned off the police radio while Logan was inside the motel purchasing rooms for the night. They were in Ft. Smith near the bus station, the yellow Regal 8 sign burning brightly over the office. Ft. Smith had a population near 100,000 people and he had seen a hooker and a john leave a room a few minutes after Logan went inside.

Logan had not wanted to stop in Mena and they forged on to Ft. Smith. It was where Logan had felt driven to go and Scott's urging to stop at a motel had went unheeded until they arrived.

He could see Logan at the desk, a young Arab man pointing toward the closest wing of the motel, talking rapidly. Logan nodded, took two keys and walked out the door to the truck. Opening the door, he pitched Scott a key. "Here. I got us a seven AM wake-up call."

"Joy," Scott muttered unenthusiastically. "Are all werewolves iron-men?"

Smiling softly, Logan said, "We are more resilient than humans. We still need sleep."

"I was beginning to wonder," Scott said, rubbing the back of his neck. Logan parked the truck and the two men go out, walking toward their separate rooms. Scott stopped, turning to look at Logan. "Logan, I apologize for not telling you more about my suspicions. I did not mean to endanger your daughter. If I had known he would come after your daughter . . ."

"You could not have known," Logan said quietly, his hands together in front of him, his bag over his shoulder.

Shaking his head, Scott said, "No, I could not." He looked into Logan's eyes, the deepness of them sending shivers up his spine. "I did not even know he was the man I was hunting. It is hard to explain, but there was tampering . . . with evidence . . . victim's remains. We knew that, but I had a hard time believing it was Phil. There was another man it could have been and I suspected everyone. If I had been sure it was Phil, I would have put a tail on him."

The man was sincere and Logan felt a weariness flow through him. Nodding his head, he said, "Forget it, Scott. It is over now. Just help me catch him before he kills more people."

A faint expression of understanding touched Scott's lips as he took a better grip on his clothes bag. "Sure Logan." He opened the door to his room and went inside.

Logan Denton sniffed of the night, smelling the exhaust fumes of the buses across the block and a dozen unknown scents of the city. The night called to him, but he could not succumb to that call tonight. His eyes searched the sky.

"Where are you?" he asked quietly. He heard the sound of air brakes and the grinding roar of a bus leaving the station. He had not expected an answer as he slid the key into the door to his room. He did not expect the night to answer him, but he felt it speak in his heart. Phil Sturgis would kill again tonight if he could. He prayed that it would be impossible, but he just did not believe that Phil would be unlucky tonight. He could not describe what told him that in his head, but he liked to call it instinct.

He had watched the truck leave him in the yard as his right leg and left shoulder healed from multiple fractures. The truck had snapped the leg above and below the knee when both tires had went across his body. Standing, he lifted his head, howling his anger and frustration in a guttural howl that was harsh, frightening and powerful all at once. He started to follow, then his mind reasoning that it might be dangerous. They would undoubtedly bring more people against him, more than he could handle though he wondered if there was a number that he could not face victoriously.

Part of him relished that thought. More prey to satisfy his hunger. Yet, his human portion of his mind knew that enough people might overcome him. He was too unsure of his limits though he no longer feared guns while he was in this form. Touching his chest, there were no holes or even rough skin to indicate a scar where the bullets punched through him.

The soft breeze made his fur bristle and he chuckled, changing into a wolf and loping into the woods, instinctively knowing where he had parked his vehicle. This becoming was intriguing as he learned his new powers. His stomach was sated and he had learned much about himself tonight. His failure tonight to kill all his prey would be his last ever. The days of learning were not over, but he knew enough to be confident in his attacks, even when his prey was armed. The guns would only hurt him momentarily. He ran with his head up, his nose sifting the wind for the information it carried. It was a surprise when he found the car pulled off the road, the young man inside sipping a bottle of homemade whiskey. The spirits were strong, but they did not dull the mask of death that ripped open the door, nor did it lessen his screams as he died. Phil ate, filling his gullet with the flesh of his new victim before heading toward his car again.

He changed when he got to the car, rolling on the ground as the bones snapped into place. Standing, he swiped the hair from his body, frowning at the dried blood on his torso. His thoughts went to the nubile teenage daughter of Logan Denton and he smiled ruefully. Phil knew there was a river a few mils down the road where he could rinse of quickly and he would drive sensibly so he did not have to answer questions as to why he was driving naked. He remembered the almost naked girl in the back of the Cadillac. If he had been at his peak powers, she would never have escaped. Before he got into the car, he touched his erection, chuckling to himself. The power in him cried for flesh, but he still wanted the girl like he had taken his original victims and the hunger refused to be denied her body. It was time to travel North.

CHAPTER ELEVEN

"Damn!' Logan cursed vehemently, throwing his folded shirt at the TV as the cameras showed the bagged bodies being carried out of the farmhouse on the state line between Oklahoma and Arkansas. The Feds were there already and he could see a dozen officers moving around in the yard as the news cameras tried to capture the scene. He had struck again and he had killed three people in this orgiastic killing spree.

Rolling to his feet, he felt a terrible dark rage building inside that he knew stemmed from the helplessness he felt at his inability to stop this monster so far. His dark hair was wet from the shower and he could smell the soap on his body. He dug in his bag for his deodorant, applied it beneath his arms and slipped on a Navy blue T-shirt with a tail long enough to hide the Milt Sparks beneath the waist band holster and the .45 ACP he was carrying. Adjusting the collar, he combed his hair and pitched the gear on his bed inside the bag. He had brushed his teeth earlier.

He had sat on the edge of the bed when he heard footsteps then a knock. "It is unlocked," he said loud enough for the person outside to hear. Scott stepped inside, a polo shirt hanging loosely over his jeans, his Ray Ban sunglasses hanging at the neck.

"You heard?"

"Splattered all over the news," Logan said succinctly, tying his bootlaces on the last boot.

"Hell of a way to put it," Scott mumbled, squinting at the bright sun of the morning. "We drove right past him last night."

"I know," Logan replied, another pang of disgust going through his body. "You talked to your team?"

"Yes," he answered, hands in his pockets. "The locals are going nuts over some kind of monster that ate and dismembered the victims like a lion.

One of the survivors is pretty gnawed up and they got him in a hospital in Broken Bow. They say a lot of his wounds are superficial and will require some plastic surgery, but he should make it. The other survivor had minor scrapes and bruises. They have all but used the term werewolf. Think the police are afraid to say it cause the media would splash it all over the screens and make them look like fools. The survivor did, however, have animal bite marks."

"Damn!" Logan repeated for the second time this morning. "If he bit the survivor, he will be going through a very distinct change in about a month or so."

Scott's face turned pale. "You mean . . .?"

Grunting, Logan nodded, slinging the bag over his shoulder. He glanced around the room, satisfying himself nothing belonged to him. Looking into Scott's face, he said, "You loaded?"

"Yes."

Logan dropped the key in the ashtray along with a couple dollars, shutting the door and testing it to see if it locked. The morning traffic through down town was louder this morning and the fuel fumes of the buses more noticeable. Putting his bag in his toolbox, he opened his door, hitting the door lock for Scott to get inside.

"We going to the site?" Scott inquired, adjusting the vents on the dashboard to where they were directed out of his face.

"I guess so," Logan replied, his voice sounding a little unsure this morning.

Yawning widely, Scott said, "I am hungry. I could eat a horse."

"We can eat on the road or there is a Shoney's with a buffet down Towson Avenue near the Phoenix Village Mall. Will not take long to eat there," Logan suggested, his own appetite non-existent. He could use some orange juice.

"Their deaths are not our fault, Logan. No man can stop every murder," Scott voiced, taking Logan's manner as meaning he was blaming himself for those people dying.

Logan rested his right hand on the ignition, jingling the keys for a moment. "I am not wanting to stop every murderer today, Scott. I just want to stop him." He turned his face, his seriousness covering his face like a stolid mask. Scott nodded one time and Logan started the truck, pulling it out of the parking lot and onto the road to drive by the old courthouse. Scott knew that Logan was being driven by the Law of the Wolf to destroy this guy before he revealed to the world that they shared this planet with another intelligent species that legend said were monsters. He knew Logan was not a monster, but Phill Sturgis was a monster. Looking out the window, tapping his jaw with his forefinger, Scott knew Phill had been a monster long before the force that turned him into a werewolf ever entered his blood stream.

‡   ‡   ‡

The recliner had been his bed for several nights and he opened his eyes slowly. He lifted his head, feeling the cool butt of the .357 magnum revolver in his lap. Placing the gun on the coffee table, he sat up, stretching in the sun shining through the multi-paned window to his right. Looking toward the front door, he scowled as he saw a faint shine of white outside. Loren gripped the pistol and stood, walking to the door and looking at the car. Grunting to himself, he recognized the truck as belonging to Corrie and Vivian Denton.

Opening the front door, he heard the pad of feet behind him, glancing over his shoulder as Randy descended the steps. "What is it?" she asked, alerted by his posture.

"Looks like we have company," Loren replied, sticking the pistol in his waistband. He moved to the side of the door as Randy looked at the truck.

That belongs to Vivian," Randy confirmed, tying her robe tighter as she stepped outside. Loren followed her out to the sidewalk. The shop light was on and Randy could see someone moving around inside the workout room.

They walked across the yard, Randy pausing outside the door, looking at Loren for a second before she knocked.

"Come in," replied the feminine voice behind the door. Randy stepped inside and saw the sleek, female form of her sister-in-law making the bed.

"You came in quietly," Loren said, his tone almost grudging.

"I saw you sleeping on the recliner and did not wish to wake you," she said, her words aggravating him even more at himself. Looking at Randy, she smiled. "Knew this bed was out here so I did not think you would mind if I slept here."

Taking Vivian's hands, Randy smiled, hugging her finally. Stepping back, she said, "I am glad you are here. Are you going to go find Logan?"

Vivian wet her lips as she tucked in the last corner of the sheet. "I do not think so unless he needs me to come to him."

Randy's lips tightened despite herself. Vivian and Logan had been lovers and they shared a special bond that she often found herself envying when it came to understanding the part of them that housed the soul of the wolf. There was that little bit of jealousy, but she managed to control. She genuinely liked Vivian and they had become close friends over time.

"Move your things into the house. You can stay in the other guest room," Randy suggested evenly. Eyeing Loren with a glint of mischief on her face, she said, "Sounds like our guard is sleeping pretty heavily on duty."

Loren flushed dark red and both women laughed at his embarrassment. He knew they were teasing him, but the redness in his face did not go away quickly.

They went to the house together, Vivian taking her bags to the guest-room. Milly had woke and was preparing breakfast while pushing the girls to get all their things packed. They ate breakfast together and Milly had been pleased when Tana came downstairs to the table for a few minutes. She drank a half a glass of orange juice and a piece of sausage. Milly had felt bad enough about leaving today, but seeing Tana interacting with people had given her hope.

Vivian and Tana were good friends and when Tana left, going to her bedroom, it was only a few minutes before Vivian excused herself.

The slender blonde woman went up the stairs and down the hallway, stopping at the half-closed door to Tana's room. The girl lay on her side to where Vivian could only see the back of her head. She lay on top of a powder blue bedspread, a quilt her grandmother made for her over legs as a fan hummed in front of her bed.

"I know you sense me, Tana," she said seriously, her voice compassionate, but factual. "May I come in?"

Tana nodded her head and Vivian stepped inside quietly, shutting the door to where no one could see inside from the hallway. Pushing Tana's shoes from the middle of the floor to the head of the bed, she saw that the room was not as tidy as usual. She sat on the edge of the bed. "Scoot over."

The young woman grunted, rolling to her back as Vivian lay on her back beside her. Vivian looked up at the ceiling.

Tana looked at her curiously. "What are you doing?" she asked after Vivian lay without speaking.

Vivian folded her hands on her stomach. "I am glad you lived."

The statement shocked Tana. "Hunh?"

Calmly, Vivian repeated herself. "I am glad you lived, Tana." She placed her hand on top of Tana's arm. "You mean a lot to me and I feel like we are very good friends."

The words repeated themselves in Tana's head, the reverberating echoing inside with a lowering intensity as she considered them. "I cared for him a lot," she whispered, not trusting herself to say the words aloud to the blonde woman.

"Love is a powerful emotion," Vivian remarked, her hand still closed on Tana's arm. "It can uplift or destroy. Destruction by love is easier than you would think."

Tears coursed down Tana's cheeks as she wiggled her right foot nervously under the covers. "He died for me," she said, her voice cracking.

"No, he did not," Vivian said with a shake of her head. Tana was unable to speak for a moment. The blonde woman continued, "He did die for you in a sense, but he died for himself too." She touched her face. "Would your Tim be able to live if he had allowed the man to kill you while he got away?"

"No," she said slowly, considering the question.

"He did love you as much as you love him," Vivian said softly, "and he made his choice. You have mourned him, but do not take it any farther. Endangering your health or allowing this to change you in a major way will nullify his sacrifice."

Tana listened to her Aunt in a way she had listened to no one else. Maybe her Dad could have made her understand better, but no one else could have gotten to the seat of her fears and trepidation as quickly as Vivian.

"I . . . I will start eating and talking more," Tana promised as Vivian stroked her long, brunette hair from her face with her left hand.

"Come on," Vivian said, rolling to her feet and smiling. "You and I are going to go for a walk, then you will get a shower."

"You are pushing it," Tana said warningly.

The pretty face under the blonde hair turned inquisitive. "Am I?" She shrugged. "You can get up or I will haul you out to the road myself."

Tana was muscular and outweighed Vivian by a few pounds, but she knew she was no match for her. "Let me get dressed," she relented.

Vivian shut the door, waiting in the hall. She heard Tana get out of bed and within a few minutes she met her, wearing a pair of gray shorts and a T-shirt. They walked downstairs and everyone stared at them in surprise as they went out the door, walking down the driveway.

"Well I'll be damned," Logan Daniel said in awe.

Loren choked on his coffee as Randy turned from watching her daughter leave not only the room she had been inside the past few days, but the house as well for a breath of fresh air and exercise to glaring at her son.

The boy gulped, ducked his head and went up the stairs. Milly was trying not to laugh and Loren would not look at her.

"He got that from his father," Randy finally said as she walked toward the stairs. "Don't worry about telling Logan Daniel good-bye girls. He will be contemplating his choice of words from his bed and will not be taking visitors."

Loren finally chuckled out loud. They could hear Randy's footsteps and the slam of the door as she went into Logan's room to confront him. Loren loaded their vehicle with the bags Milly had packed by the time Randy returned. There was several hugs exchanged with Loren promising her he would be home as soon as possible. She told him to be very careful. The smile on his face did not need any words to go with it.

Waving at Vivian and Tana as she drove by, Milly felt sad about leaving, but she had so many things she would have to catch up on once she got home. Bills would be coming due and she had other business to see to before they became delinquent. It was a long drive back home as she drove towards Red Oak, headed to McAlester to hit SH-69 to IH-40 to Oklahoma City. She was glad Tana was doing better. She hoped this would be over soon for everyone.

‡   ‡   ‡

There were cars filling the parking lot around the restaurant and Logan could see an abundance of heads with steely gray hair sitting around the green tables inside the restaurant. A small van had parked in the handicapped parking area beside the door with the monogram that declared: Willow Hills, a resting place away from home.

"Looks like an old folks convention," Scott said as he walked by the windows a step behind Logan.

"It is an easy breakfast," Logan replied, realizing his own hunger had been growing as he thought about eating. The entered the door, seeing a half dozen people waiting to be seated while a woman with light red hair checked out a number of patrons. The air conditioning was cool, but it had already turned hot outside. He accidentally bumped into a gum machine, stepping to the side of it before knocking it over.

"Where to once we get to the last kill site?" Scott asked quietly. "Got any ideas?"

There were no easy answers to his questions. "Not sure. I can't track him with radar or I would do that. We will have to see."

Scott had not expected much more as he peered over the booths at the patrons eating breakfast. His stomach growled at the smell of bacon and sausage wafting in the air. He saw an old farmer in a ball cap sitting across from his wife, chattering about something important to them. Yawning, he looked toward the buffet and froze.

His eyes locked on the staring eyes of a man sitting to the left of the buffet. Scott saw Phill at the same time Phill had seen him. "Fuck!" Scott cursed, drawing his pistol while taking cover behind the wooden partition that separated the dining area from the waiting area, even as Phill raised his gun and fired.

The shot was like a bomb inside the restaurant and people screamed, none of them aware of the danger in their midst. Logan heard the bullet whiz past as he tried to ascertain the danger Scott recognized, the loud roar of the shot pounding his ears as he drew the .45 ACP from his belt. The bullet had shattered the window behind him as people dove for the floors and under the tables. In his haste, Phill had missed.

Phill was drinking his second cup of coffee when he saw Scott waiting to be seated. The serial killer had his weapon close to hand and slid it into his lap as they stared at each other. He had fired too fast, diving behind the food bar for cover.

"Get down," Logan screamed, his pistol in his hand as he ran forward seeking a better shot. Phill stood, holding his pistol in two hands, shooting twice at Logan, making him dive for cover before turning his weapon on Scott. Scott had fired a shot that gouged the buffet table, but did not strike the werewolf.

People were screaming and a pudgy black waitress ran into Logan as she made a getaway through the kitchen, knocking him from his feet as she scrambled for safety behind the counter. Phill emptied the .40 S&W, one bullet striking the cashier in the chest. The woman dropped, screaming in pain as blood splashed the back mirror. Logan glanced at the wounded woman, cursing as Phill suddenly dove through the window behind him.

"Man down!"

Logan heard Scott call to him, but he was moving toward the threat. Weaving through the maze of tables and chairs, avoiding the panic-stricken people as much as possible, he circled the end of the buffet table, leaping out the window to follow the killer. He could not shoot inside, but the parking lot was not crowded. He saw Phill racing to his car and he fired just as his target snaked to his left, his .45 caliber slug whining as it ricocheted off a window brace of a large truck.

Cursing at the near miss, Phill dove over the hood of a car, landing solidly on the warm, dark pavement, sliding in a fresh magazine. He ran in a crouch toward his car, trying to avoid becoming a target and engaging the two men after him.

Logan crossed the drive, leaping to the hood of a Honda Prelude and sending two more toward the killer, both bullets ripping gouges in parked cars.

The return fire forced him from his high perch and he dropped to the ground behind an old Oldsmobile as the bullets ripped into the glass and metal body. Logan returned fire, driving Phill into rolling under a van, putting a large enough obstruction between them to keep the Sheriff from taking more shots at him.

Cars were slowing and he heard a crash behind him as the gore-watchers ran into each other watching the two men exchange gunfire. Logan rounded the van, his .45 in front of him as he slowed, looking for his target. Movement inside a car caught his attention and he saw Phill glance at him just as the car started.

The sight acquisition took less than a second as Logan slammed two shots through the car window, spraying the inside with glass as Phill ducked down in the seat, pressing down on the accelerator before dropping the car in gear. Grabbing the shift, he pulled it down in drive, the car lurching forward and over a concrete parking stop, a shower of sparks spraying from the bottom.

He was heading into downtown as the car bounced and shimmied over another row of parking barriers. Dropping the magazine from the well, Logan leaped on the hood of another car, slamming the new magazine home and releasing the slide during the same fluid movement to aim. He fired his first round into the engine area of the car, the second one striking four inches forward of the first.

Phill swerved the car, ramming a small Ford and knocking it onto the sidewalk as Logan put two more rounds into the door. He emptied the other three rounds into the rear of the car, shattering the rear window as Phill finally got it lined out on the highway. The staccato roar of another gun caught his ears and he saw Scott was on the sidewalk near the road, shooting through the back window with steady shots. The car veered to the right and Logan jumped from the car hood, landing in mid-stride as he gave chase on foot. Scott was running beside him, both men closing on the slowing car as they reloaded on the run.

The car finally high-centered on a railroad embankment and Phill Sturgis jumped out of the car, his left shoulder slumped, a long gun in his left hand as he fired his pistol at the running men. Logan slid to a stop, raising his gun to fire, then taking cover behind a heavy trash barrel when he realized a miss would send his bullet into a group of innocent people behind Phill.

The car would not move when Phill exited, holding the searing wound on his left shoulder. He saw Scott and Logan pursuing on foot. Raising his gun, he fired, Scott diving into a ditch as Logan started to fire, then dove behind a trash can.

Cursing, Phill ran in front of a teenage girl, waving his pistol at her. She stopped, her face frightened as he circled the car, opening the door and dragging her out in the street. She was crying and begging as he slapped her to the asphalt, getting behind the wheel and taking off.

"Shit!" Logan ran to the middle of the street, screaming at the girl. "Get out of the way!! Get out of the way!!" The girl stood and ran to the sidewalk, giving Logan a semi-clear shot as he stopped, shooting through the back of the car. The car lurched, the back tire blowing out as one of Logan's bullets was deflected into it from the top. Phill was not stopping the car for the flat, but he would not be going far.

A blue Mazda truck stopped and Scott said, "Get in!" Logan ran around to the passenger side, climbing into the truck.

"Where did you get this?"

"Government business," Scott stated. "I commandeered it."

Logan pointed and Scott followed, seeing the car was losing the rubber on the rim. They could hear police sirens closing in the distance.

"Reload for me," Scott said, handing Logan his pistol. Logan reloaded the magazine, slapping it into the gun firmly. Handing it back to Scott, he reloaded his own gun.

"I want this son-of-a-bitch!" Logan muttered, leaning forward in his seat as the car crossed the opposite lane and crashed into a used bookstore, scattering bookracks across the sidewalk and destroying the front of the store.

Gunning the truck, Scott ran towards Phill as the man hastily climbed out of the car on the passenger side. He raised the long gun and fired. The two officers both ducked as the truck shuddered, the front windshield spider-webbing all the way across. Scott automatically hit the brakes and the truck spun almost 180 degrees in the road, thrusting Logan and Scott back into the seat as it came to a rest.

"Shotgun!" Logan yelled, feeling the burning in his right shoulder where one of the pellets buried in the muscle. He fell out the door with his pistol in front of him for a shot, pushing himself up, narrowly avoiding a car as it honked going past him. Phill had crossed the street and was headed into an old motel that looked to be abandoned.

The stairs looked precarious in places, but Phill did not stop to inspect them as he raced up two flights to a row of rooms, deserted with only a few items of junk or refuse laying inside. He listened, hearing the door open downstairs as the two men followed him. The shotgun would make a difference in this old motel where the distances were perfect for such a weapon.

He found a place to watch the stairs and waited. The men that followed him had been trained to search house, but so had Phill and he was good at it. He felt like his knowledge would make him a formidable opponent. Smiling wolfishly, he knew he could always resort to his other self. Neither man could stand up to that type of power.

Scott surveyed the room, his eyes covering all the darker places that concealed someone before he stepped to the side and Logan entered. There was an old counter across the room that could hide someone, but it would offer no escape. A heavy banister and stairwell wound up the front of the building and the hard wood railing was still intact. An open room through a hallway beckoned and another room they could not discern further back. He pointed to the stairwell and the disturbance in the dust marking someone's passage recently. Logan nodded, pointing towards the back where there would be another set of stairs.

Pointing to himself, Scott pointed to the front stairwell. Logan shrugged, holding his gun in both hands and aiming up the stairs as he moved under them. Scott went to the steps and started up slowly when Logan gave him the all-clear sign.

Crossing through the hallway, Logan could see no one had passed through recently though there was some sign of transients staying over night in the past. The air inside the motel was dead and dusty, clogging his nasal passages enough he was not registering a clear scent of the were-wolf.

He found the stairs. They were open and circular, winding around a broom closet or something built beneath the steps from the first floor down. Logan started up them, following the .45 as he placed each foot solidly on the stairs before moving the other. He could still hear sirens and he hoped the police did not come barging up the steps though he expected it at any moment. Listening, he heard the creaks of an old building and whining of the summer breeze penetrating a place where the caulking had dissolved or the mortar cracked. It was not silent, but death awaited somewhere upstairs.

He had been good at hide-and-seek as a child. Strange that he would remember those happy times when he was about to eliminate his two biggest enemies. Rarely had he been "it" during a game. Some of the children teased him because he took it so seriously, but Phill had always taken things more seriously than others.

The shadows moved and he lifted the shotgun, slipping the safety off quietly as he saw Scott's head on the stairs. He put the gold bead on his forehead, tightening the trigger.

The steps creaked and the play of the lights through the old windows made Scott nervous as he ascended the stairs. He had seen nothing on the second floor and the marks had gone up the stairs so he followed. As he reached the third floor, he stopped, taking a breath before looking over the steps. He dropped to the steps as something struck him a wicked blow above the ear, the roar deafening as it blew a hole in the wall behind him. Scott lay on his back, blood dripping around his ear and onto the stairs as he cursed. Turning, he scrambled up the stairs, his Commander in his hand.

Logan tightened his lips when he heard the shotgun. He was on the second floor, almost directly beneath the shots. He looked up at the floor, wondering how thick it was between floors.

"Give it up, Phill!" Scott yelled, wiping the blood from his scalp. "We have you outnumbered!"

"Go home, Scott," called the voice down the hall. "Go home and pray the God of the Night does not decide to pay you a visit!" He laughed, chuckling loud enough that Scott could hear the insane laughter.

Lying on the hard wood stairs, Scott took a long breath, looking around to see if he had anything he could use to his advantage. The wall behind him had a few windowpanes in it and one had a gaping hole beside it where the shotgun charge that almost removed his head struck.

"Phill, give up and we will get you some help. Some professional help," Scott promised, easing up the steps a few more feet.

"You would help me right into a court and jury determined to give me a death sentence!! I don't need help," the voice said thickly, sounding almost petulant and childlike in nature. "I am more powerful than you will ever be. What I am is like a god, Scott, a god!!"

"You are delusional and sick," Scott reiterated. "Let me help you!"

Phill laughed, his voice changing. "I know you are here, Denton. You are the hunter who seeks me," he yelled, his tone different as though taunting the man, yet fearing him at the same time.

Listening, Phill heard no answer and smiled to himself. Logan was a hunter and it was fitting that a god did battle with a god.

Logan was listening to the two men and he had a good idea where Phill was hiding. He hoped he could force the issue to his advantage.

Logan started to shoot through the floor when he heard Phill exchanging words with Scott, but the silver bullets were soft and might not punch through the flooring effectively if it was thick. The hard wood slats were enough to deform the bullet and there would be other material between them to where he could not be certain of his success.

He went to the back stairs, going up them silently. Logan hoped Scott kept Phill talking long enough for him to find the madman. There would be no hospitals or evaluations. Phill would be killed and Logan's vow to the Council of the Wolves would be complete.

After a bit, he heard Phill call his name. He was on the third floor with the man. Phill did not sound sane and Logan hoped he did not change into a wolf. Logan could see killing Phill while in the wolf form and sending in people to bring him out. It would cause an uproar they could not hide from the media.

"I could smell her, Denton. Your pretty girl child had been fucking like a whore," Phill said, his voice thick and growing guttural. "She had been having sex and her scent reeked through the car, Denton. If I had been evolved, I would have killed her and devoured her sweet flesh like I did that whore in Texas."

There was no sound other than the sounds outside. The police were there and Scott figured they were putting up a police line around the building.

The mad man's voice rang out, echoing through the forgotten hallways of the motel. "She would have been made immortal!!" He laughed. "I would have fucked her first, Denton . . . gave her what she wanted, what all sluts like her want! I would have made her moan in ecstasy and scream in terror! I would be her alpha and omega."

"You wouldn't be shit," Logan muttered from behind him.

Phill did not turn to attack as he pushed off with his legs through the door as the .45 slug slammed into the wall where he had been. Phill spun, pointing the shotgun with one hand and pulling the trigger.

Grunting, Logan spun against the wall as the shot hit him in the right arm and chest, splinters from the door facing spraying his face. He fell, digging at his eyes and cursing the slow response of his human body to repair wounds. In the form of the wolf the wounds repaired in minutes, as a man it could take hours, even with his heart stopped. As a wolfman, the wound healed in seconds.

Scott stood, firing his pistol three times as Phill went into a room across the hall, leaving the shotgun in the hallway. The FBI agent yelled, "Logan?!" He heard a groan and ran forward a few steps. The slug hit him low and he lurched, dropping to a knee and shooting twice at Phil as the killer ducked, rolling across the floor, triggering his last round through Scott's chest.

The FBI agent stiffened, his face growing pale as he staggered forward a few steps, collapsing in front of Phill as the killer shook his head. "Mess with the best, die like the rest," he said, repeating the axiom he had read on the T-shirt of mercenary types.

Scott was facing him, his mouth open as he gurgled, trying to talk. Phill moved to his knees, taking Scott's pistol. Tossing his own to the side, he searched Scott and found two more magazines of Hydro-shok ammunition. The FBI agent moaned and Phill slammed a powerful fist behind Scott's ear, the blow cracking like dry wood as the dying man stiffened, then relaxed. "Shut up you, bastard," Phill muttered as he retrieved his shotgun.

Walking back into the room where Logan had almost killed him, he stopped when he saw the body was not in the room. There was blood splashed on the wall where he had taken a hit and the .45 ACP lay on the floor, but no body was to be seen.

"Where are you?" Phill asked in a whisper. Then he heard the faint sound of something clicking on the hard wood floor.

Understanding came to Phill in an instant. "You know don't you?" he said, holding Scott's pistol in front of him as he went into the adjoining room. He walked through it and into the small kitchen. The sound of the claws was no longer audible and he knew Logan was waiting. A pile of clothing lay in the floor and he nudged them with his foot. "You came for me that night I was after your daughter, didn't you?"

He listened, hoping as he goaded the man to push him into betraying his position. "She has a great ass, Logan."

Silence.

"That boy was scared shitless!"

Phill went through the door to the hallway just as Logan launched himself from the shadows. The silver bullet in Scott's gun slammed into his shoulder and he roared, careening into a wall with enough force to knock a sofa size hole though the sheet rock. The pistol was empty and Phill cursed as the large werewolf rolled, pushing itself toward the stairwell, a greenish ichor oozing from the wound.

"You are not so powerful," Phill taunted, lifting the shotgun. Logan was gripping the stairs, his body seeming to flow for a moment before he changed into a man. The excruciating pain on his face made Phill laugh and he triggered the buckshot into Logan's chest, the heavy shot charge pitching him off the stairwell to tumble two floors, crashing into the old broom closet in a tangle of limbs and old handles still in the closet.

Walking to the stairwell, Phill looked down at the body of the second man. "You are not so powerful, Denton," he said in a conversational tone. "I thought you might be a god too, but you aren't. I shall take your daughter now, but it shall be different. She will not join you for I shall consume her." He started to turn, then looked over the stairs again into the splintered hole where Logan lay. "I shall ravage her, Denton, as I did all my works before I got this power. Then I shall devour your family and everything you love will be mine. Pray to me in your death for I am their future."

Phill dropped Scott's gun on Logan's twisted body, followed by the two magazines. He could hear the police on a bullhorn outside.

Walking to the pile of clothes, he took Logan's wallet and his keys. He went up the stairs to where he could gain access to the top of the building. Taking off his clothes, he changed into the form of a wolf, holding both wallets and keys in his mouth. Sniffing of the old tar and gravel, he walked to the edge nearest the other buildings. One was close enough and they would not be able to see him jump. Gathering himself, he leaped, landing on the other building lightly.

Panting happily, he went to the next building and jumped to it. He could still hear the police on the bullhorn as he went through the access door as a man, changing into a wolf once he was inside. It was an old storage section of a store beneath the floor. There were old clothes and he chuckled as he put on a pair of overalls along with a white shirt. There were several pairs of old boots and he found some that would fit. He donned the clothing, dropping the wallets in different pockets before walking downstairs. The store was still in business, but he slipped unnoticed through the office areas and into the main part of the store easily.

On the sidewalk outside, he smiled at a pretty lady who was looking up the street where the police had barricaded the old motel. She said, "No shots for over a couple minutes now."

He nodded. "Reckon I better go home," he said, shoving his hands into his pockets. "Too much excitement in the big city for me."

The lady shook her head in agreement as Phill meandered down the sidewalk, whistling a tune he heard his daddy whistle when he was a child. He needed a vehicle and he was going to see if he could find the vehicle Logan and Scott had been driving. He knew Logan's truck and he would take it without a second thought. There was an appointment he needed to keep and he intended to keep it tonight.

CHAPTER TWELVE

"Damn!" Loren said as he listened to the voice on the other end of the receiver. He took a deep breath and looked away from the people in the living room. When he hang up the phone, he went to where Randy and Vivian were talking. He turned on the TV to Channel 5 news out of Ft. Smith.

"*. . . two men killed. The shoot-out started in a nearby Shoney's restaurant on Towson Avenue where authorities say the gun battle left one innocent dead. There were three men involved in the shoot-out and two of the men identified themselves as FBI agents to the patrons after the gunfight began. Sources say a patron near the buffet table opened fire, one of his errant bullets striking assistant manager Maria Stevens in the chest as she stood behind the register. She died on the scene. The fight ensued outside the restaurant where it caused a small pile-up of vehicles and numerous scrapes and bumps. The two men chased the first man to the old Mandle Motel where the gun battle left two dead and the third missing. The identities of the men have not been revealed pending notification of the families. Word is that the man who started the gunfight may have been the same man linked to a number for murders across the country. The two dead men have been taken to Sparks Regional Medical Hospital where the families will identify the bodies.*"

The screen had shown the after math of the scene and the Mandle Motel as well as the car jutting from the large window of the Pony Express Bookstore. Randy asked, "Who called?"

"It was Bill. He heard it over the radio. The Feds have had the Ft. Smith police to wait before releasing any information or contacting family of the deceased."

"Do you think it was Logan?" Randy asked worriedly.

Shaking his head, Loren said, "He didn't know, Randy. I don't think so. It would take a silver bullet or decapitation to kill Logan and I don't see that scum having time to prepare silver bullets." He paused. "Doubt if even a mad man could handle your husband in a fight."

"I can't believe this! The shooting in Ft. Smith and the killings by Big Cedar!" Randy ran her hands through her hair. "How is he getting away with it?"

"I'm not sure, but I bet Logan was at the state line. Those two federal boys just happened onto that guy and got killed in the process," Loren surmised.

Standing, Vivian said, "He will call tonight. If he went back to where the killings happened down South, he will be in Ft. Smith tonight. When he calls, we will make out plans then."

The calmness of the slender blonde woman was infectious and Randy's nerves settled. "You are right." Her lips pursed. "Still, the killer is back in this area. He came here for some reason."

"It is me," said the soft voice from the stairs. They saw Tana standing there in her shorts and T-shirt. "He wants me."

Randy stood, walking to her and hugging her. "He can not have you," she said fiercely, kissing the top of Tana's head.

Vivian went to the picture window, peering out at the yard, the flowers. It was beautiful outside and Logan Daniel would have been playing outside except for his small blurb at the breakfast table. The mountains in the background were small in relation to her home in Idaho, but they were nice mountains. She would like to run them one night while she was here, but this was not a social call.

"What will we do tonight to prepare?" Tana asked, accompanying Randy to the sofa.

"Nothing different except I shall sleep upstairs tonight with you," Vivian said, her eyes going to Randy. "Let Logan Daniel sleep with you."

"I'll be downstairs with this .357 Magnum full of silver bullets," Loren said decisively. He looked at Vivian. "You carrying a gun?"

"Yes," she replied with a nod. She raised her shirt and showed him the butt of a small automatic next to her flat belly behind her waistband.

"A Mustang?" he asked.

"A Mustang II," she replied. "It is a little bigger on the grips and holds more rounds."

"It hasn't got much stopping power," Loren said with a shrug.

"The size of the bullet does not matter as much as the content," she said rhetorically, lowering her shirt back in place. Her hair was loose over her shoulders and she looked to be in her early twenties or younger.

Tana stood, walking to the TV and turning it off. She folded her arms in front of her as she faced the adults. "I want a gun," she said seriously.

"No," Randy said adamantly.

"I can shoot," she argued, looking at Loren for support.

"You can shoot and you are responsible," Randy said, "but you are wanting it for revenge. Not for defense."

Tana scowled angrily. "Mom, I . . ."

Vivian touched her arm, looking into her face. Tana closed her mouth, looking at the floor for a moment before finally nodding her head. "Okay, I want to kill him," she admitted.

Standing, Loren placed his hand on the pistol on his belt, the other on his belt. "Revenge is not an easy thing to live with sometimes, Tana. We are not here to kill him." He glanced at Vivian. "At least your mom and I are not."

"What I am to do, I do to protect my species." She released Tana's arm and sat on the recliner. "Killing people makes for dark dreams at night. You are not the only person to see a friend ripped to pieces or pummeled to a pulp. Maybe that sounds harsh, but we have each seen tragedy and we have experienced the emotions you are experiencing. Revenge does not soften those feelings. Revenge only gives you another bad thing to dream about at night."

Shutting her eyes, Tana said, "Okay. You got me." She moved to the sofa and sat down, her elbows on her knees.

"It could be a coincidence," Loren said, though he did not believe it either. "If we prepare for the worst, we will not be surprised."

"Sounds good," Randy said. Changing the subject, she glanced at Tana. "What do you want for supper tonight?"

Smiling a little, Tana said, "I could go for some stir-fry. Beef, broccoli and bean sprouts."

"How about some egg rolls? I have the wraps."

"I'll help make them," Tana said. Randy smiled, a silent thank you in her eyes to Vivian. The blonde woman smiled, looking back out the window. She believed that the man would come for Tana too and that is why she came here. She had been a werewolf much longer than Logan and her instincts were very good. Vivian loved Tana as though she were a younger sister and she knew that she would stay here to protect her.

The blonde werewolf did not think Loren and Randy were capable, but neither of them thought like her. Randy had shared the soul of the wolf for many years, but she was still alien to the instincts, which could easily cause her to hesitate in a crucial moment when hesitation meant death. Vivian would not.

‡   ‡   ‡

Sparks Regional Medical Hospital was a good hospital that served much of Western Arkansas and Eastern Oklahoma's medical needs. It was a large hospital that sat on a hill one block off the road where the gunfight occurred. The medical examiner's lab was downstairs and the coroner had already declared both men dead. The room was cold for the obvious reasons and the steel tables were just large enough for the cadavers. It was not a popular place and the architects had the foresight to put it in an area that was isolated from the more traveled routes in the hospital.

The coroner had placed a tag on the big toes of the two men indicating John Doe #1 and John Doe #2, though they had found identification on one of the men. The other had been strangely naked with a horrendous bullet wound through his shoulder that sizzled when the technicians first recovered the body. A white-red mixture oozed from the wound for over an hour before it stopped. The shotgun wound had opened a hole through the entire body in the thoracic region. The man did not have a chance.

The man with the identification had indications of trauma to the head from multiple shotgun pellets and from a blunt instrument. The bullet wounds in the torso were the ones that appeared to prove fatal. The medical examiner had not had time to do more than a cursory check of either man before he was called away.

How long he had been aware of the cold, he was not sure. His left eye opened and he felt frozen, his mind sluggish and dull. There was so much coldness, his flesh felt like glass as he told his muscles to move. They did not respond to his brain.

He knew he had been wounded badly because he hurt more than he ever hurt in his life. There was a dull fire burning solidly in his shoulder and he remembered the bullet that seared through him like a lance from hell. The bullet had been from Scott's gun and it had been silver. He took a breath, wheezing somewhere inside his chest. It was the first time he recalled taking a breath since he became aware.

How could he live without breathing?

The microbes in his blood had kept him alive. They had provided the oxygen required to keep his brain from dying, his muscles from atrophy and degeneration. They had made sure their host had not died.

He called himself a host, but was he truly a host? The change in his blood was not parasitic.

At least his head was working. He tried to move and could not even move his neck, his consciousness slipping. With a huge push of his mind he got his body to respond and he felt the table slide from beneath his as he fell to the cold tile floor with a dull thump. He shook, his eyes closing as he left the world of consciousness. The world went black again.

The intern was pasty faced as she flew up the stairs, barely avoiding an orderly with a tray of test equipment in her haste.

"Sorry," she mumbled as she passed him, running to the emergency room. One of the doctors on call was walking from one of the emergency cubicles. His name was James Rutherford and he hoped tonight was not going to be a busy night.

"Dr. Rutherford!" she called breathlessly. He caught her by the arms as she slid to a stop in front of him.

"Nancy, you are as cold as ice!" he said, holding her, trying to ascertain what was causing her excitement. Two RNs were looking at her skeptically. He had known Nancy since she arrived and found her attractive. She had short, flaxen hair and she wore glasses that gave her an innocent schoolgirl look that others besides him had noticed. "Where have you been?"

"The meat room," one of the nurses said matter of fact. "She ain't the first one that has spooked in there."

"I'm not spooked," she said, shaking her head. "One of them is alive. He is not on the table." Her voice trembling with excitement.

Dr. Rutherford had seen the two dead men come in before the medical examiner looked at them. They were both deader than hammers. "Ms. Hull, Nancy, sometimes the dead have muscle spasms. He would not be the first one to spasm off a table."

"No," Nancy insisted. "Dr. Rutherford, he is in the floor and he *is breathing*!!"

Rutherford seen another doctor come in. He was a scientist from Colorado that was working with one of the cancer units and the rescucitation department. He in his early forties, fit and trim. He had the reputation as a lady's man and was rumored to have slept with two nurses and a candy striper on the night shifts. His name was Shields and despite those rumors, he was one of the most eminent men in his field.

"Doctor Shields?"

The man stopped. "Yes, Dr. Rutherford?"

"You heard about the shooting today?"

Nodding his head, he said, "Two men killed. Tragic. I worked on them and they could not be revived." His voice was so calm, so certain.

"One of them is alive," Nancy Hull said, breaking into the conversation.

"Balderdash! Those men were dead meat when they were brought in here," he argued.

Nancy was flabbergasted. "Come with me!!" She grabbed his hand, tugging on it. Shields frowned, but followed, indicating he wanted Rutherford to go as well. The young intern led them down the hallway quickly and down the stairs. Opening the door to the lab, she could hear the raspy breathing again.

"Dear God!"

The voice belonged to Shields and he pushed his way through, kneeling over the supine body of the man who was breathing. He gripped Logan's arm and Logan felt it as he turned his head. It was a magnificent strain as Shields grabbed him, hollering at Nancy. "Get us a gurney! Now! Help me Dr. Rutherford."

Rutherford lifted the man's feet as they lay him back on the table as Nancy left the room in a run. Shields looked into Logan's eyes, examining the chest wound. "Unbelievable! Incredible!"

"What is it?" Rutherford asked.

Indicating the wound on Logan's chest, he said, "This was an open wound all the way through him, now it is not. The organs were gone, now they are there." He looked Rutherford in the face. "This man has regenerated his internal organs, doctor. I am willing to say this man *is not human*!"

Rutherford could not speak as he looked at the man dumbly, the steady wheezing rowing less audible.

Nancy returned with the bed and an orderly to help lift the wounded man onto the gurney. They wheeled him upstairs. She was looking down at him when he opened his eyes. They pushed him into one of the special lab rooms for the rescucitation unit.

"Hook him up on an IV. I want fluids in him," Shields ordered. "No pain relief. Only liquids. Get me blood and tissue samples. Bring them to the lab!"

He stalked off, a mad gleam in his eyes as Rutherford and Nancy went to work. Logan opened his mouth. "Back off," he whispered.

Rutherford ignored him. "Give me the strap." Nancy handed him the strap and he buckled it across the man in case he tried to give them any trouble. Sliding a needle into Logan's arm, he filled the vial with blood, then a second one. Pulling his lip back, he took a scraping inside his mouth, depositing the tools in a small sterile bag.

Logan shook, the table rocking. "What are they doing?" he asked the intern who was watching him.

"They are getting samples for some tests," she assured him.

Logan was thinking well enough to believe that the tests would not be good for him. He tugged at the strap and the bed rocked.

"Calm down," Nancy said. "Calm down or they will give you a sedative. They may use more straps."

Closing his eyes, Logan thought about his chest. He had forced the change on certain body parts in the past much like he changed his features for Scott to verify his identity. Black hair sprouted from his chest and shoulders. He heard her gasp as the wound closed visibly, the flesh turning pink. Nancy covered her mouth as the pink flesh gradually turned normal and he had no scars.

"Release me," he said, his eyes pleading with her.

"No," she whispered, shaking her head side to side.

The power was coming back and Logan triggered the change, even as Nancy stiffened and passed out. The strap was designed to hold a human with no mental restraints on the amount of strength used. It did not work with a werewolf. The leather snapped, the wounds healing all over his body except where the silver bullet penetrated his shoulder. It was healing, but slowly. Changing back to a man, he gripped Nancy by the collar as an orderly stepped in. He had heard the commotion. He glanced at Nancy and Logan, moving to confront Logan.

The man reached for Logan's arm, but the naked man grabbed his wrist, pulling him forward while kicking his feet out from under him. He landed on the bed and Logan struck him twice in the back, stunning him. He found the other two straps and strapped the man in place, gagging him too.

Looking at the man, Logan decided his clothes would fit and he stripped the man to his skivvies, wearing the loose green scrubs without any shoes. Nancy was beginning to come around. He lifted her to her feet. She looked at him fearfully.

"I won't hurt you," he promised, "but I have to have those samples they took. Where did they go?"

"The lab," she said, her voice full of fear.

"Take me," he ordered, pushing her ahead of him as they left the room. He followed her down the corridor to a small elevator. They got inside the elevator and went up one floor. The door opened and they got out. The elevator only went to the lab and back down to the lower floor. It was obvious this room was isolated.

Grabbing her shoulder, he pushed her in front of him, making her lead the way as she went through the door of the lab. Rutherford and Shields were standing together over a microscope.

Logan said, "I need those vials of blood, Gentlemen."

"What are you?" Shields asked, holding a pair of glasses at his side.

"A man," Logan replied. "Only a man."

Shields laughed in disbelief. "Men do not come back to life. Men do not heal themselves after they die." He shook his head. "No, you are not a man."

Logan pushed Nancy hard, Rutherford catching her. He saw Shields reach for the vial and he dove across the table into the man.

Shields swung a ponderous right fist at his head. Logan went under it, slamming a shoulder into Shields' chest, knocking him on his back. A quick right-left combination had him talking directly with the sandman. Rutherford was reaching for the vials when Logan punched him savagely across the jaw. The doctor wilted, Logan catching him to prevent him from smacking his skull on the floor. He took the vials, walking to a sink and pouring them down it, running water in the vials and down the drain.

The young woman watched him, her eyes curious. "You are not a monster?"

Logan smiled cynically. "I hope not."

He took the tissue samples and burned them with a small burner on the lab table. Pitching them in the trash, he turned, walking to Nancy. He took her by the shoulders, kissing her deeply as she tensed, then responded. He stepped back. "What do you think?" he asked.

She was breathless for a moment. "You kiss like a man," she finally said.

"I am a man," he said with a smile. Pointing at the two unconscious doctors, he added, "Tell them I am sorry."

"I will," she replied, her curiosity piqued by this man. She watched him curiously as he removed the shoes from Doctor Shields' feet. Sliding them on his own, he grinned, his face becoming boyish and handsome. Nancy laughed.

"I need some time Nancy. Will you give it to me?"

She nodded her head gravely in agreement.

Logan went to the elevator and pushed the down button. He climbed inside and rode it to the ground floor. A woman in purple scrubs entered the elevator and he left it, walking toward a sign that read south lobby. Some people looked at him as he walked through the lobby, but no one said anything as he went out the doors. Walking to the parking lot, he ran to Towson, heading for a Burger King across the road. Standing on the hill, looking toward Arkhoma, he could see the sun was going down soon. He was not sure how long he had been "dead", but it was most of the day.

Scott was dead. He had seen him take the hits and remembered seeing his corpse in the hallway. He regretted it, but there was nothing he could do about it now.

Sturgis would go to his house tonight or the next. Logan hoped it would take him at least two nights to find his house and he could be there waiting on him. He needed a ride and he suddenly remembered the spare key for his truck in the back. With a happy chuckle he jogged along the road toward the restaurant where everything started this morning. He would get in his truck and be home around nightfall. Logan was feeling better as he felt his strength growing. Sturgis had drawn serious blood today and Logan intended to pay him back in spades.

CHAPTER THIRTEEN

The four-wheel drive rode higher from the ground than his personal truck and Phill thought he could grow to like the sensation. He had found a .22 Long Rifle caliber pistol beneath the seat and it was lying on the seat next to him. The magazine had nine rounds of Stinger ammunition in it and he knew the pistol was very accurate simply because he had fired this type several times in the past. There was a box of ammo under the seat too, but he did not bother to lay them in the seat with the gun.

The radio was on 93.7 and he was listening to Jewel singing as he tapped his fingers on the steering wheel. He thought about the entertainer, smiling smugly as he thought that no one was immune from his power. The power beating in his chest was immutable unless it was the ability to grow. Where would his power end?

Denton had been a werewolf too, yet he had fallen easily under attack. Phill was convinced he was more than a werewolf, more than a mortal in either species.

Some men were destined for greatness, destined to change the face of the world and how man views his existence. He believed he was reaching the next plane of existence -- the plane of existence that most men would eventually attain. Evolving was a painful process and it took the toll on those less fortunate, but Phill knew it was necessary, that all changes for the better of man required sacrifice. Sacrifice was required by most religions so it was a good thing even if he and his peers had no understanding of what they were doing or viewing. He smiled in reflection of his thoughts.

Did he truly have peers?

What creature could judge him or his actions when they were beneath him? Should he select a mate when most of the women he had encountered were unworthy of living?

Phill decided that fate or destiny would select a mate for him. He relaxed as he suddenly knew this would be the answer. He had driven through Spiro and Poteau, winding around the back roads. It had taken a while, but he found Denton's house. He had driven in front of it only once. He did not want anyone to recognize his vehicle as belonging to the late Sheriff Denton. It had occurred to him to go to the courthouse and question the blond he started to kill at that club one night. She would know where he lived, but he would probably encounter law officers that knew him too. The drive had been relaxing and he wanted nothing to prevent him from completing his mission.

The news on the radio had not identified the dead men and he doubted that they would until tomorrow morning. He wondered who had been placed in charge.

His mind had been on the pretty teenager he had chased before he had fully evolved. He could remember the scent of her, the sight of her firm, delectable buttocks as she ran from him in fear. Feeding from her sexually would only be heightened by feeding from her in the new way his inner soul demanded. How do you explain the need he felt?

Tomorrow, he would go west, driving north first and finding victims in the more desolate places in the United States. Once he reached his full power, discovered the full potential of his abilities, he would go to the East Coast.

Dining coast to coast! He chortled at his impromptu thought. He was a king and his subjects would be chosen at random.

He drove to the gas well where he had killed the boy and almost killed the girl, parking the truck. Climbing out of the truck, he slid the .22 pistol in his pocket before he walked around. The scents were gone though he could see the ruts where they had towed the car away. Shattered glass shone like diamonds when he pulled in here, but they were invisible under the starry sky. He wanted it to be dark when he went to the Denton house. The dark was his friend and he felt an urge to howl.

Lifting his head, he howled, a pitiful, whining sound from his human throat and Phill choked up laughing at the feeble sound. He pulled off his shoes, ignoring the sharp white rocks on the well pad as he let his features flow, his muscles changing as he stretched the clothes he wore. Lifting his head, he howled, a coarse, gravelly sound that filled the night. He changed back, putting the boots back on his feet. Looking at his watch, it would not be long before he fulfilled his plan. The only thing he regretted was that Denton would not be around to view the aftermath. It would be a fitting punishment for an inferior being to view.

‡   ‡   ‡

The truck had been gone when he reached the dimly lighted parking lot. There were sheets of plywood over the broken windows and a sign declaring that the restaurant was closed until further notice. It had taken him longer to get to the restaurant than he expected and the truck was already gone. Nancy had given him some time, but there had been two hospital security trucks drive by and he had no doubt they were looking for a light green set of scrubs on a tall man with dark hair. Logan had broken into three houses before he found clothes that would fit. He was dressed in jeans and a muscle shirt, a Raiders cap pulled low to hide his features.

With the news of the killer on the radio, he had decided hitchhiking would do nothing but get him questioned by police. He had no identification on his person and he was not sure what report the hospital would make about his appearance and subsequent disappearance from there.

He considered stealing a car, but he had no tools to use. Nearing Pocola city limits, he decided that he would be better off changing into a wolf and move across country on four legs. Logan changed his mind there too after figuring it would be late in the morning before he arrived at his home. He crosses a number of fields and behind the Tri-county Speedway racetrack, crossing a wide creek before crossing the highway to a large convenience store. The telephone was near a number of trashcans.

Cars were passing by on the road as he lifted the receiver, making a collect call to his home. The number was busy and he scowled. Dialing a second number, he spoke to the operator and she identified him when the other side answered.

"Where the hell are you?" Bill asked, the worry evident in his voice. "Thought that might have been you in the shoot-out!"

"I was in the shoot-out," Logan replied, "but I survived despite what might be playing on the nightly news. What has the media been saying?"

"Two men dead along with a woman at the Shoney's. Who are the dead guys?"

"I was one of them, but they made a mistake," Logan said quickly. "I'll explain later, Bill. You got to trust me on this one."

Coolly, Bill said, "That has never been a problem. What is going on?"

"I want you to come pick me up. Send a car over to the house. I think he may be headed in that direction." He hesitated. "Bill, I need you to stop by the office and get my .44 Magnum Redhawk from my desk. There is a green box of bullets at the left, back corner of that drawer. Bring them too. This is important, Bill. Tell the deputy you send to my house to arm himself with a shotgun and fire at the head. I'll relieve him myself."

A low whistle came through the phone. "This sounds damn serious, Logan. Wish you would tell me everything."

Logan sighed. "I will eventually, Bill. You are a good man. I am at the Corner Mart in Pocola, but I am heading for the Poteau River Bridge to get out of the lights. Stop on the West side coming from Spiro and I will be there close."

"Sounds like you have the police after you too," Bill commented.

"Maybe," Logan admitted, "but I do not have time to answer questions or make an explanation right now."

"It'll take me around 45 minutes to get there, but I'll hurry," Bill said. "You armed?"

"More or less," Logan replied.

"Okay. See ya' in a bit," Bill said, hanging up and walked through the house. His wife looked at him expectantly. "Logan needs some help. I'll be back shortly."

"You be careful," she said seriously.

"I always am," Bill said with a smile, leaning over and kissing her forehead. He would call one of the deputies from the radio in his car. Slinging the gunbelt around his hips, he dropped in the seat and started the car. It would not take so long to get there except he had to stop to pick up Logan's gun. He owned extra guns, but Logan was adamant about picking up the .44 magnum revolver from the office.

‡   ‡   ‡

The stir-fry had been excellent and Loren sat at the table drinking tea, talking with Vivian and Tana while Randy spoke on the phone to Vitoro. Vitoro had heard the news today and called to see if Logan was in the middle of it. They had not heard, but she was hoping Logan would call tonight. They had talked for almost an hour while Tana and Logan Daniel cleaned the kitchen. Logan Daniel had been much less rambunctious since his faux pas at breakfast.

Loren felt strange wearing his pistol all through the house, but he knew if he needed it, he would need it suddenly and without warning. He kept watch on the windows and the sliding glass door. He tried to do it subtly, but he seen Vivian was doing the same thing.

He had been pleased with Tana's recovery. She had eaten more this evening than she had eaten all week, a smile covering her face from time to time. She reminded him of Sandy Trent, her mother, and he meant that in a good way. Sandy was a beautiful woman. She was not cut out for being a mother and responsible for children when she was younger. She had remarried recently and he had spoken to her a few times in passing. Maybe she regretted leaving Tana with Logan for the time she missed, but Tana had been the person who gained from her mother's decision. Tana was intelligent. Logan and Randy had taught her respect -- for herself and others. Logan believed that respect for anything began with a respect for yourself. Loren believed the same ideal.

The pretty blonde was a fascinating creature and he listened to her tell stories of her youth. Hiking the mountains, fishing trips in the cold mountain streams for brookies and camping in some of the most remote sections of the country as though there were no worries in the world. He could see why Logan had liked her, but he could also see why he ultimately chose Randy.

The tall, dark-haired woman was his soul mate in all things not of the wolf. That was the appeal and in reality, Logan's man-self controlled the direction of his life. Vivian was his soul mate as a wolf and Loren was willing to bet the wolf-self still yearned for her. He felt strange as this understanding came to him like the plot of a slow story he might watch on television. If the wolf half of Logan was the driving force, he would have stayed with Vivian indefinitely. It was a rather heady realization.

Vitoro understood so much, yet he kept it to himself. Loren blamed it on his Native American heritage and old age stubbornness, but he knew the old man might have ulterior motives in making them seek their own answers, answer their own questions. People learned in such ways and he believed Vitoro wanted them to learn for themselves.

With the dishes cleared, they retired to the living room. He saw that it was nearly 11 PM and Logan Daniel was wearing down. Randy had turned on the television, flipping the channel to M*A*S*H for a few minutes before it went off.

"I'm sleepy, Mom," Logan finally said, rubbing his eyes like a child several years younger than his age.

Randy looked knowingly at Loren. "I guess we will go to bed."

"Okay," Loren replied with a nod. He looked at Vivian and Tana. "You two might as well hit the hay too."

Randy took Logan by the arm and hey walked up the stairs together, Tana a few steps behind. Loren could sense the hesitancy in Vivian.

"I'll be all right," he said with a smile on his dark, handsome face.

"Why are you so dark complected?" she asked, returning the smile.

Loren grunted, cocking his head to one side a bit. "Part Cherokee. Not much, but for some reason I am darker complected than my . . . than anyone else in my family."

Vivian lifted her shirt, withdrawing the Colt from her waistband. "Take this. You might need it tonight," she said.

He shook his head, but she insisted. Loren took the gun and stuck it in his back pocket where it was hidden. "If I can't stop him with this .357, you will need something."

Her face turned gloriously savage for a moment. "I have something."

"Yes," Loren agreed. "I guess you do."

Vivian went upstairs, Loren watching her, silently appraising her very feminine figure and cursing himself for it later as he blushed. Sitting in the recliner, he did not feel sleepy. The shower started upstairs and he heard the women preparing for bed. Laying the Smith and Wesson in his lap, he glanced at the doors. The man was a werewolf and he had came back to this area. Logan had not called tonight. Loren took a deep breath and felt suddenly tired. He had faced death and danger before -- it was nothing new -- but he had honestly prayed he would never face another night in danger of a werewolf attack. He could have gone home and left his friends here to fend for themselves, but he was not that kind of man. Besides, construction was only exciting during tax time and for some reason, it just wasn't the same.

CHAPTER FOURTEEN

Jim Tucker had been the closest officer on duty and he had drove from the Winding Stairs through the back roads to the paved road going to Logan's house. He had thought Bill's orders were a little sinister and vague if it was dangerous enough to need a shotgun. The road to Logan's house was not traveled a lot and he saw the headlights of the four-wheel drive pick-up coming from the opposite direction. It looked like Logan's truck and Bill told him Logan would relieve him.

Recognizing the truck, he hit his flashing lights, pulling over to the side as the truck rolled up beside him to a stop. Rolling down his window, Jim grimaced as the window rolled down on the truck and Logan shone a flashlight in his face.

"It is me, Sheriff. Jim Tucker," Jim said, squinting into the light. The light was lowered, but he was partially blinded. "I'm just now getting here. Most of the boys are patrolling the eastern side of the county tonight looking for that killer." He could not see into the truck cab very well, but Logan was not speaking. "Logan?"

An instant arrow of pain into his neck preceded the flash as he jerked from the pain. The roar of the pistol was like thunder and he felt the fiery arrows slap repeatedly into his face and chest as the flashes and thunder became steady. Jim Tucker slumped to the passenger side of the car, shot to pieces by the .22 pistol in Phill's hand. The car rolled forward as Jim's foot relaxed on the brake, angling into the ditch where it dropped noisily into a deep wash and caught on the frame there.

Phill climbed out of the truck whistling softly, walking to the car, reaching inside and turning the ignition off. Turning off the lights, he pressed the pistol against Jim's temple and fired the last shot into his head. Jim jerked and Phill reached inside, removing his weapon belt. Hefting the pistol, Phill saw it was a .40 S&W Glock. He put it in his pocket, carrying the .22 semi-auto back with him along with the gun belt.

He noticed that Jim Tucker had been wearing a bulletproof vest. It had not been much protection from a headshot or the higher angle of the truck to the car. Tough luck for him. Good luck for Phill. That was the way it should be in his opinion.

‡   ‡   ‡

"You look like hell," Bill growled as Logan stepped from the shadowy ditch, climbing into the car and shutting the door. He saw the .44 magnum revolver lying in the seat and checked the ammunition in the cylinder.

"Feel like hell," Logan agreed. "You get someone to go to my house?"

"Jim Tucker is headed that way. We did not have anyone close."

Logan was satisfied. "Jim is a good man. Take me home, Bill."

"You going to tell me what this is all about?" Bill asked as he turned the car around in the middle of the road. He glanced at his friend speculatively as he headed back towards Spiro.

"It is a long story and one that will seem unbelievable at times, Bill. It involves a secret you will have to take to your grave." He waited a second to let his words sink in. "Still want to know?"

Bill knew Logan did not exaggerate. "I think so."

Leaning back in his seat, Logan began his story when he received the invitation to go to the gold mines Milly owned in the mountains of Idaho. He did not go into detail on everything, but he definitely held Bill's attention.

‡   ‡   ‡

Jumping in surprise, Loren came awake all at once in the recliner, his hand closing over the revolver in his lap. Something woke him and he was unsure what had done it. The women were in bed. He remembered the last shower shutting off . . . how long ago? He looked at his watch and saw he had not been asleep for over ten minutes. Standing, Loren walked to the large multi-paned window in the living room, checking the front yard. Walking to the back door, he saw a light on in the shop. He wet his lips, unsure of whether he should leave the house without waking Randy or Vivian. Moving to the front door, he relaxed when he saw the big four-wheel drive in the driveway.

Logan's truck.

"About time," he muttered, opening the front door and stepping out on the front porch as he holstered his pistol. He could not believe that someone had driven into the driveway without waking him. At least this time he had woke from something. Crossing the end of the driveway, he saw that the light was the on in the small bathroom, but he could not see anyone moving around inside the room.

"Logan?" he called as he reached the door. He heard a grunt from inside and opened the door. Stepping inside, he looked toward the bathroom, catching the movement of the shadow to his right from the corner of his eye.

The man struck him with a barbell bar across the shoulder, knocking Loren down as his shoulder went numb from pain. Loren kicked out with his right leg, causing the man to trip forward. Landing on the concrete floor, Loren felt the man tumble on top of him. His arms were like a vise and Loren elbowed back with his left arm, dislodging him for a second as he scrambled forward. The holster was set up for his right hand and the bar had struck his right shoulder. He clawed for the revolver when the deep, guttural growl was emitted from the rapidly changing man in the floor. Gripping the gun, he was pulling it free when the werewolf sprang, its maw open and lunging for his neck. Loren jammed the gun in its mouth as it slung its head, ripping the gun from his hand and breaking his index finger.

Loren landed on his back upon the bed, pitching the werewolf over him with his feet before spilling to the floor, trying to regain his footing. The revolver was near the weight bench and he dove for it, his shoulder sending a deep, sharp pain all the way through him as he sought to attain the firearm. Over the weight bench he dove, struggling to get the weapon that could save his life. He got it in his hand, turning to face the werewolf and caught a massive forearm across the face, slamming him into the wall. All his breath left his body and he felt a rib break when the wolf grabbed him around the chest, heaving him over his head and through the back window into the yard.

Hurrying to the window, the werewolf looked at the crumpled figure of the man lying immobile on the blood-covered grass. He snarled, walking to where the pistol lay and picked it up. Opening the cylinder, he ripped it and the main arm from the gun, pitching both pieces out the busted window that he had thrown the man through.

Phill turned and loped out of the shop and across the yard to the front door. He peered inside the small door window, then moved to the front window, looking inside. No one else was awake and he growled contentedly, his olfactory glands swelling as he swayed back and forth as though he were listening to music only he could hear.

A single reading lamp near a recliner lighted the inside and he heard no noises inside through the walls. He could hear so well in this form that it amazed him that he could hear people talking when he was circling the farm house near the state line. The door was not locked and he pushed it hard, the door swinging in to thump gently against the doorstop. He could smell the potpourri in the kitchen as he sniffed inside the room, moving in slowly, cautiously as he growled in the back of his throat.

The smell of females was intense and he could smell something he liked about two of them. He walked through the carpet in the living room, looking at the pictures. A small mirror surrounded by brass wheat straw hang beside the fireplace mantle and he saw his face. Moving closer, he cocked his head, inspecting the widened snout and long fangs protruding from his mouth. It was the face of a god!

Raising his head, he inhaled, bounding to the kitchen through the hallway. His long claws clicked loudly on the hard wood floor. Looking out the sliding glass door, he could see the corner of the shop. They were upstairs and he could smell her, scent her lingering essence through the room.

Randy jerked as she felt the hand close over her mouth. She opened her eyes to look into Vivian's face. Her face was taut with fear, though she was very calm and she pointed toward the hallway. Randy listened and she heard a faint, rhythmic clicking sound emanating from downstairs. Her eyes grew wide as realization crept into her mind, her face showing terror as Vivian placed her index finger across her lips, motioning for Randy to wake Logan Daniel quietly.

The clicking was louder and Randy put her hand over Logan's mouth, shaking him awake. He awoke, his eyes getting scared, but Randy lifted him over her, handing him to Vivian. The younger woman took the boy and moved stealthily out the door. The ominous clicking of the claws had stopped.

Rolling to her feet, Randy opened the night stand drawer slowly, cursing when she saw the pistol was not in place. Why hadn't she checked that last night? Seeing the green luminous numbers on the clock radio, she saw she had not been asleep long. She had worn a T-shirt and shorts to bed last night and she walked barefooted to the hallway, glancing toward the top of the stairs.

Listening, she heard the faint clink of the window in the back guestroom. A faint growl came from somewhere toward the stairs. Stepping cautiously into the hall, she gasped as the werewolf landed at the top, his feral eyes locking on her. With a scream, she dove into her room even as he closed the distance in less than a second. She slammed her door, feeling the bones in her body pop as she initiated the change. Her door burst into a thousand splinters as the werewolf crashed through, his head looking at her in surprise before she ran past him on four legs. He swiped at her, his claws tearing her shoulder as she yelped in pain. She was quick and around him before he could react, running headlong down the stairs.

She had never taken the form that combined man and wolf, the sensation too strange for her to be effective fighting the rogue wolf. Following her family, she saw the window was still open and she went out of it, her front paws catching the windowsill before she jumped on the small outside balcony. Running down the stairs, she almost collided with Vivian, the slender blonde in the very form that Randy felt so odd in taking.

The window shattered, a large, hulking shadow flying through the air as glass rained down on them. The rogue wolf landed on his feet, going to all fours before whirling to face the two females like a primeval wraith.

Phill had heard someone moving upstairs before he leaped to the top. He was sure he would surprise whoever was moving around and he had accomplished his goal when the brunette tried to escape to her room. He followed and had been momentarily shocked when he saw she had changed into a wolf. That crucial second of inaction allowed her to get around him. He started to follow, but he stopped in the room that was filled with Tana's scent. He had found some of clothing, lifting it in a clawed hand, inhaling the fragrance of her as the hunger bellowed in agony. He and it needed her!

She was gone and he smelled another female that had the smell he associated with the brunette. In his mind he realized if they were all werewolves, they could be outdistancing him. With a lurch, he gave chase, jumping through the large window frame to the ground below. The two females were waiting and he turned, going to his haunches as the blonde wolf struck him from the flank, her claws savaging his thighs and chest as she sought to sink her teeth in his throat. The dark wolf hesitated and Phill clutched the blonde wolf around the neck, lifting her high as he heard the bones snap and her body go limp. Pitching her into the log house, he turned his attention to the dark wolf. It bowed its back, growling loudly as it backed around to place itself between him and the blonde wolf.

Tana looked under the seat for Randy's extra key and she could not find it. Logan Daniel sat in the back, his face filled with wide-eyed wonder. "Is mom going to be okay, Sis?" he asked.

"I think so," Tana said, her voice desperate as she looked under the passenger side mat. "Damn it!" She felt so helpless. Logan Daniel dropped to the floorboard, digging his hand under the seat to help her. He knew that the monster that killed Tana's boyfriend was here and he was scared.

"Where is Uncle Loren?" he asked, his voice muffled behind the seat.

"I don't know," Tana said, her voice cracking as she felt the fear building in her. There were no keys!!! Grabbing Logan's hand, she said, "Come on!" Logan climbed over the seat, running to the shop with his older sister leading the way. They were almost there when Tana heard a low moan. She ushered Logan Daniel inside before she ran to where Loren lay.

He was covered in blood and his right arm was stiff as he tried to push himself to stand. Tana was horrified, but she lost no time in bending over to help him to his feet.

"He is here," Loren mumbled weakly.

The sound of a fight was coming from around the house and Tana glanced over her shoulder before turning to stand beside Loren as she helped him inside the shop. Pointing to a small door on the floor near the toolbox and air compressor, she went to it, opening it as Logan Daniel took Loren's hand.

Loren grimaced, the dried blood cracking on his face as the boy inadvertently squeezed his broken fingers. Tana reached inside, turning on a light. The heavy metal door was held by a brace once it came up and Tana helped Loren and Logan downstairs.

"My gun?" Loren said, his words were slurred, but his eyes were clear.

She remembered seeing it laying beside him in the dewy grass, the cylinder missing. "It was destroyed," she said with a shrug as she climbed the steps, closing the door and sliding a huge metal bolt into a metal plate set into the concrete. Loren had looked at it appraisingly and it was a hell of a bunker.

"Will the door keep it out of here?" Logan Daniel asked nervously, sitting close to Loren on the cot. There were several cots leaning against the wall. Logan had bought them for using in this bunker during storms. They had been down here once during a really bad storm and Logan Daniel did not like it then. He did not appear to mind so much this time.

"I think so," Loren said hopefully. He tried to stand, his face going red with strain, sweat popping up on his forehead. "Damn," he cursed weakly, looking up almost ashamedly at Tana. "Your mom needs help."

"I will go," Tana said bravely, looking around the room for a weapon. Loren got a strange look on his face, reaching into his back pocket. The small automatic appeared and he handed it to Tana.

"I had forgot about it."

She took it, pulling back the slide. She saw the quizzical look on Loren's face. "Aunt Vivian has had me shoot it several times," she explained. The slide felt a little rough, but it seated easily enough. Turning to her brother, she said, "When I go out the door, you lock it behind me. Do not open it unless it is someone you know."

He nodded his head seriously and Tana unbolted the door. She felt strange going back into the night to face the terrible monster that killed her boyfriend and put her through hell. It was much stronger now and it was here to kill. Yet, she was strangely calm, the slim automatic in her hand as she peered out the door. She could no longer hear the fighting and she prayed she was not too late as she cleared the door so her little brother could lock it. She heard the bolt fall into place before she left the shop. Now she heard some fighting again.

Something had happened to Miranda Denton as the fight wore on. She felt a change inside as the wolf instinct urged her to attack, to push the weak side, to gain his attention to keep him off Vivian. She felt more natural, more powerful as the wolf in her controlled the way she fought. The slender blonde wolf had been hurt badly twice and Randy knew it was because of the ferocity of her attacks. Vivian knew what it took to kill this monster and she was determined to get her teeth in his throat so that her powerful jaws could sever the neck and provide the killing stroke to take him down for good. She had taken horrible wounds and Phill had almost killed her more than once.

Randy had used the form of the wolf to attack, slashing the male wolf's thighs, almost hamstringing him once. He roared in pain, turning his attention to her. He pounced on her and Randy felt bones snap and shatter as he brought his powerful fists down on her body. She yelped, whining with pain as she tried to scramble from beneath him. His claws dug in her throat, the fetid breath spewing in her face as he lunged for her neck. She pushed away, gaining enough footing to break free though her body ached from the pounding she took.

With a surge of willpower, Randy changed, taking the form that was the most powerful of all. A low growl emitted between clenched teeth signaled the change and Sturgis found himself between two sets of sharp, rending claws. Randy's long claws dug at his stomach, her teeth biting at his shoulder.

Launching himself into Vivian, he and the smaller wolf rolled into the balcony posts, cracking one of them with the force of impact. He caught her by a foot, slinging her into the broken post, her back snapping as Randy attacked with a deadly snarl. Sturgis ducked, clawing her belly open as she went over him and rolling into a ball beside Vivian. Sturgis grabbed a 2X4 bracing and slammed it through Vivian's body, pinning her to the ground.

The young werewolf raised her head, howling in horrendous pain, the board through her spine and chest. She nipped at it, clawing at the board, but she could not pull it out without the leverage of her feet.

Randy was stunned for a moment, then Sturgis landed on top of her, his claws lashing her face. She bit him, ripping his forearm and throwing him off her body. Sturgis faced her in the back yard, circling around her as Vivian mewled painfully, the stake-like board clawed to shreds at the end.

He was strong and she knew she could not best him on strength. He had proven that he was stronger than both her and Vivian as well as being almost as quick. It had been years since she had battled for her life and the memories of the Idaho mountains came back in vivid clarity. She felt sadness and anger building within her, the anger feeding upon the sadness as though fuel for a fire.

Suddenly, Randy changed in her human form, standing in front of Sturgis, tall, slender and nude -- a breathtaking sight. Sturgis took a step forward, halting for a second before changing into a man. The leer he seemed to have as a werewolf was still present as a man.

"You are not what you think you are," Randy said softly, her eyes on the eyes of the killer.

He smirked. "And what am I?"

She felt his eyes on her body, but she did not let that intimidate her as she replied. "You are a sick, insignificant man who can only feel like a man when he is carving up someone else. You are a plague upon this planet that must be cured. You are nothing."

Phill laughed, holding his stomach. "You are a fool!" he spat wickedly. "I am a god!" He waved his hands around as though to indicate everything around him. "This means little to the universe, yet I will change this world and how it sees people."

"You are a killer, a taker who has never given back to the very race you belong to," she said, seeing that Vivian was still working at getting the board out of her body.

His face turned ugly. "Being human is not necessarily a good thing. I have seen what we do to each other. Men to women. Women to men.

Each of us to each other," he said, stepping towards her. "Sometimes people require a sacrifice for their sin, the moral laxity. Your daughter is such a sacrifice. The hunger desires her as payment and it will not be denied."

Shaking her head, Randy said softly, dangerously, "You can not have her."

"She is no longer yours to give," he said patiently. "She is mine and I shall have her." He was within arm's length of her and stepped closer. Randy looked at him defiantly as he put his hand on her chest, moving it to her right breast.

Like a striking snake, Randy brought her knee up, crushing his testicles with her knees as he howled in pain, dropping to the ground as she started the change. Phill was changing too and she closed her fangs on his neck when he struck her with his elbows so hard it dislodged her, breaking all the ribs on the left side of her chest. He kicked her, smashing her with his fists and claws as she tried to get away. Her trick had almost worked, but all it served to do was enrage him.

Randy felt the hammer-like blows, tasted a smoky flavor in her mouth as Phill ravaged her body with blow after blow. She sensed him lifting her before she went flying across the yard and into a tree. The sharp pain of bones breaking made her cry out.

Phill Sturgis advanced on her, his head low as he approached for the kill.

"Hey!"

He turned, startled by the youthful voice filled with anger and defiance.

There she stood, the reason he came here. She was dressed in a pair of shorts and a T-shirt and he remembered the nakedness of her he had seen that night she almost became a sacrifice.

"You were looking for me," she stated, walking around the house toward him. Phil bounded once toward her, stopping and looking her over. She was taking slow steps toward him and he sniffed the air.

Lifting the gun, Tana shot. The bullet sliced through his shoulder and Phill back flipped in agony, screaming obscenities in a voice that carried through the night like a lion's roar. Tana fired two more times, cursing lightly as the rounds struck the dirt around him. He was flopping around wildly and she could not hit him.

Moving closer, she fired again, the bullet clipping his small toe off. He roared, charging into her, knocking her down and the gun from her hand. She rolled across the grass as he turned, standing erect as he plodded toward her as she slowly pushed herself up with her arms.

"NO!" Randy screamed, throwing herself into the battle again. Phill had forgotten about her as the teenager held his attention. Randy attacked him from the right flank. She bit into his side and he ripped a hunk of flesh from her back. Throwing her again, he grunted in satisfaction as she lay still after sliding down the trunk of a tree. He had thrown her into it head first.

"It's over," Tana said, firing the Mustang.

The slug hit him in the hip and Phill fell to the ground. He howled and screamed as Tana stood, stepping closer. She aimed the pistol at his head as he looked at her with hatred in his eyes.

"This is for Tim you son-of-a-bitch," she whispered. She pulled the trigger and the gun clicked. Her face in shock, she eared back the hammer to fire it again and Phill knocked it from her hand. He stood, his face twisted in anger, agony and madness. Tana walked backwards as he slowly changed into a man.

"I can not die!" He stalked toward her and she kept back. "I was given the power of a god for a reason!" His eyes were yellowish. "You must die, Tana Denton! I shall kill you tonight and all will be complete."

Tana darted to the side and Phill just laughed as she grabbed the gun again. Opening the slide, she saw a round in the magazine. Pushing it up, she heard it click. She pulled the trigger and the hammer clicked again. Working the slide, she saw him changing, bunching his legs under him to leap and she knew she would never get it around in time.

All things went into slow motion. Randy was no longer calling out to her. Vivian was not struggling to her left. It was simply her and the werewolf as the pistol swung toward it. The werewolf was almost on her when she swung the pistol around, her finger squeezing the trigger. The roar was loud and she saw him swiped out of the air as though swatted with a giant bat.

Sturgis had a massive bullet hole through his chest and he fought to stand but he could not move his legs. The agony took his breath away and he open and shut his hand trying to get his claws on Tana.

"Not this time Sturgis."

Tana looked toward the voice and she saw her Dad holding his big pistol in his hand, Bill walking a step behind him with a shotgun.

"Step back, Tana," he said, walking closer, his eyes on Sturgis.

Sturgis was gasping, his eyes watery profusely as he stared at Logan. "I-I k-k-killed you," he growled gutturally.

Shaking his head, Logan said, "No. It takes silver to do that and you did not have it, Sturgis." Showing him the .44 magnum, he added, "This pistol is full of silver bullets." Looking Phill straight in the face, Logan smiled. "You are dying, Phill and nothing can stop it."

"No!!!!" He lurched, but he could not move his legs. "No!!!" he cried out pitifully, changing fully back into a man. He reached for Logan and Logan did what he felt was best. He shot Phill Sturgis between the eyes.

The man who thought he was God pitched back with the impact of the bullet, his brains blown across the grass as he sprawled on his back. Logan holstered his gun as Tana came to him.

"Oh daddy!" she cried, holding him as he hugged her tight, the dead man's eyes glazing over as he lay on the ground in front of him. He kissed her forehead, stepping away and going to Vivian. She watched him as he gripped the 2X4 and heaved it out of her. She sighed, her body beginning to heal immediately.

They hugged each other and then Logan was kissing Randy, his arms full of naked woman as she encircled him tightly in her arms. Bill was blushing, turning his head.

"I am sorry, Bill," Randy said, chuckling as Vivian changed back into her human form. The two women stood naked and Bill turned red as a fire engine. They went into the house to put on clothes, Tana taking Bill with her to get Logan Daniel and Loren out of the bunker.

Logan had told Bill to park near the road and he was glad he had the foresight to keep from warning Phill of their approach. He knelt over the dead man, weariness going through him. How many more times would he have to enforce the Law of the Wolf?

Logan and Randy Denton watched as the body was zipped up in the body bag and loaded into the county van. Bill patted Logan on the shoulder. "No one will know. I'll tell Dr. Patterson to tag him and we will send him on."

"Tana go with Loren?" Randy asked.

"Yes. He would not ride in an ambulance so she and that blonde girl went with him." Bill looked at Logan. "You never told me your whole family was those things."

Chuckling, Logan said, "We aren't. Vivian was born a wolf."

He shook his head, watching the van leave Logan's yard. "Your secret will be safe with me always. Both of ya'," he promised, holding out his hand. Logan took it gratefully, then Randy.

"I knew it would," Logan said with a smile, hugging his wife as Bill walked away. They turned, looking at their house and the repairs they would have to do when Bill stopped and turned.

"I did not turn in your badge, Sheriff," he said gruffly, a candid smile on his face. "So you have your ass in to the office to file your own reports."

Logan and Randy looked at each other with a grin as Bill walked to his car, chuckling with every step.

"Shall we go to the hospital and check on Loren?" Logan asked, placing his hands on his wife's hips as she turned to face him. He kissed her passionately. She stepped back after they broke from the kiss, her hands going to her jeans.

"He will just be grumpy if we check on him," she replied, stepping out of the shorts as they fell to her ankles. She slid the panties down to join them. "I want to run with you tonight." Motioning toward the dark mountains behind their house, she said, "Up there." Her blouse lay beside the other clothes and her bra joined them in less than a second.

Logan took off his clothes, smiling as his wife changed into a pretty wolf, her coat dark and glossy. He changed, nuzzling her as she licked his face. They turned together, trotting into the darkness that called to their hearts.

Vivian and Tana helped Loren out of the truck as Logan Daniel opened doors for them. They were walking into the house when they heard the dual sounds of two adult wolves howling to the moon, singing wolf song through the night on a mountain somewhere in the night. Vivian smiled at Tana.

"What?" Loren asked, the finger brace on his broken fingers already irritating him.

"They are together," Tana said knowingly.

Loren listened to the echoes and nodded. "That is the way it should be." They helped him inside and made him comfortable. The pain pills put him to sleep and Tana went with Vivian to the living room.

They stood together near the window, Logan Daniel curled up on the couch asleep. Vivian put her hand on Tana's shoulder. "You did well tonight, Little Sister."

"Why do you call me that when we are alone?" Tana asked.

"Someday," Vivian started slowly, "your heart will take the path of the wolf and you will understand everything so clearly. Your heart is like your father's."

Tana smiled proudly, hugging her Aunt Vivian as they stood looking into the night. Across the far open field they could see two furtive shadows making their way toward the house. The two wolves were mates . . . and they were coming home.

The 737 jet was leveling off as it reached cruising altitude, banking to the West as it headed for Denver at an altitude of thirty-three thousand feet. Dr. Shields liked the first class accommodations as he pulled out his lap top computer from beneath his seat, waiting as it booted to the Windows screen. He opened a file to his journal and typed in the title: **A New Beginning**.

Underneath the title he wrote Logan Denton's name. Leaning back, he thought about what he knew about the man. It was very little, but he had been able to convince the other personnel in the hospital to refrain from turning over information he wanted to keep secret. No one tried to explain a dead man who got up and walked away a few short hours later, but it happened. Only a handful of people were aware of the spectacular miracle, but he knew Rutherford would keep it to himself. He feared ridicule too much in a small community to spout off about men rising from the dead.

He saved the file, then turned off the computer, placing it back under the seat. A man could win every prestigious award in medicine and science if he could expose this mystery. A man could write his ticket to any university or lab. Shields smiled as he reached in his pocket, looking at the small vial of blood in the miniature cold packet. Inside was the key that would unlock a new universe. The blood was a first step, but he knew they would eventually need more than just the blood. He remembered the speed the man displayed as well as the fighting skills. Logan Denton had a background and he was going to investigate into his past first -- in an attempt to find some answers. He leaned back in his seat, methods for obtaining the information he would need going through his head. There was much to do and he must consider every aspect.

The long, grayish pony-tail whipped in the wind behind his head as he stood in the sparsely crowded terminal as the Boeing 737 landed on the tarmac, smoke billowing from beneath the wheels as it landed with a loud, mechanical thump he could hear in his memories. The black jeans were stiff with newness and the Western shirt and jacket were accented with the black and turquoise tie at his neck. He stood with his hands crossed casually in front of him as he watched it taxi to the terminal. The old man preferred the open air terminal here as opposed to the seats inside.

Some would think he would be comfortable meeting these people, but he did not feel the ease he would have liked to have felt. The questions did not disturb him because he had answered similar questions in the past for dozens of others coming to him for answers. It was the reaction. One never knew how the reaction would be when people came face to face with a new beginning.

The terminal in Boise was not very crowded and he watched the passengers departing -- children and parents, a schoolgirl coming home from abroad.

When they entered the terminal he knew them. The nervousness, the tenseness around the eyes marked them with the desperation they felt inside. He saw the parents looking around, but the boy looked around for only a second, then peered directly at him.

He knew.

The instinct was strong within him and he could sense or smell the werewolf across the room. He picked up his pace and walked to Vitoro as his parents followed closely behind him.

"Mr. Vitoro?" he asked, his youthful voice unable to mask the curiosity, the fear of what he had became as well as the opportunity for answers to those questions. In the timbre of his voice he could hear the indecision, the unanswered questions behind his eyes, stirring incessantly in his brain. He was exactly as Logan described him and could see that Logan had been right about him. This one would need some direction before he went back home to live this new life thrust upon him by a madman.

Smiling pleasantly, Vitoro said, "Yes, please, call me Vic. So many people do nowadays."

"Dolphus Campbell, Mr. Toro," the father said, his big hand callused from hard work as Vitoro shook it.

His white teeth flashing, Vitoro said, "The same request I made of your son is made to you as well. I am known as Vic to most people and I answer by it readily enough." He took Mrs. Campbell's hand, bowing slightly. "Nice to make your acquaintance, Mrs. Campbell."

His almost European manners startled Jessica Campbell, but she muttered a response that was intelligible. They followed him to the luggage terminal and he helped them carry their things to a dark blue, late model Suburban, the windows tinted dark in the back. Dolphus and Jessica climbed in the middle seat. Ray took the front seat beside Vitoro.

"I understand you are a logger," Vitoro said as he buckled his seat belt around him. His passengers noticed and did the same before he started the vehicle.

"Yes sir," Dolphus replied. "I drive a bulldozer."

"I have managed to obtain you a position with a crew building a small dam on one of the nearby rivers. Would that suffice?"

Dolphus glanced at his wife. Well, I . . . yes, it would."

Glancing in his rear view mirror as he started the truck, Vitoro said, "Mrs. Campbell, I understand you are a seamstress, a dressmaker as well as master craftsperson."

She smiled elegantly. "I do all right," she said.

"We have a large store where we sell our local crafts. I am sure you will do well with it," he said.

Vitoro pulled the truck from the parking lot, going through a gate and to the highway that would lead to their new home. The blue mountains were ahead of them in the distance and he saw Ray was looking at them. Vitoro ignored the adults as they settled back in their seats for the ride.

"There is much to learn," Vitoro promised, his eyes on the road.

Ray looked at Vitoro for a moment before nodding his head. "I thought I was a monster when it first happened."

Smiling wolfishly, Vitoro said, "You can be or you can be what destiny calls you to be. Destiny is ever changing, Ray."

"Will you teach me?" Ray asked. "Is that why Sheriff Denton sent me here?"

"I will guide you along your path, but I will not teach you. You will learn for yourself. It is the way to enlightenment that does not fail to make the lessons memorable."

Ray opened his mouth to ask a question, but he closed his mouth with it unasked. His brow wrinkled a bit as he looked to the mountains. Things were going to change for him -- they already had changed! It was going to be a new world out there and he would be looking at it with a new per-spective, a new outlook on reality.

Life was not a static line. It was changing, flowing into different pos-sibilities he had never even considered. He had known he would never be the same after he talked to Sheriff Denton and the pretty blonde woman. He was a werewolf like them. He did not answer to the call of the moon, but he believed he would -- as surely as his veins flowed with the blood of the wolf.

David Falconer grew up in Eastern Oklahoma, running the creeks, rivers and lakes near his home. An avid outdoorsman, his love of the outdoors is only equaled by his love of reading and surpassed only by his love of family. He has written numerous outdoor humorous short stories for the outdoor E-zine www.backwoodsbound.ocm including Armadillo Warfare and The Hunter's Peril as well as more serious essays such as OLD MEN and Tippy. He considers himself lucky to have been raised in the company of old men who taught him the fine art of Southern language, outdoor wisdom, a love of history and the ability to know what is important in life. David owns a small ranch in Eastern Oklahoma near his hometown but maintains his residence near Sherman, Texas with his wife, Sheila. They have one daughter who is attending college. He has an older daughter that lives in New York where her husband serves this great nation in the US Army.

Printed in the United States
109070LV00004B/310-339/P